legends
of the man
with the aura
of green

Volume 2
The Blue and Red Knights' Tale

Deborah J. Corker

i

Legends of the man with the aura of green
 Volume 2: The Blue and Red Knights' Tale
Copyright 2025 by Deborah J. Corker

Published April 2025

Cover design by Art Painter
Cover art: Lightscape, Tromso, Norway, July 11, 2018
Unsplash

ISBN – 13: 978317019006
ISBN – 10: 1477123456

Library of Congress Control Number: 2018675309
Printed in the United States of America

For those who quest and overcome

CONTENTS

ACKNOWLEDGEMENTS

To my beta readers: Candace, Carole, Janet, and Karen. Thank you for your patience, wisdom, wonderful ideas and suggestions. Two volumes down, so man more to write!

To my readers: I hope you've read Vol 1 so you already know and love the knights and other characters. I want to share just a few of my idiosyncrasies so you can indulge fully in the story.

In the first book I used primarily titles: The Blue Knight instead of a name, which were always capitalized. I have continued that practice but interchange names and titles freely, both capitalized.

I use minimal commas but often use . . . a pause. Think of the speaker stopping and waiting before continuing the story, something hard to communicate with the written word.

In the book hand language is visual and represented by a different font. When a person is communicating in both hand language and speaking the different font will be bolded.

Finally, forgive me for giving you a cliffhanger. The story of the White and Green Knights is coming shortly. There are many legends of the man with the aura of green.
I hope you want to learn (read) more.

Closed hand to heart. Thank you. Deborah April 2025

The Blue & Red Knights' Tale

PART ONE

Legends of the man with the aura of green – Volume 2

The Blue & Red Knights' Tale

Homecoming Struggles

Preface

The Storyteller sighed, looking around the room to see if she had everyone's attention.

"It is always difficult to tell a tale starting in the middle.

Our four knights have failed their quest to find the man with the aura of green.

Now the princess is gone from the castle, and the king has fallen into madness.

Two generals have gone out into the land to 'protect'.

An evil spreads throughout and poses a threat not yet fully realized and mostly unseen."

INTRODUCTION
THE RED KNIGHT, DESERT FOLK, BLUE KNIGHT & MOUNTAIN FOLK

Allow me to introduce the Red Knight, Bartholomew, and his wife, Beatrice. Beatrice has always been a songstress. For their wedding, she had composed and sung her vows to her beloved. Bartholomew is no stranger to music either. Unfortunately, his voice was not always as true as the musical notes he wrote for his small chamber orchestra. So, while their souls were in harmony, his voice was often not.

Together their Keep and surrounding lands were always filled with music. Fesitvals never failed to include troubadours, small and large groups of singers, and collections of diverse musicians with a wide assortment of instruments. The fact that the Red Knight's quest for the man with the aura of green took him into the desert lands where he met the Caretakers, who were also filled with music, could not have been by pure chance. Think not . . . that this was a mere accidental meeting but an indication of forces moving far beyond our ken.

It did not take long for Desert Land Caretakers, Hmway and Allayu, to become part of the musical symphony of the Red Knight's lands and people. Surprising, you might think, because they stood a head taller than most, wore long flowing garments of bright colors, and had the whitest smiles in their dark faces. Individuals whom most, if not all, the Red Knight's people had never seen or met before. Their acceptance boded well for the Red Knight's people and ill for those who did not. The confrontations with those who held ill will were few, but the more interactions they had within the kingdom, the more the conflicts grew. These conflicts were one of the many subtle signs that an underlying evil was spreading throughout the land.

~~~

The Blue Knight, Rupert, and his soon-to-be wife, the Head Counselor of the Mountain Folk, Minerva, were a bright and merry pair. They were wed in their souls long before their eyes or bodies met. Rupert was a man of his people, never forgetting a name or face. Each day he sought out what was good and right in the world and strove to make it even better. Minerva, on the other hand, came from hardship and grief. She viewed the world with intellect and compassion - Seeing, anticipating, preparing, and rolling her way through life with a soft voice and stern smile (when needed).

To find one's life mate after a failed quest and a kingdom on the edge of chaos seemed ill-fated. Then again . . . this was not mere happenstance but a fortuitous event creating a strong force to combat the rising evil.

Reminders of Volume 1
THE KING IS LEFT ALONE (ALMOST) AT THE CASTLE

The handmaidens and Head Cook waited until the King had exited and began cleaning up the table. They were an efficient team. Quickly, everything was cleared away except the four goblets of the knights.

Just before they exited down the hidden stairway, the White Knight spoke to them. "If it had not been for you," she paused trying to find the right words, "our King and Princess would have been lost to us. We owe you our gratitude and thanks."

All four knights rose and placed a closed fist upon their hearts. "We need your continued support and wisdom to restore our Kingdom," she finished. There were a few moments of silence, then the knights sat.

The knights watched the handmaidens depart. Head Cook brought back a full pot of hot tea and refilled their cups, brushing aside the Blue Knight's assistance, leaving without a look back. Things had taken an unexpected turn with the taking of the princess by the man with the aura of green. All who remained at the table knew that a life-changing, even world-changing, moment was upon them. Each knight took time to contemplate what their role might be in that changed and altered world. All the knights wanted to wait for their king to awaken from his stupor, but soon realized they could not wait, it was time to act.

King Nicholas had remained withdrawn. He was not as out of touch as the knights believed. He just didn't want to face reality. His daughter was gone. What did it matter ... the future? There was no future without his daughter and wife. All he felt was rage toward the man with the aura of green. How dare he take the princess and demand he, *the King*, heal himself.

After the meal he had finally gathered enough strength to leave the throne room, ignoring the knights, and went to the Princess's room. He sat in the chair beside her bed that he had occupied for so many days, weeks, months. But tonight was different. There was no fire lit and burning bright. No food or drink at the bedside table. The flowers were wilted. The room was empty. Empty of her, the princess, empty of life.

"Why, why, why!" He pounded upon the empty bed and then collapsed, all strength and hope failing him. As he lay there the events of the night repeated in his head. Listening to the knights and castle staff talk about him as if he was not present. Hearing how everyone thought him mad. As the story unfolded, he had finally realized that Head Cook and the handmaidens had been the only ones caring for the princess and himself for many months, unseen, unnoticed, unacknowledged. Then to hear that his generals and army had deserted him. He was repulsed by the soldiers who had remained and *sat at his table* barely behaving better than wild animals. He had made sure not to make eye contact with any of them but had their faces engraved in his rage.

He had left without giving the knights any indication that he even was aware of their presence. He heard them say they were leaving the castle tonight and would be bringing the rest of their parties back. His brain couldn't piece together what he had heard. He thought they said they were traveling with people they had met on their quest. The knights had FAILED their quest. Why would there be people with them? Why would they be here?

"So what." He mumbled. "What does it matter?" "Why." He fell asleep asking himself why, what had he to live for, why. He didn't notice when one of the handmaidens covered him with a blanket and lit the fire. He remained lost in his own despair. He wasn't aware of the moment when only he and the head cook were the last ones left in the castle. He failed to understand that his life and world had permanently changed.

The man with the aura of green stood silently watching the king restlessly sleep across his daughter's empty bed. He took one step forward and laid a gentle hand upon the king's head. His hand glowed green and the glow seemed to move through the King, stilling his restlessness and making his breathing easy and deep.

He shook his head sadly. The power within King Nicholas was still buried deep but it seemed to reach out to the man with the aura of green, burning a bit brighter. The king was hopeless now, but the power within would soon find its time. The man with the aura of green hoped it would be soon enough.

Chapter One
KNIGHTS – WHERE DO WE GO FROM HERE?

The knights left the castle in the early evening and returned to their encampments, each caught up in their own thoughts. What lay ahead was truly beyond their ken in this moment. None was sure of where even to begin. Each was grateful that they had people they trusted waiting for them.

People with whom they could hopefully share this burden and responsibility. People they never would have met if not for the King's quest. People whose fates were now intimately bound with their own and the kingdom's.

Chapter Two
THE GREEN KNIGHT & THE KING

The Green Knight knew he had to remain with King Nicholas. With the Princess gone the King had no reason to live. In fact, departing this life might just seem like the easiest course for the bereft king. But that was not a solution that anyone wanted and definitely not what the kingdom needed.

It was early morning when the Green Knight and Festus, his groom, mounted their horses and started their return to the castle. The other three camps were just beginning to stir, fires rekindled, meal preparations begun. White Knight Alexandra came out of her tent and stretched. She saw the Green Knight moving and went to intercept him on the road to the castle.

"Morning," she lifted her hand in greeting, standing on one side of the road.

"Sir Knight, you rise early," the Green Knight responded, stopping his horse and sliding out of the saddle to stand before her. They clasped hands to arms silently.

"Returning to the King?" She knew where he was going but hoped he would offer his thoughts.

"Aye. I think I can serve best by helping Nicholas return to himself." The White Knight nodded and waited. "My son Gerald will take over for me at home." Again, the White Knight nodded and waited. The Green Knight lost all semblance of control, "Alex, what if he . . ."

Alexandra had not released his arm, now she squeezed it and drew him in closer. "He will come back to us. Charles, *YOU* can be the father he needs right now." She hoped her voice was filled with more confidence than she felt as she looked steadily into his eyes. "Each of us has a role. I believe this is yours. No one else could even get him to respond but you." She waited till he nodded. "Charles, knowing you're here will allow the rest of us to return home and make proper preparations before we face what is ahead."

She waited until he acknowledged this statement. "We are all safer because you are here." She watched as he moved through uncertainty to frustration and then drew on his years of experience to find a new conviction within. He unclasped from her and put a closed fist to his heart.

"By my oath and honor as the Green Knight, I will safeguard our King until your return."

"By my oath and honor as the White Knight, I will safeguard our kingdom and return." She took a step back, closed fist still upon her heart.

The Green Knight remounted and nudged his horse forward. The White Knight nodded at Festus and whispered, "Take care of him." Festus looked very serious, nodded *I will*, and followed his knight toward the castle.

Chapter Three
GERALD, THE BLUE KNIGHT & THE HEAD COUNSELOR

A final check of the Green Knight's camp, a tightening of bundles on his horse, then Gerald turned to the Blue Knight's camp that was closest and seemed to be the most awake at this moment. *Maybe he can tell me more about the princess and the man with the aura of green.* He took his horse's reins, "The whole world has gone crazy," he said aloud and walked the few steps to the Blue Knight's fire, his horse shook her head and reins as if agreeing. Gerald gave the horse an affectionate pat on her neck and whispered in her ear, "Do you have any answers?" but got no response.

"Morning Gerald," Simon said as he continued to build up the fire, "you had breakfast yet?"

"No, can I help?" Gerald tethered his horse and stood by the fire, appreciating the warmth.

"Can you fill that pot with water and set it on the fire?" Simon pointed with a stick then adjusted the fire with it before tossing it on top. "I've got eggs and bacon for breakfast. Plenty to share." His work with the fire complete, he turned to their food stores pulling out the eggs, bacon and a large pan.

"Shall I wake the knight, counselor and engineer?" Gerald asked as he set the filled pot on the fire.

"Nay, as soon as they smell the food they will come." He drew out four plates and then dug in the bag to find a bowl for Gerald. "I'm surprised you can't hear them arguing," he paused, sighing deeply, "I mean discussing." He looked over his shoulder at Gerald. "They never stop, I don't know what they can always be talking about," he paused to stir the eggs and turn the bacon, "until last night ..."

13

Gerald waited but Simon did not go on. Sitting down next to Simon he said, "I know, everything changed last night when my father, I mean the Green Knight, returned."

Simon lifted the pan from the fire and turned to look directly at Gerald. "The silence last night was eerie. Even when the knights were gone the counselor and engineer kept talking." He looked searchingly at Gerald. "I thought the worst thing that could happen was the King would reject the counselor and engineer. But this . . . is so much worse." He put the pan back on the fire after flipping the whole contents of the pan over in the air.

"Engineer, I've told you before, the king is not possessed by evil spirits, he is just broken of spirit," the Blue Knight came out of their tent behind the engineer and immediately turned toward the counselor's tent. Holding a hand out toward the engineer he stopped at the tent's doorway and said, "Madam Counselor may I offer my assistance?"

"Yes Rupert." Her voice as always was pleasant, but she sounded tired. She and the Blue Knight had stayed up most of the night talking, but her weariness wasn't from lack of sleep.

The Blue Knight entered her tent and soft words could be heard, then silence. Simon turned to Gerald and mimed a kiss, puckering his lips dramatically, causing Gerald to let out a laugh which he immediately stifled with one hand.

The Blue Knight exited the tent with the Head Counselor in his arms. This morning she rested her head upon the Blue Knight's shoulder and her eyes were closed. The engineer hurried over to ready her chair and grabbed a blanket which he laid gently over her shoulders once she was settled in her chair.

The Head Counselor pulled the blanket around her more tightly and smiled at the engineer, "Thank you Mud." The engineer bowed deeply and dropped into his place by the fire. She looked up to the Blue Knight and extended a hand, which he took immediately. "Rupert, don't worry. My body sometimes betrays my spirit. I'll be okay."

The Blue Knight dropped to sit beside her and kissed her hand. "I'm sorry, my heart." All pretense gone. "I don't want to lose you now that I've found you."

She stroked his cheek fondly, "I like your stubble, it's so soft." He leaned into her hand.

Chief Engineer Mud cleared his throat speaking far louder than needed. "Simon, as always a bright fire and hot fast break," reaching for the plate of eggs and bacon he was offered.

Simon held out a plate to the Blue Knight and Head Counselor, both finally aware of others around them. "Gerald is joining us this morn. The Green Knight has already returned to the castle." He handed Gerald the last plate taking the bowl for himself. He passed out the mugs and pulled the water off the fire. Swallowing a bite he said, "I was out of tea, you'll have to steep your own, if you have any." He poured himself a full mug of steaming water, set it beside himself and pushed the pot toward Gerald.

"Gerald, good morning." The Blue Knight smiled warmly in his direction. "The Green Knight has a task ahead of him. But he is the right man for the job." He took a bite of food then took the pot and filled his and the counselor's mugs before passing the pot on. "He'll have to draw on all his experience as a father. I think that is the only way to reach the King now, by family, or some semblance thereof." He took another bite and then looked at the Head Counselor who hadn't eaten anything yet, a look of concern filling his face.

Seeing the Blue Knight's concern, the Head Counselor picked up her spoon and took a reasonable bite. "Hmm, Simon, you are a good cook. I think these are the best eggs I've ever tasted," she took another bite and indicated to the Blue Knight to go on with his own meal. The Blue Knight hesitated only a moment before taking a big bite, smiled, eggs and bacon showing in his teeth. "Honestly, Rupert! Exactly how old are you?" The Blue Knight kept smiling until she took another bite. Only then did he close his lips and clean off his face, returning to be the well-mannered knight.

Again the Chief Engineer cleared his throat, "Honestly you two are worse than adolescents." He snorted and eggs went flying across the fire and struck Gerald in the chest. The engineer jumped up and rushed to Gerald. "No ill will sir, my pardons! I'm so sorry. I . . ."

Gerald finished wiping the eggs from his jacket and lifted a hand to the stammering engineer, "No harm friend, be still. No offense taken." He smiled broadly, "if you hadn't been so upset I'd probably be laughing right now." Still the engineer offered apologies. "Chief Engineer, far worse has befallen me, for less cause. Be at peace."

Softly the Head Counselor said, "Mud, sit down and finish. We are all equals here."

Gerald's head turned quickly to look at the Head Counselor. Puzzled he asked, "Head Counselor, may I ask a question?" She nodded. "Why did you say, I mean I think it true, but why did you say, we are all equals here?" The look on his face and the tone of his voice made it clear that it was only understanding he sought and there was no offense taken.

The Head Counselor smiled at Gerald, took a moment to adjust the blanket on her shoulders while the engineer finally resumed his seat, still embarrassed and swallowing down more apologies. Looking from the Chief Engineer to Gerald, she spoke softly but with authority, "In your world Gerald, we," she waved a hand toward the engineer and herself, "are not even considered people."

The Blue Knight started to speak but she silenced him with a soft touch. "But here, with the knights," she smiled warmly at the Blue Knight, "here we are not only people, but treated as equals, a rare and unfamiliar occurrence. It is hard not to worry that we cause offense by any of our actions." She looked at the engineer whose head was hung, "Much less spitting food on a knight's son like Mud just did."

The Chief Engineer jumped up and began apologizing again.

"Mud, I jest. Peace Chief Engineer." Her voice altered slightly into the Head Counselor, leader of her people, and the Chief Engineer stilled.

Gerald took that moment to throw his last piece of bacon at the engineer hitting him in the cheek where it stuck in the stubble the Chief Engineer proudly called his beard.

Everyone was dumbfounded. After a few long moments the Chief Engineer took the piece of bacon from his face and popped it in his mouth. "Aah, just what I wanted to finish my meal. I was a little *short* on bacon."

Another momentary silence, then they all burst into laughter, drawing stares from the other camps which were all stirring now. When calm finally came, Simon gathered the plates and cleaned them with a bit of sand and water. The Chief Engineer added another log to the fire, heightening the warmth.

The Blue Knight made sure the Head Counselor was comfortable then turned his full attention to Gerald. "Can you share the plan?"

Gerald balked a little under his stare. He was always amazed at how regular men, people he corrected himself thinking of the White Knight and Head Counselor, became knights or people of authority merely by a slight altering of their presence. For many this may have been intimidating, but for Gerald it was reassuring. In his heart, he trusted those who were knights, he trusted his father. If the knights chose to stand by the king and kingdom, there was hope. He took a breath and told the short of the tale.

All four listened closely and nodded approval of Gerald's return to the Green Knight's lands for management and the Green Knight's return to the king and castle. They expressed surprise that the Green Knight had called his captain of the guard but considered it thoughtfully. They waited with bated breath for more, but Gerald had nothing to offer.

When the Blue Knight was sure Gerald had nothing more to say he rose, closed his hand into a fist, laid it upon his heart. "By my oath and honor as the Blue Knight, I will safeguard our kingdom and return." They all looked at him, saying nothing. After several more moments of silence the Blue Knight sat down. More time of quiet reflection passed.

Chapter Four
THE BLUE KNIGHT, HEAD COUNSELOR, AND MAN WITH THE AURA OF GREEN

Finally the mood lightened, just a bit, the Head Counselor laid her palm on the Blue Knight's cheek.

"Have I ever told you how sexy you are when you get all knight...y?" She gave him a smile that melted him in place.

When he gathered his aplomb he said, "Um, that's not very counselo...ry of you to say." But everything about him, from the blush on his cheeks to the quaver in his voice told everyone he was touched by her comment and deeply moved for being called a sexy knight by the woman he adored.

"Sorry, love, I couldn't resist." She smiled warmly, disarming everyone now, "It's too soon to get serious. We have a lot of work to do and need to include the Red and White Knight." She looked around, then toward the Red Knight's camp, "I think they are ready for early morning visitors."

Simon rose, "I'll go talk to the Red Knight."

Gerald was already up and turning, "I'll go talk to the White Knight."

The Blue Knight pointed to the communal fire, "We'll meet there shortly."

Both nodded and strode away with purpose. The Blue Knight looked from Chief Engineer to Head Counselor. "Is it fair to ask you to stay?" He kept his focus on the Chief Engineer because he knew his eyes would be pleading for the Head Counselor to stay if he looked her way.

Chief Engineer stood, all of his three feet six inches emanating a formal nature, "Sir Knight, it is with regret that I must return. I have many who are accountable to me and it is my . . ." Here he hesitated searching for the right words, "honor, to maintain and continue to expand the road you helped build."

The Blue Knight remained seated and reached out to grasp the arm of the engineer with his own waiting for the engineer to do the same. Slowly the smaller man firmly grasped the arm of the Blue Knight, easing up his grasp as he noticed the knight wince. The Chief Engineer smiled warmly. "I've never knight fasted." He shook their arms just a bit. "Guess I don't know my own strength."

The Blue Knight tried to remain serious, but the twinkle in his eye always betrayed him. "And I have never knight fasted a Chief Engineer." Both shared a brief smirk before the Blue Knight went on, "I'm sure you are valued at home as much as you are valued here." Each gave a final squeeze and released one another.

The Blue Knight turned toward the Head Counselor, concern crossing his face before he schooled it into an appropriate version of a knight on a mission of great importance. "Head Counselor? What is your intention?" He refrained from touching her because it would have weakened his resolve.

The Head Counselor pulled herself a bit more upright and looked from engineer to knight. "I fear my ambition has been betrayed by my body."

The Blue Knight went up onto one knee, all formality gone. "My lady!"

She gasped as she shifted. "I'm afraid if I undertook the journey home, I would be in need of the man with the aura of green myself." She took a deep breath and tried to give the Blue Knight a brave smile, but no one was fooled.

As if the mere admission of her illness made him manifest, the man with the aura of green appeared around their wagon. As he passed the fire he picked up an unused mug and filled it with the remaining hot water, dipped into a pocket, pulled out a packet of herbs and poured them into the water before kneeling before the Head Counselor. He removed another small, wrapped packet, unfolded it, carefully pulled out one single leaf from the pile. He handed it to the counselor, indicating she should put it in her mouth, which she did without hesitation. As she chewed, her relief and easing of pain was evident to all.

The man with the aura of green stirred the tea. He looked at the Head Counselor and shook his head in a chiding manner. "You wait too long."

She smiled, sincerely, "I missed you."

He chuffed and handed her the mug. "All of it now." His voice was gentle, and his look concerned, but she knew he was not to be ignored.

She blew across the tea and sipped cautiously, then grimaced.

The man with the aura of green's look was unflinching, "All."

She shrugged and the blanket fell off her shoulders, which the Blue Knight jumped up to replace immediately, tucking her in more snugly and kissing the top of her head before returning to his seat beside her. She grimaced again but drank the rest of the tea down.

The man with the aura of green swiped his finger in the air as if he was wiping the inside of a mug.

Head Counselor sighed and followed his action, wiping the remaining herbs up with her finger and into her mouth. She shivered from head to toe, not cold or pain, but in reaction to the foul taste of the herbs. When she had recovered enough to speak she said, "You could add some mint or something to make it less repulsive!"

The corner of one side of the man with the aura of green's mouth quirked up and his eyes twinkled. Whatever he was thinking he kept to himself. He pulled out another larger packet and handed it to her. When she took it from his hand three fingers went up.

"Three more times?" her voice hopeful but knowing.

He made a circle with a finger and thumb and moved like the sun moving from sunrise to sunset.

"Three times a day," now her voice was resigned, "how many days?"

A full hand was held up, fingers spread.

She groaned, "FIVE days!" She looked to the Chief Engineer who shook his head and took a step back, clearly saying without words: Don't look at me, I'm not getting involved. She sighed and looked to the Blue Knight, who smiled warmly, nodded in support and affirmed the instructions given. "Men," she said but with no enthusiasm. She looked back to the man with the aura of green. "May I have another pain leaf? I promise to use it only if I need it!"

He looked at her for a long moment, withdrew another leaf and handed it to the Blue Knight. "Don't let her wait so long." He watched the Blue Knight as he searched for a safe place to store the precious herb and observed the counselor watching *her* knight. He carefully refolded the packet and placed it in his pocket.

The man with the aura of green stood and moved to the back of the Head Counselor's chair, rubbed both hands together vigorously and then slid them down her back, pressing the heel of his hands into the small of her back and down her hips. Involuntarily the Head Counselor groaned then bit her lip, she endured several more rubdowns before she released her lip and sighed with relief.

The man with the aura of green stepped to one side and indicated to the Blue Knight that he should take his place. Together they went through the hand rubbing and the massage motions on the counselor's back before he was allowed to touch her. Not until the knight felt the counselor relax and lean into his hands did the healer indicate he could stop.

The Blue Knight left his hands against the counselor's back and leaned down to lay his lips upon her head. "My love," his breath puffed lightly against her hair. Her eyes were closed as she leaned against him with an intimacy reserved for lovers.

After a few moments she leaned forward, "Thank you, both of you." She looked over one shoulder at the man with the aura of green and the other at her Blue Knight.

"How many times a day should I do this?" the Blue Knight asked. The healer raised three fingers. "Three times a day?" A nod. "Before or after the tea?" The counselor shivered involuntarily and both men smiled.

"After." The man with the aura of green laid his hand upon the Blue Knight's shoulder and waited until their eyes locked. "Take care of her." It was said softly but with such conviction that the Blue Knight knew if he did not take care of the counselor properly, he *would be* accountable to the man with the aura of green. He nodded and fisted his hand against his heart in a silent but irrevocable commitment. As quickly as he had appeared, the man with the aura of green slipped around a tent and was gone.

Chapter Five
BLUE KNIGHT, HEAD COUNSELOR, WHITE KNIGHT

After several quiet moments, "He's gone isn't he?" It wasn't really a question, but the Head Counselor knew they needed something to break the trance the man with the aura of green always left on those he healed and met. The Blue Knight and Chief Engineer nodded.

"So for now, you're with me." The Blue Knight tried not to let too much happiness coat his voice. He leaned down to look into her face and he stole a kiss.

"You're incorrigible! You know that?" she said with a smile.

He kissed her longer and more passionately until the Chief Engineer cleared his throat again, saying LOUDLY. "I'd tell you to get hand fasted and get on with it, but we don't have time for that right now." The Chief Engineer turned away in false disgust, a smile crossing his face as he walked back into the tent, that for now, he still shared with the Blue Knight.

The Blue Knight and Head Counselor looked at each other for long moments. Just as he was about to speak, she lifted two fingers and laid them upon his lips. "Rupert, now is not the time," she said softly.

"Who knows when it will be time. Our whole world is about to be turned upside down." He looked searchingly into her face. "Your world may no longer be safe." She gritted her teeth but did not look away. "Why not now?" He went down on one knee and took one of her hands in both of his.

She shook her head no. "Rupert" He held onto her hand and eyes. More softly she said again, "Rupert" this time reaching up with her free hand to stroke his face. Once more, lovingly she said, "Rupert."

A female voice from behind them startled them both. "You two make a cute couple. A wedding might be the right way to start a new world." The White Knight smiled, no hint of humor or mocking in her voice. "You could do a simple hand fast now and a proper celebration later . . . when things get sorted out." She took a step forward and lowered her voice, "But for this morn, we all need to join and share details of each other's courses ahead." She leaned in even closer, "When we're done, I'll hand fast you myself with my husband as witness." Both started at her offer. "Just don't scandalize Simon too much on the way home." She smiled wickedly and straightened. "Come now, we have a kingdom to save." She turned on her heel and walked to the communal fire, back straight, face sober, only a slight upturn of her lips and the wink she gave her husband as she passed by hinting at anything but the seriousness of their situation.

Chapter Six
THE RED KNIGHT & DESERT FOLK

The Red Knight's camp seemed to be waking slowly this morning. Two women were walking among the animals, making sure they were watered, fed and healthy. They stroked the animals and hummed softly, in perfect harmony. Occasionally one would alter the melody and grin widely as the other harmonized without hesitation.

The women, wives of the Red Knight and Hmway seemed to be bound together by some long-lost ties or family relations. Although one was dark and one pale, one was tall and one short, one was thin and one plump, one had thick curly hair and one fine straight hair, when they smiled or sang you could not tell them apart, except when they made harmony. Which united them even more.

After they had finished with the animals they joined the others at the fire. Hmway handed his wife a bowl of porridge with nuts and berries and a mug of mint tea. The Red Knight handed his wife a plate of eggs, bacon, a warm yeast roll and a mug of mint tea. They sat down in unison, clinked their mugs and dug in. Hmway rubbed his eyes sleepily, even his morning hum was drowsy and lacking its usual joy.

"Understand kingdom politics now?" his wife asked smiling sweetly. His hummed response was dejected at best and sorrowful at worst. She picked up his bowl and handed it to him, encouraging him to eat. "You'll feel better." He took her hand, bowl and all, and brought it to his lips giving it a kiss before taking the bowl.

"You always heal my soul, even if you can't heal my aching head," his low voice rumbled. Now his hum was a bit more uplifting and his strong smile began to show.

"Hun, stop stirring the fire. You made a lovely fast break for us. You should eat too." The Red Knight's wife held out his plate.

The Red Knight reached out and wrapped an arm around his wife. "You could not take better care of me dearest," he paused and smiled, "unless I was a horse, then ufffff." He withdrew his arm and grasped his side where his wife had planted a swift elbow at the horse comment. "That was a compliment to the horse you know," he groaned.

She leaned in and kissed him lightly on the cheek. "I know, I just couldn't resist!" Then she dug in with earnest, finishing her food quickly and looking for more.

"We have good fortune. Hmway and Allayu are going to stay with us." The Red Knight dished the remaining food onto his wife's plate. "I think their way of caretaking and working together without a king could give us a different way to move forward with the coming changes." He looked toward Hmway hopefully.

The women looked at each other, something unspoken passing between them.

The men rose. "We need to join the others at the communal fire and share our plans." Both extended a hand to their wives, drawing them up. Arm in arm they headed toward the others.

Chapter Seven
COMMUNAL FIRE

As if a silent bell had rung, all the knights and their parties gathered at the communal fire. The three remaining knights stood together waiting for all to settle in.

"As you may all already know, the King is alive but not of right mind at this moment. The Princess has been taken by the man with the aura of green. We assume for healing. He left King Nicholas with instructions to heal himself before the Princess could return." The White Knight finished speaking and looked to the Red Knight.

"The King's troops have been divided and have left the castle. We fear that the generals may have plans that will not benefit the kingdom. So not only the king is at risk, but so is the kingdom." The Red Knight turned to the Blue Knight.

"Ummm," the Blue Knight cleared his throat, "We, the Knights of the Kingdom, believe that our world is at a point of change." He looked toward the other two knights, who both nodded. "We think that we need to play a role in the changes and the world to come . . ." He looked at the Head Counselor and Chief Engineer and then seemed to lose his way.

The White Knight spoke up smoothly, "And we would like all of you to assist us." She placed an open palm on her chest. "I have been changed for the better, by knowing all of you and meeting new friends. I think together we can make a better kingdom," she hesitated, "for all of us - Those now part of the kingdom and those who've always been excluded."

Each knight seemed to stand a bit taller and slowly made eye contact with everyone present. One by one everyone rose.

28

"I think I speak for all present," the Head Counselor looked around the group and received smiles and nods, "you, the Kingdom's Knights, have shown us what the people of this kingdom can be. If we can help all the kingdom's people to act, think and believe as you do, we join you without hesitation."

A Brief Interlude

The storyteller paused, took a long, draught of her warming ale and looked around, observing her listeners, and contemplating. "Before I can go on telling you about the knights and what they did to try and save the kingdom, we have to go back in time. Let me tell you how the generals, who deserted the castle, came to be there in the first place. And how the evil found its way into the kingdom."

~~~

For many long and fruitful years, the kingdom had operated with more success than failure. There had been no threat from without because they were surrounded by frozen land to the north, desert to the south, ocean to the west, and a vast wilderness to the east that few crossed willingly.

Now their greatest threat was an evil growing within. It had come hidden in seemingly good actions that actually came from ill will. It spread insidiously, infecting the unwary or weak of heart. It posed even a greater threat than the two wayward generals.

The two generals who had left their posts in the king's castle had very different motivations for doing so. Although one said what people wanted to hear his intention was hidden and self-serving. The other spoke from truth from his heart. Superficially the reasoning from both sounded the same. Both men had earned their posts by protecting the kingdom from danger and threat. Yet even those paths were guided by different motivations and actions.

Chapter Eight
GENERAL CONRAD BEAR
(CONNIE TO THOSE WHO KNEW HIM BEST)

General Bear grew up in the farmlands where his family had lived for generations. When bandits from the east started hijacking caravans bound for market or the king's castle, Conrad and some of his like-minded friends began providing protection for the caravans. Conrad was wise beyond his years and he found a way to harness the wild energies of young men frustrated by a life of hard work and little adventure.

Many years ago Conrad had been returning from the market with one of the king's soldiers. They were discussing a soldier's life and the training needed when five bandits set upon them and demanded the coin received for their goods plus any food that remained. Conrad's inclination was to talk them away from their plans and find a compromise.

The two leaders seemed to be listening while three moved to the back of the wagon to see what they could find. Unfortunately for them, they found the soldier lying in wait. You see, he had fallen back off the bench into the bed of the wagon when he saw the bandits. He lay still and soundless, pretending to have fainted in fear when the bandits fell upon them. Before a cry could be heard or a warning sounded, all three thieves lay dead and the soldier stood before the remaining two, his sword bloodied.

Conrad took that moment to lash out with his whip, catching one bandit across the face. At the snap of the whip the soldier struck and the other bandit lay dying. The whipped bandit turned to run. Conrad cracked his whip again, catching him around the knees and toppling him face-first into the dirt. The soldier was upon him quickly. He asked a few questions that received no answer. The soldier made him only one offer, "Answer or die." The bandit chose death.

"Did you have to kill them?" Conrad asked, still thinking he could have talked the bandits into letting them leave with some of their money and goods.

"Yes," the soldier said without hesitation or emotion and with no opening for further discussion.

The remainder of the journey was quiet. Little of the lively conversation that had preceded the encounter returned. Conrad finally spoke before leaving the soldier off at the livery, for he had come to buy a horse.

"How long did it take you to train so you could fight like you did against the bandits?"

The soldier stayed beside Conrad in the wagon as they halted before the livery. "I've trained for many years," he replied. Seeing Conrad's crestfallen expression he hurried on, "But I learned my basic skills in about three months of constant practice under hard taskmasters who weren't afraid to put you down if you started getting cocky."

Conrad pondered, not sure how to ask his next question. "Must you become, or commit to becoming, a soldier to get such training?"

Slapping Conrad upon the back, the soldier asked, "Ah lad, you looking to become a military man?"

"No, no." Again Conrad hesitated, "I just need some training. It's not the first time I've encountered bandits. With you and your sword, this was an easier outcome." He paused but his own moral standards made him continue. "I would like it to have been accomplished without everyone dying though."

"Ah," the soldier stroked his chin. He looked thoughtfully at Conrad, contemplating the boy's character and commitment. "Would it just be you wanting to learn some," here he picked his words carefully, "defensive skills?"

"Nay, sir. I think most all the young lads, some of the older men, and maybe even a few lasses would like to be able to protect themselves." Conrad looked at the soldier hopefully. "Do you know how or where we might get some training?"

"Have you spoken to others about this?"

"Aye, sir. My father, who owns the livery," he pointed to the man now exiting the building and coming toward them, "and some of the farmers I haul for when they need me."

Jumping agilely down from the wagon bench, the soldier extended a hand to Conrad's father. "Well met. I seek a horse and am told you have some of the best stock around."

Conrad's father shook the extended hand firmly, nodding, "Aye, tis true."

"I also understand that you may be seeking a teacher of the defensive arts."

Conrad's father looked at Conrad then back to the soldier. "Aye, tis also true."

"Then my friend, let us see if we can strike a deal." The soldier laid a hand upon the man's shoulder, motioned for Conrad to join them, and soon the deal was done.

For three months, in the dead of winter, when the fields lay fallow and cabin fever soon encroached, the soldier would return to the village and train all who came in the defensive arts. This continued for three years in exchange for one of the village's finest battle steeds and, if he succeeded in outliving the horse, its replacement.

So it began the first winter only young men of Conrad's age (and selection) trained, with ongoing practice through spring and summer after their field and craft work was done. With these trained men, Conrad formed two groups from alternating farms and trade crafts who now escorted the caravans to and from the market. The price for an escort: a tenth of the total profit taken in either goods or coin and split by the escorts after successful completion of the journey. No success, no payment and never a charge for Conrad's services.

For the most part this was a successful venture. Less and less often were the caravans troubled by bandits. Fewer and fewer escorts or caravan travelers were injured when they did have an encounter. Since payment depended on a successful journey, sometimes the escorts were a little too energetic in their defense of the caravan or drove the caravan harder than necessary to complete the journey. Conrad learned that with any venture there is always a learning curve and not everyone is suited to the task, even if they have the skills.

In the second year, the soldier identified the three or four who, as he called it, had a soldier's leaning and seemed hungry for the fight. After discussion with their parents, he offered them positions in the King's army, effectively removing the threat of most of the unnecessary violence and finding lifelong roles for those ill-suited for farm life or escort duty.

Also in the second year, more of the general populace attended training. Some of the older men and women learned how to use their strength or wits more than the sword. A few of the women showed great promise both with sword and defensive fighting skills, using their wit to create strategies that prevented the need for both. One young woman, named Alexandra barely sixteen, even agreed to spend a year with the soldier's troop to learn more. The soldier, as did others, saw something special in her. Their instincts and faith in the girl were confirmed when she later became the White Knight.

The third year found the whole community gathering for defensive training. More soldiers were found for the King's army. The soldier himself found a wife, a sister of Conrad's, who fought by his side for many years until he met his death, not in battle, but in old age. By this third year, the problem of bandits was all but resolved. The protectors were vigilant and the caravans were profitable. Conrad took his idea and his skills to other parts of the kingdom, offering to set up and train community defense teams where needed.

No longer a boy, Conrad had grown into a bear of a man, with a brave and gentle heart. He was recruited by the same soldier whom he first queried about training several years later to join the King's army. This time he chose the soldier's life, quickly moved up in rank and soon was known as General Bear with responsibility over the castle's army. Where he had dwelt happily until the Princess's unfortunate illness and the King's madness.

Chapter Nine
GENERAL MALLORY (MALICIOUS TO ALL HE TORMENTED)

General Mallory had fought his way to the top. A young man full of violence and anger, he had been given an option at the age of fifteen to join the army or spend the rest of his life in a mine as an indentured servant with little chance of reprieve. He chose the army with such enthusiasm that the judge wondered if he had made an error in judgment.

Mallory came from some of the poorest in the kingdom, a family with no real skills, land or prospects. When his father died when he was ten, he became the man of the family. He supported his six-year-old sister and mother who worked tirelessly at menial tasks for others to keep a roof over their heads and one meal a day on the table. Whether by hook or by crook, Mallory brought home food and occasional trinkets that brought such joy to his mother and sister that he forgot for a moment how he had obtained them - usually by theft or violence.

By the age of twelve he had his own gang that ran roughshod over the city. His gang extorted merchants for protection money, helped facilitate illegal trading of banned goods and, quite by accident, ran the fanciest brothel in the area. At eleven, Mallory had paid for his first sexual experience and the brothel's madam had taken him under her wing. When he saved her from a vicious attack by a client, she named him her heir. Now the Madam lived a life of leisure running the brothel, but no longer working in it. Mallory and his gang were the protection that provided her girls with safety and a steady income from some of the finer gents in the county. He also had set up his mother as cook and his sister as a maid in the brothel, ensuring a better life for them and taking that burden and day-to-day responsibility off his back.

36

But Mallory's anger could not be contained and no matter what his gang or he accomplished, he could not refrain from violence. His time in the army began after he had almost beaten a man to death with the man's own whip because the man tried to stop Mallory from whipping a horse lame just for being poorly shod, underfed and overworked. Both horse and owner died shortly after Mallory left for the army. All three were a loss to no one, except Mallory's gang, which soon came apart without his shrewdness and brutal control.

The army seemed made to handle both Mallory's ferociousness and his keen mind. He learned quickly and worked harder than anyone else in his troop. He also assimilated easily to the army's hierarchy, acknowledging his officers with deference and complete obedience. As he rose in rank, he humiliated or beat those he considered his inferiors into submission. His rise to general was sometimes suspicious, sometimes auspicious, but always carefully orchestrated by Mallory's desire to get to the top and to be in control.

When it had been decided to divide the military troops into the four regions overseen by the knights and the king's castle, some disbursed gladly, some retired, and only a small number remained at the king's castle as the standing army. Mallory managed to influence the king into appointing two generals and dividing his troops into inner and outer guards. No one was surprised by Mallory's shrewd manipulations except Conrad who did not understand the need for double troops or perceive Mallory's true intentions. Likewise, when the princess' illness drove the king to madness, Generals Mallory and Bear's departure from the castle grounds came from very different motivations.

General Bear saw the absence of the knights and the lack of guidance from the King as a breeding ground for trouble. When he proposed taking the army out in small groups to patrol different parts of the country, he saw it as prevention and protection for the kingdom and its citizens.

Mallory took time to digest Bear's proposal. When he had finally crafted a plan that worked to his benefit, he made an alternate proposal. Both generals would take half the troops and set up two bases from which they could send out patrols. Mallory proposed that this would provide more consistent coverage, the ability to mobilize more troops quickly if needed and put less hardship on the citizens required to support the troops. Conrad was quick to see the benefits of spreading their protection wider and putting less stress on the local support. Although leery of Mallory's intentions, he could see no real dangers. How wrong Bear was.

Chapter Ten
PROTECTION? OR SOMETHING ELSE A FOOT

General Bear agreed to protect the lands between the Green and White Knights. This was his homeland; he could readily secure land for the outpost and would be able to provide some of their food and livestock with a little investment of time and coin. In fact, he and his troop were welcomed with open arms. His family helped supply horses and prepare land for crops. His old friends, the soldier and his wife, helped oversee the outpost, led drills, set up mess schedules and cooking assignments, and provided general caretaking.

The impact they had on the surrounding area was immediate and helpful, because it was Bear's philosophy that troops should be independent and able to provide all their own needs. General Bear also believed that if a soldier was not working to protect, he should be working to build up his community. Bear's troops found little to protect against because both the Green and White Knights oversaw their lands with fairness, honor, and a quick response to trouble. Bear's soldiers contributed to the community helping with farming, rebuilding, and other tasks needed in the area. For the first time, in a long time, General Bear, Connie, was home and seriously considering retiring, because the world seemed to be at peace. But alas, that was not to be his near future.

General Mallory and his troops took a more barren, inhospitable area between the Red and Blue Knights' lands, just skirting the edges of the Green Knight's land. He immediately began making demands. He required quarters built by the locals, a fully stocked larder, and when food was scarce, he demanded payment in rubies and sapphires - an unheard of practice because only the king was paid in gemstones.

His soldiers did more harm than good. They drank too much and destroyed property. When they did find criminals or possible activities that could be a threat to the kingdom, they dealt with the individual with such punitive punishment that the purported criminals were rarely seen again. Or the 'soldiers' simply took the stolen goods and added the thieves to their number. Many felt Mallory was trying to set up his own kingdom and raised their voices crying for the return of their Knights and King.

~~~

The Storyteller paused again. Looking at what should be a thinning crowd. She sighed and stretched, "I think that's enough for one night."

An outcry came from the crowd: "Just a little more." "What about the evil?" "Is General Mallory the evil?" "What about the King?" "What about the Princess?" "Where is the man with the aura of green?" "Please we want to hear more!" A slow chant started and gained volume and speed. "More, more, more, More, More, More, MORE, MORE, MORE!"

The Storyteller raised her arms and quieted the chanting. "All right, all right. Just a little about the king's distress over the princess and how he let evil in . . ." She took a breath and scanned the room again before saying, "And then that's it for tonight."

~ ~ ~

Chapter Eleven
THE FALL OF A KING – THE RISE OR EVIL WITHIN

King Nicholas paced back and forth. "How many of these fools do I have to suffer before my daughter is cured?" he yelled at the Minister of Healing kneeling before him. "Why do you continue to bring in these charlatans, thieves, frauds, and men who only do her more harm!" He lashed out with one arm knocking over the stanchion beside his throne.

The Minister flinched as the stanchion fell beside him, a mere breath away from striking his head, but did not rise or move away. "Your m-m-m-majesty, we are searching everywhere. We've even reached out to our neighbors."

The King stopped pacing and looked down upon the man trembling before him. "What did you say?" The coldness in his voice froze everyone in the room.

"My Lord," the man bent even lower to the floor, now fully prostrate. "There is a healer coming from a neighboring kingdom." The man flinched as the king sucked in a breath. "He doesn't know about the Princess." He rushed on then paused, waiting for a blow, but none came. "He is coming to consult on our plans for a hospice and to teach some of our healers-in-training." Again he waited, not knowing if this would be his end or another brutal punishment. His breath came out in shallow gasps as he tried to remain still.

The King began to pace again. *Too much, too much!* he thought. With all his fears for his precious daughter, now he had to worry about another kingdom trying to take over. His mind wandered back to the day he'd come to this kingdom. He'd been apprenticed to the Green Knight. He smiled briefly recalling how good it had been to be part of the family: the Green Knight, his wife and son. Together they'd worked the land and grew crops that they sold at Center Town. That's where he'd met his wife, the Princess Ivy. A tear fell as he felt the surge of love for her and the joy their life had been until . . . until his daughter was born. He had anticipated such joy at becoming a father. His anger rose again because he remembered his father - his cruelty and greed. Someone who saw his son as merely another piece of property to barter with to use for his own purposes. *NO! I will not let my people be used like that!* His people, this kingdom, he couldn't let them be subject to that evil king, even this sorry man before him, he was still one of *his* people. He couldn't let this happen! He paced faster and faster as his mind and thoughts spun out of control.

"Sire?"

The King stopped pacing before the man again. "From where?" His voice chilled the air.

"Kurdusk, Sire." The man dared to get onto his knees, head still deeply bowed. "He and his entourage should be here within the week Sire." He dared to lift his head slightly. "Then, perhaps, the Princess will be healed."

The King lifted a foot and set it upon the man's shoulder. The minister slumped down slightly. The King pressed a little harder and the minister was again prostrate. "Never, NEVER," he paused to make sure he was clearly understood and to regain his calm, "act without my direction or permission." He barely resisted the urge to press harder and hurt the man. "Do you understand Minister?"

Everyone in the room could see the Minister breathing hard, sobbing? "Yes, My Lord."

The King removed his foot and stood surveying the crowd of ministers, soldiers, courtiers, servants and gawkers. "If you have no purpose here, leave!" He watched people scurry out of his sight, which decreased the numbers by almost half. "Ministers and soldiers prepare the Castle; we have foreign visitors arriving." That left the room barren save a few servants who bowed low and took up the tasks that had been interrupted by the Minister's announcement.

Ruby, the Head Cook, approached the King with a platter of fruit, warm bread and tea. She sat it on the small table beside his throne and waited. The King looked at Ruby and away, not acknowledging her. Ruby continued to wait.

Without looking he said quietly, "What is it Ruby?"

"You need to eat."

"And who are you to direct the King?" He spoke without force.

"Your Head Cook."

Now he turned toward the old woman who stood still but with ultimate confidence in her position and her request. For several long moments they stared at one another. Then the King reached out and tore off a chunk of the warm bread, picked up the tea, ate and drank. Ruby smiled, bowed slightly and left his side, disappearing. The King sat down and took another bite of bread and sip of tea. He picked up the apple and took a bite of the crispy, juicy flesh. Under his breath he murmured, "Some king, taking orders from his cook."

Ruby stood behind the tapestry next to the throne, listening. She snorted softly when she heard the King's comment and turned to go down the hidden staircase that led to the kitchen. "A good king, if you heed," she said softly.

One of the other servants in the kitchen heard Ruby's comment as she entered and asked, "What's that Head Cook?"

Ruby waved her off then clapped her hands. "Everyone, we need to prepare for royal guests from another kingdom." Pointing

44

to two of the younger girls, "You two, get some more fruit from the garden." Pointing at the man bringing in firewood, "You, down to the stores, I need at least two bushels of grain." Looking around to find another person to assign a task, "You, find our butcher. We need half a cow, no, let's start with a lamb." Slapping the table in the center of the kitchen, she said, "Vegetables. Lots of vegetables!"

Meanwhile, the King had gone to his daughter's room. The Princess lay on clean linen, a low and warm fire burning, aromatic fresh flowers on the table beside her. His chair sat beside her bed, a full pitcher of water and two glasses beside the flowers. He poured water into both and sat. Lifting one toward his sleeping daughter he asked, "Thirsty, my precious one?" He held out the glass waiting, waiting as he had done for months, for his daughter to reach out and take it from him.

Slowly he set the glass down and took the other, rolling it between his hands. Head bowed he began to speak, relaying the events of the day to his daughter, asking her questions that remained unanswered, waiting for her laughter, tears, or any response, any at all. And, as he had done for so many nights, he draped one arm over her form and folded the other beside her, then laid his head down and slept.

Chapter Twelve
THE MAGICIAN

The Magician and his entourage had been encamped on the Green Knight's Forest lands for many months. Since the Green Knight's wife had died, his lands and people had received little attention which had allowed the Magician's group to move in. He had been ensconced before the knights were sent out to find the man with the aura of green. He'd had time to send out scouts to various parts of the kingdom, searching for something, anything, that would give him an opportunity to gain wealth, influence and power. He had been tasked with discovering a way to end the current king's reign.

The Magician had been hired by the father of King Nicholas. A father who had his own kingdom, but now wanted to annex these lands and all the wealth therein for his own use. The Magician had endured many long hours listening to his employer bemoaning his fate, the injustice of the world, on and on. His oldest son had proved to be a wastrel, unfit to take on the throne, and worse – seemed to be set upon the destruction of his father's kingdom by inciting wars with neighboring kingdoms. Time and time again, the king had interceded to prevent a war or cover a crime, finally sequestering his son in the northern lands in an attempt to end the needless conflicts he had caused. The Magician knew that he had seriously considered having his son killed, but even that king's petty little heart hadn't shrunk that much.

That king had told him that he'd married off his third son to this kingdom, hoping to make a treaty with them. But the Magician knew the truth. He had sold his son into indentured servanthood to the Green Knight. Instead, the Green Knight had made Nicholas an apprentice and part of his family. When his son, now a man, had met and eventually married Princess Ivy of this kingdom they had been living contentedly far away from him. Over the years father and son had reunited occasionally when treaties needed renewing, but the relationship between son and father was nothing more than a historical fact used to cement or prevent current conflicts. There was no love lost between them.

The Magician's employer had thought it was the wisest move to remove the problems before they began. He banished his oldest son, sold his third son to the Green Knight, and was now grooming his second son as his heir. Little had he known that *the third* son was the cream of the crop who'd rise to the top. First as a shrewd farmer, then as a businessman. When Fate moved and he met and fell in love with the king's daughter Ivy, everyone was surprised their love match was also a ruling match; Nicholas was part of a royal ruling family. His business acumen was matched by his wife's compassion and insightfulness. Together it was an excellent match for ruling a kingdom. When they assumed the throne together, their kingdom had thrived. They ruled with justice and vision, thwarting the traditions of class and wealth. Creating a kingdom not based solely on class and privilege, but on the common good of all. Their kingdom had been known for its innovation and care for the masses with healing, training, and basic necessities for all.

Then tragedy struck. The queen had died in childbirth. The light in his life had gone out with the death of his wife. The king lost his center. His love for his daughter was unmistakable. But without the compassion his wife had provided, the darkness in his heart led him to make black and white judgments favoring punishment rather than justice. Innovation and new ideas were quashed. When his daughter became ill, all the healing arts became focused only on his daughter.

The Magician sighed, rolled his neck and stretched. He knew he could abandon his assignment. He was far enough from the king who had hired him. It would be easy to leave his employer's designs far behind because he had an agenda of his own. If this kingdom was as seriously compromised as had been implied, then it was ripe for the picking. Why shouldn't he take this opportunity for himself? He could make this his own kingdom. He knew all the weaknesses of his employer's kingdom. He knew he could not overturn the petty politics of class which still ruled within it. Once he'd ensconced himself in this kingdom's court, he'd ferret out its weaknesses and then... maybe he'd make it his own.

Anyone watching the Magician would have thought he was conversing with someone because he cocked his head slightly to one side and smiled with a single turned-up lip. His thoughts shifted, as the new ruler he could negotiate with the man who would be his former employer. Instead of annexation, he would keep the kingdom and make a new treaty with himself as king. His smile widened. Did he want to be "KING?" His smile turned shrewd. Yes, yes he did! He rose and slapped his hands together. "Devin, it's time to stop lurking in the trees and meet the King!"

The next few days saw a flurry of activity in the camp. Not only had the Magician sent out messengers to gather his people back to him, but his entourage was being transformed into a magic traveling show with a side of royal healing powers. He was always pleased when the theatrical side of his crew came out. His people seemed to flourish under the spotlights. They enjoyed showing off talents rarely used, or desired, in day-to-day existence. He paid well and his people, he was sure, would do almost anything he asked of them. He was not inclined toward violence or killing, but he didn't have a problem inciting either in others. In fact, it was a specialty of his.

Chapter Thirteen
BECOMING A ROYAL ENTOURAGE

The Magician walked among the wagons. Stopping frequently to chat with people, reinforcing the story: "We are a group of healers from Kurdusk, here to help train healers and open a hospice. We bring the entertainment with us to ease the spirit of the sick and lighten the weight of illness and despair. We need to gain trust. We can't place the blame on the king, even though we all know he's responsible for this turn of misfortune in their kingdom. If all goes well, we can move into the King's court and become his most trusted advisors. Then will have the freedom to act and the king will get credit for all our good works." He smiled, a bit wickedly.

He knew much more about the situation than he shared. He knew all the upheaval revolved around the King's sick daughter and that she'd been sick for many months. The King was becoming unhinged. After the death of his wife, it was only a matter of time, but now, if he lost his daughter too, it would unravel more quickly. Without a king to lead, there was only despair and doom ahead for this kingdom.

~~~

The Magician also wondered where the man with the aura of green was. He was sure he could have healed the princess. Why hadn't he? Had he even come? Would he, could he, interfere with his plans? Most often the man with the aura of green healed the body. But the Magician knew that he also healed the soul. It was a slower, deeper healing that most failed to recognize. Those who failed to open themselves also to this spiritual healing, never really healed physically. There was always some remnant of their physical injury - A limp, a restricted function in the damaged area, something that always reminded them of their injury. But those who embraced the totality of the healing the man with the aura of green offered, healed completely – body and soul, regardless of physical damage done.

This always puzzled him. When he had been healed by the man with the aura of green as a child while his family was trading here in this kingdom. His innocence allowed him to embrace the healing fully and he bore no scars, either external or internal. It frustrated him now, because no matter how much of the healing arts he learned, how many magical tricks he mastered, it seemed he never again could touch that part of his soul. The soul that was pure. The soul that longed for love. The soul that did not strive to destroy. The soul that didn't see a lack or void, only abundance. The soul that did not desire to steal from those who had what he didn't.

As he moved through his camp, the germinated seed of unhappiness and discontent began to grow.

He snapped at a few workers hanging drapes, then paused to take a deep breath, and apologized. "Remember, we are a *Royal* caravan. Sent by our kingdom as representatives and honored healers. If we need new drapes, get them. Money is not an object in this campaign." He turned to leave, then turned back, speaking with his most solicitous smile and sweetest voice. "BUT, waste not, if the coin spent does not go to our greater goal." He faced all the workers with steely cold eyes. He made eye contact with each one before he went on, all sweetness gone, "I will get reimbursed from those who wasted the coin." He paused long enough to make sure his true intention sunk in. Then he brightened his smile and voice. "Go on, get the new drapes and some carpets. Oh, and some more royal crests of Kurdusk. That *is* our home country." He winked and strode away.

When he returned to his own vardo, he was surprised to find a visitor. The man with the aura of green sat just inside his door, unseen until he spoke.

"Devin."

The Magician was startled but after years of practice, showed only slight surprise and opted to react with outrage at the intrusion rather than pleasure. "Do you always let yourself into people's private residences?".

"Yes."

Despite thinking he'd gotten the higher position, this took him aback. He started to speak but stopped himself until he could re-establish his power, at least in his own head.

The man with the aura of green waited, but not long enough for Devin to regain his aplomb. "Don't do this."

Again, the Magician was put off balance and before he could prevent himself, he spoke, "What? Do what?"

The man with the aura of green only looked at him with sadness in his eyes.

"Why are you here?" The Magician spoke in anger, his voice rising. "Who do you think you are?" Now he stood and shook his finger at the man with the aura of green. It was only when he noticed his entourage looking at him that he reclaimed his calm, taking a step back, straightening his clothing as if he'd been in a physical altercation with the man with the aura of green. He looked around and flicked his hand which spoke clearly to all: "Nothing to see here, back to work."

The man with the aura of green rose and stepped out of the wagon. He laid one hand upon the Magician's shoulder, turned and was gone.

It took several minutes before the Magician stopped staring behind the vardo where the man with the aura of green had seemingly disappeared. Finally, he let out a deep shuddering breath. "No," he whispered and entered his vardo shutting the door, but not shutting out the world he was going to change.

Chapter Fourteen
REPORTS OF SPIES

The Magician was not surprised by the network he had established. He knew his business and hired people who could infiltrate and seamlessly become part of any community. As he listened to their reports, he was amazed at how easily it had been to become part of this kingdom. The people were still open and trusting, believing the King and Princess would recover and the kingdom would return to the thriving, positive place it had been before the Queen's death. But he was also aware that this was a good place to live, and it was not due solely to the king or the people's loyalty to their king.

The knights did not "rule" so much as facilitate their people's lives. The knights were well respected, loved even. He doubted that many people would be easily turned away from their Knight. It would be much easier to turn the people in the kingdom away from their king. The knights changed things significantly. Instead of one, he'd have four "kingdoms" to overcome. His plans to work solely within the King's court faded away. The King was no longer the force that served as the foundation for this kingdom. It was the knights. But how do you undermine four separate kingdoms within a kingdom? The knights were the cornerstones of this kingdom. Each loyal to their King but able and already ruling their own lands and peoples. He needed another source of disruption.

Another problem began to manifest within his own camp. They had intentionally settled in the Green Knight's forest lands. After the Green Knight's wife had died he'd stopped paying attention to the fringes of his farmlands and forests. Especially the fringes that bordered other lands where people could come and go invisibly. The forest also protected and provided shelter for those who chose to thwart the norms and rules of the land. He had caught more than one thief attempting to steal from his own camp.

The first time he caught a thief, he'd taken back what was his and let the thief go with only a warning. The second thief left with a broken hand and a warning that the next thief would leave with no hand. This had slowed the attempts, but the people surrounding his entourage were desperate to attain anything they hadn't earned. They felt they were entitled to things they thought they "should" have and felt justified in taking them wherever they found it. The third thief left with no hand. The fourth was never seen again.

He embedded his own people within this disenfranchised group. Their reports were tiresome and troubling because he realized how much of his resources he had to waste on this distraction and dishonesty. But here he also found the other source of disruption he needed. He could take these thieves and plant them within the knight's lands, knowing they would be as bothersome to the knights and their people as they had been to him and his.

The biggest opportunity came quite by surprise. A general in the King's army, encamped at the Castle. General Mallory was not the typical soldier and the more the Magician learned about his past and his current position the more he saw in him as a possible solution. If he could get the general out of the castle, he believed he would be a very useful tool to create an uprising. The Magician even had a forest full of people to send General Mallory's way once he was out of the Castle. People who would love to cause problems, steal, harm, maybe even kill . . . just for the fun of it. It was an added bonus that he would be ridding himself of most of the horde of wasted, wicked, wayward troublemakers tormenting his entourage.

He sighed heavily. On top of everything else, he was surprised to find out that he had lost some of his own to the lure of a "good life" under a knight, particularly the Blue and White Knights. But that was a problem for another day.

Chapter Fifteen
THE MAGICIAN MEETS THE KING AND THE PEOPLE

The Magician approached the Castle with a much smaller caravan than he'd planned. News had come to him during his final preparations that King Nicholas was much more volatile than anyone had anticipated. The stories about what the king had done to the previous healers attempting to cure the Princess curled his toes. There was no reason or rationale in the King. Devin questioned whether or not he should even offer to try to cure the Princess. Playing Magician, hospice founder, and healer trainer might be the safer course, but would it give him intimate access to the King? He needed to find the fine line between professional and confidante that the King would confide in.

His spy in the court reported that, for the most part, all associated with the King were very loyal. However, the Royal Guard was divided. General Bear served at the pleasure of the King and would protect and serve him with his life. General Mallory served the King but his motives were questionable. The spy cautioned that while Mallory might be the best source to incite a downfall, the General could not be trusted.

Devin, the man, questioned whether he wanted to include this man most called General Malicious in his plans. Devin, the Magician, knew this was exactly the sort of person who could become the cause that brought down the kingdom. But what kind of problem would General Malicious then become instead?

They approached the Castle and King dressed in their finest robes, their caravans dressed with royal colors and crests. As they got closer, the Magician sent out some of the performers, jugglers, and sleight of hand artists to prepare the King's people for his arrival. He intentionally placed the healing caravan near the end of the troupe. He would be the last to arrive after the others had introduced themselves and entertained. His interlocutor would be moving through the crowd, testing the attitudes and atmosphere. It was the interlocutor's job to interpret when the mood best suited the Magician's arrival and whether it would be a show or a subtle introduction.

The people of Center Town welcomed the caravan with cheers, laughter and shout-outs for more! As they neared the Castle the mood shifted significantly. Those who were allowed entry into the Castle were reserved and focused. The guards at the gates did not suffer fools or let any mere petitioner enter the gates. After a quick consultation with his interlocutor, it was decided that only the Magician and the Healer's Caravan would approach and try to gain an audience before the King.

Entry into the King's court was a bit chaotic, almost bringing the Magician to strike out, if not physically, but with words of rebuke. "How has this kingdom survived this long operating like THIS!" He mumbled under his breath. He brooded for a few moments and changed out of his fancy finery into a more sedate and serious robe. He took off the elaborate hat and smoothed his hair down, trying to look as serious and credible as possible.

Then, he stood before the King, alone.

The Magician noted carefully who surrounded the King. His personal staff and servants were attentive and wary. The soldiers were of two different ilk: one upright, well put together, with military bearing and responses. The other seemed put-upon, their uniforms untidy, responses and actions lazy. Each wore a patch that represented their unit, a bear for the well-disciplined, a broken sword for the other. It did not take long to identify General Bear and his men versus General Mallory and his. The Magician selected a couple of his men to take some flasks of cheap wine to the barracks to see if they could find someone who would like some drink and conversation.

This might be easier than we anticipated with Mallory onboard, he thought. *Now I have to impress the King.*

Silence descended upon the room slowly, both King and Magician remained still and quiet. When all attention had finally focused on them the Magician bowed slightly, not a formal bow he would have performed in formal court for he sensed something different was needed here.

"Your Highness, I come humbly before you today both as the architect of your new hospice and perhaps the instrument of healing for ... (He refrained from saying- the princess -only at the last moment, somehow sensing it would be the wrong thing to say.) ... those in need." He bowed his head again and kept it lowered, hands tucked in his robe, a solitairy figure offering no threat or ill-will, only a humble man here to serve the King.

The King sat in a huff, slumping and scowling. "From whence do you come?"

"Kurdusk, my liege."

"How do you come to be here, now?" His tone sounding a bit curious, not suspicious.

The Magician took a deep breath as if to start a long and intricate tale. The King raised his hand. "I have not time for stories, speak truth with brevity."

The Magician smiled, but only slightly, having correctly anticipated and manipulated his response. "Of course. Having served my Lord of Kurdusk for many years and with great favor, when the request came for help with a new hospice and training of healers, my Lord asked if I would serve." He waited but the king remained silent. "I agreed readily and truly. Wishing not only to serve but heal as the opportunity presents."

He kept his head up using his peripheral vision to watch those around the king while he waited. The court still contained too many sycophants and wannabes. Only a smaller number of those loyal to King and Kingdom remained. They served with heart as well as body. His thoughts were interrupted when the King finally spoke.

"What do you know of the Princess?"

The Magician considered his words carefully but spoke without hesitation. "As most know, my Lord, she has fallen ill." He paused a moment before continuing, "How fares she? If I may be so bold." This was the real test, would the King answer, answer honestly, or strike out.

The King rose and turned to a few of his counselors, motioning them toward the Magician. "Attend to the hospice. If you succeed and do well, you may have the opportunity to meet her." He strode from the room without another word.

The Magician looked after him, mildly surprised, but satisfied that he had succeeded in his first mission of gaining an inroad into the kingdom. The counselors ushered him out a different passage and into a planning room where conversations about the new hospice and healer training programs could be discussed. Surprisingly, the Magician enjoyed these tasks. He had a clever mind, with an architect's eye, and the ability to assess a situation, quickly finding flaws and strengths. The sun was setting when he was finally dismissed from the room with instructions to return before the fast break in the morning.

When he left the Castle the Magician sent his carriage and people on ahead. He wanted some time alone to think. As he wandered back to where the caravan was encamped, he realized he was being followed. Although the Magician appeared to be a harmless cleric or scholar, he was well armed below his robe and prepared for almost any confrontation. Observing his followers he decided to spend a little more time wandering around Center Town. He hadn't really had the opportunity to look around much during his entry. The town was well laid out around a central square.

Currently, the two rows of canvas shops were closing up. He could see fruits and vegetables being sorted for stew pots or tomorrow's sale. Cloth was being folded and sorted, checked for damage and theft. He saw jewelry, tools, books, children's toys and more. This was a fine market with a good trade. It indicated how well the kingdom was doing. He couldn't be sure until he checked tomorrow, but if there was little scarcity, his task would be harder to accomplish.

Just as he finished his turn around the square and was about to head toward his encamped caravan he was confronted by the three men who had been following him.

"Evenin'," said the first.

"Lost?" asked the second.

The third only laid his hand upon the sword in his belt and smiled.

The Magician took time to examine each and commit their faces to memory, also noting that the two who had spoken had clubs, not swords.

"Evening, gentlemen." He kept his voice relaxed, showing no fear or hesitation. "I'm heading to my camp." He pointed over their shoulders to where he could see his carriage. "I just finished my counsel with the King." He watched them carefully, gauging their reactions. "We've got a job to start in the morn." He did not move, remained relaxed, and waited.

"What be your business?" Asked the first.

"I'm here to build a new hospice and train healers," he responded evenly.

At that, the three exchanged looks and seemed to come to some kind of unspoken conclusion. The second spoke. "When be the new hospice open?"

"Soon, my friend. I think we have the building already." The Magician realized that these men were not criminals, just in need. He continued, "Tomorrow we will put out the word for new healers. Training will be at the King's expense and a promise of work will follow successful completion."

He was surprised at how quickly the demeanor and attitudes of the men changed. Now they were eager, curious, hopeful.

The second man looked at him hopefully. "My wife be a healer," he held up his hands as if in apology, "not like ye, kind sir. Might she be trained?"

"Absolutely!" the Magician replied.

"My son's kinda lost soul, doesn't know what he wants to do. Can he be trained?" The first man asked hesitantly.

The third man's response was completely different. "When will ye heal the people?" He said angrily. He stuck a thumb over his shoulder back towards the Castle. "Rather than just royalty?"

The second man gave him a slight shove.

"Have a care man!" He indicated the Magician. "He works for the King."

The Magician leaned forward, a bit conspiratorially, before answering. "I am a guest of the King, Sirs." He then looked to his left and right before continuing. "The hospice is not in the Castle. There will be," he paused to raise one hand, "Power willing," he tucked his hand back in his robe, "room and money enough for trainees and all successfully trained healers to outfit three if not more hospices."

All three men smiled broadly. "Good on ye then." The first offered.

The second offered a hand which the Magician shook.

The third took a moment to make eye contact. "I will see you soon."

The Magician nodded his head and started toward his carriage, unhindered.

As soon as he entered his carriage, his two strong-armed people asked, "All good Devin?" almost in harmony. Devin did not respond. When the carriage crossed over the imaginary line of his encampment, he tapped the roof indicating he wanted it to stop.

He finally answered his men. "All good boys. Just meeting the neighbors. Mostly good people." He paused and turned away from his own vardo. "Where is the healer's vardo?" One of the men indicated a wagon on the other side of the camp so he headed in that direction.

The elder of the two men spoke out of the side of his mouth to the other. "I think the boss is getting soft."

"Huh?" the other questioned.

"Once upon a time he would have not wasted a breath on men like that." He shook his head in disgust. "He'd have taken them down, quick as a wink, no hesitation."

The younger man looked after the Magician and thought to himself *Is he getting soft? Or wiser?* Out loud he said, "First night mate, first man." As if this explained why the Magician had been so easygoing.

The older man huffed again and strode off. The younger man took one more look toward the Magician and then followed.

Chapter Sixteen
HOSPICE AND HEALERS

The work of creating a new hospice went quickly. Because the Magician's people had been scouting out the kingdom for months, he was also able to make suggestions for two other locations that would serve the people outside Center Town. Both had abandoned buildings that could be repurposed with only minor repairs. Not surprisingly, the healer training program had an overwhelming response. As is always the case, it was immediately evident that about a third of the applicants were unsuited to be healers. Again, the Magician's preparation for this journey allowed him to make connections with local trades and merchants, so he could make suggestions for a different course of trade for those unsuited to healing without making them feel rejected.

Very quickly, the Magician and his team of healers were becoming known and respected. They, via the grace of the King, were creating jobs for builders and tradespeople, in addition to training new healers. Unknown to the King there had been quite a bit of healing going on also. The man with the aura of green had made an appearance at each of the three new hospices. He tended to those who were beyond the training skill of the new healers. He never spoke to Devin directly, but the Magician felt his smile - that slight upward tilt on one side of his mouth - and his approval every time he appeared.

Devin, as he allowed most of the hospice and healing workers to call him now, was beginning to enjoy the routine and consistency of rebuilding the hospices and training new healers. For the first time in his adult life he found the routine pleasurable. He liked having people greet him, offering a smile or kind word. He surprised himself by joining groups after classes for a drink now and then. But when he returned to his camp, he became the Magician again. Respected, feared a bit, alone.

The more time he spent in this kingdom, the more he liked it. He saw what it had been before the King's wife had died and his daughter got sick. He'd even had a brief interaction with the Green Knight's son, Gerald. Another possible problem situation turned positive. The "wranglers", as Gerald had called them, were the discontents who hid within the Green Knight's forest lands. They had been stealing from the emerald mine and lumber fields and taking their loot across the border to trade. It had become a very profitable business. Then they got lazy and got caught.

The Magician had forced these particular wrangers, whom he thought were traders, to alter their routes, to go around his camp, far around. It had taken more than simple conversation or negotiations. He had set up roadblocks and took the goods from the thieves. But the wranglers were slow learners. It took five stops before they altered their route and changed their routine.

Unfortunately, these changes finally alerted the Green Knight's people to what had been happening and Gerald was sent to sort it out. Gerald wasn't really equipped to handle a band of thieves. Gerald's first encounter with the wranglers ended with them leaving with everything they had stolen and Gerald left only with puzzlement. For the second encounter, Gerald was more prepared and confiscated some of the goods, still, the wranglers came out ahead. The third encounter turned violent and that's when the Magician's people interceded. By then the Magician and his caravan had to be formally introduced and explained to Gerald.

The Magician had approached the Green Knight and offered a generous rate for the land the caravan occupied. Gerald had become well-informed about the hospice building and healer training. In fact, the two men found they had quite a lot in common and soon became friends. Friendship was not something Devin had really ever known. This country was becoming a bigger problem than he ever anticipated.

Devin had to get back to the King. The Magician had to make his appearance soon. He had to see if he could do anything for the princess. Devin had to make sure his people were sowing the seeds of discontent within the Castle.

He made a conscious effort to stop attending classes he was not teaching. He also stopped monitoring the hospice building efforts. They were almost finished. All that remained were the final touches: finishing the edges and dedications to the king. "Dedications to the King," he murmured.

"What's that Sir?" A stray worker asked as he passed the Magician.

"Just talking to myself," he chuckled, "at least I'm not arguing with myself and losing."

The man stopped and looked at the Magician. "Sir, you okay? You've been working really hard." With his hand he indicated the camp, "Everyone says so. Is it almost time for the big move?"

The Magician was taken aback by both the acknowledgment of his hard work and the lack of movement on his original plan, for which they had come here. He smiled, "Soon, soon," and proceeded to his trailer.

Chapter Seventeen
MEETING THE PRINCESS

The summons from the King came without warning and only by the luck of the draw was the Magician available and ready immediately. His suspicious nature and the awareness of his true mission here had kept him on his toes. The summons was a mere alteration of his routine, not a disturbance.

As he exited his trailer he found the man with the aura of green waiting for him.

"You can't heal the princess."

"Why do you say that, have you seen her?" Devin asked a bit perturbed at his presence and presumption.

The man with the aura of green did not respond.

"I have a meeting with the King. We've completed the hospice and the healer training is almost over." He straightened his robe, brushing away non-existent stray hairs. When he met the man with the aura of green's eyes, he was mesmerized and couldn't look away.

"Devin, don't put yourself in this position. The princess can't be healed by you." The man with the aura of green laid a hand on Devin's arm. "Please." He lingered a moment longer, then was gone.

Devin, the Magician stood dumbfounded, long after the man with the aura of green left. *Why had he come? What was he trying to tell me? Does the man with the aura of green know why I'm really here?*

If he was due at the Castle in less than half a candlemark, he would have tried to follow and get some answers. But there was no time. "Curse him!" He said out loud and started to move toward the

Castle, stopping to call his aides and the carriage they had arranged for him to present himself to the King. He had to make a good showing. Especially if he was finally going to meet Princess. He had to be THE one who won the King's trust and hopefully begin the Princess' healing.

The Magician was uncharacteristically nervous when he approached the castle. He was used to being the one in control. The one who had all the answers and anticipated all the possibilities long before the first card had been played. But now, with the man with the aura of green telling him there was no possibility of healing the princess, he was off-put before he began.

He took a moment to center himself. The carriage was moving slowly as he'd instructed, so he had a few moments to gather his thoughts and re-evaluate his game plan. First, he would humbly present his progress on the not one but three hospices he had rebuilt. Then he'd discuss the healer training program, which has been a huge success. Enough people had been trained to staff the three hospices, and lay healers had been trained with basic skills, so minor aches and ills could be handled by the people themselves.

He *would not* mention how successfully his people had undermined the confidence of the kingdom's people. Discontent could be sown with a simple question to someone: "Why does HE deserve that?" Or a statement that undermines confidence: "Well, you tried your best, too bad it isn't good enough." They had been planting those little but insidious doubts and encouraging dissent over the mildest slights. Subtly changing the underlying attitude from positive to negative. From hopeful to doubtful. By the time the Knights returned from their quest and to their lands, the seeds were growing and the discontentment was now becoming visible, having moved from internal thoughts to external actions.

He was surprised that it hadn't become more pervasive. The people of this kingdom lived in a positive and uplifting place despite their king's decline. Thank goodness General Mallory existed. He was making this job so much easier.

~~~

The Magician was ushered into the King's Court. It had a much different atmosphere around it now. There were far fewer courtiers; the servants and staff, even fewer, were much more subdued, and the King was volatile. He bowed low.

"Your Highness."

The King and his kingdom were enervated by the constant drain that came from the king's sadness and the evil undertones that the Magician and his people were feeding the people.

The Magician waited.

"Why are you here?" the King asked angrily.

"As you requested, Sire." He took the chance of standing upright. "To continue the good works you commissioned of me."

The King rose and paced. One of the two remaining advisors spoke softly to him. "Ah, the Magician. I hear you've done some good things." The King continued to pace and waved a hand at him, which the Magician took as a directive to continue.

"Thank you, Sire. We have rebuilt three hospices." He paused but got no response from the King so continued. "Our, aah, *your* healer training program has grown. We have been able to staff the three hospices and have many semi-skilled lay healers now." Again he waited.

The King stopped pacing. "Healers?"

"Yes." The Magician responded. Pleased to have finally gotten the king's attention.

68

"You've been training healers?"

"As per your direction, Sire." He tried to sound confident but the king's stance and attitude gave him anything but confidence.

"Why have you been wasting time training when you should have been healing the Princess?" The King turned his full attention to the Magician. His face was red with anger, his clothes disheveled, his hair unkempt. "Why haven't you been healing the princess?"

It was all the Magician could do not to take a step back. He felt physically assaulted by the King's anger and frustration. "My Lord, as you directed, in your wisdom, to prove my skill." He paused, not knowing if he'd be struck, thrown out or allowed to continue. When the king remained silent, he continued. "I come now, humbly, to ask permission to see the Princess. And with the Power's grace and all the skill I possess bring her back to herself." He chose his words carefully. Too many had stood in his place and failed. Some never heard from again, some beaten, some serving in the lowest positions in the castle. He also could not forget what the man with the aura of green had told him: "You can not heal the princess."

Abruptly the king turned and left the room. From the hallway he shouted, "Follow." The Magician rushed to do so.

By the time the Magician reached the Princess' room, the King was already sitting by her bedside, holding her hand. He took a moment to take in the surroundings. The fire, burning brightly but not too hot. The fresh flowers on the table by the bed. A pitcher of cool water with drops of water condensing on the outside. And two glasses.

"Nothing you have done," the King stroked his daughter's hand, "is as important as her."

The Magician remained silent. For the first time really witnessing and comprehending the king's despair and grief.

69

It was a whispered cry, "Please, heal her."

Again the Magician waited, when the king had composed himself he asked, "May I be alone with her to assess her condition Sire?"

After several long moments the king rose and turned to him. "If you harm one hair on her head, place one mark on her body, you will die." He stared the Magician in the eyes, making sure he understood the truth of his statement. "How long do you need?"

"Two candlemarks Sire. That should allow me time to discern what I need to proceed."

The King turned and left without another word. He closed the door softly. Outside he spoke to a guard posted at the door and then was gone.

The Magician sat down beside the Princess and looked very carefully. Visually she was beautiful. Even the months of sleep had not taken away her youthful glow or solid constitution. He leaned closer and sniffed. Many illnesses had their own distinct odor. All he could smell was the lavender soap used on her sheets and sleeping gown, a light floral scent on her skin and hair, and the cedar logs burning in the fire. He stood and circled the room. It was barren and clean. No lingering scents or remnants of something that could be causing her to sleep and not wake.

He shrugged off his robe and opened his bag. He began with all the basic physical measurements. Her breathing, her heartbeats, he looked and smelled her eyes, ears, and mouth. He felt her limbs for coolness, which would indicate that her blood was not flowing, but they were warm and responsive. He was about to roll her over and inspect her back for bites, stinging or scratches that may have let some poison into her system when the door was flung open.

An older woman bustled in with a tray of warm water and a cloth. She turned back to the guard, "I've got ere right, boy. I do this every day!" Then she turned to the person beside her whose arms were bundled full of bedding. "Don't dawdle, I've got things to do." After they were both in the room, she kicked the door shut with a foot and turned to the Magician.

"Devin, correct." It was not a question. "I'm Ruby, Head Cook. I've been taking care of the Princess all her life." She set the tray down on a shelf on the other side of the bed. With one hand she motioned where to put the bedding. "I know who you are." She looked him up and down. "I know what you've been doing." She put up a hand to silence him. "For all the good, you've done something ill too..." She walked around him, looking him up and down, then huffed. "He doesn't look that dangerous to me!"

The Magician had followed her with his eyes. Now he turned because it was evident she wasn't talking to him anymore. The shock would have tumbled a weaker man. Beside Ruby stood the man with the aura of green. He hadn't taken notice of the individual carrying bedding. He reached out, found the chair and eased himself down into it. "W-w-wh-why are you here?" He managed to mumble out.

Ruby gave out a short "Ha" and tapped the man with the aura of green's arm. "You told me he'd be surprised. But I didn't think *this* surprised." She looked the Magician over even more carefully. "So why are you ... "

But the man with the aura of green touched her arm stilling her. "Devin, you can not heal her."

"I, but, there is nothing wrong with her that I can see," the Magician said hurriedly.

"Ruby has provided all the care she needs," he turned and smiled at her and she blushed, "but her healing is not within her or your power."

71

Devin started to rise. "It is not time." Devin sat back down. The man with the aura of green sighed sadly. "You have planted your evil seeds. **It is** time to go. You and your entourage."

Now Devin did stand. "But we've still got healers to train."

The man with the aura of green looked at him with such pity it almost hurt.

"I've done good things for the King and Kingdom." Now he was sounding a bit indignant.

The man with the aura of green shook his head negatively. "And all undone by the evil you've planted."

The Magician persona, not Devin responded. "I have accomplished the rebuilding of three hospices, trained hundreds of healers and lay healers. I have . . ."

The man with the aura of green cut him off with a raised hand. "Undermined all, by the foundation of ill-will and discontent you've sown."

Devin puffed up but could not respond because it was true.

"It's time to go." The man with the aura of green gathered up the bedding and turned to leave.

"Grab your bag and let's go Magician," Ruby said as she picked up the tray. She waited until he had collected his bag and robe and stood before her at the door. "Open it."

Which he did and the three departed the Princess' room.

Two women were waiting outside the room. One immediately took the bedding from the man with the aura of green and departed.

Ruby cocked her head toward the Magician, "Him, out."

The other woman held out an arm for the Magician to follow and took him to a side door which led him out to the courtyard, near his waiting carriage. She waited until he had entered the carriage and the horse began to move before departing.

The Magician sat stunned, speechless. He had to make a decision. Stay or Leave. Return to the Castle or accept the word of the man with the aura of green. By the time he reached his encampment, he had made his decision. He stepped out of the carriage and turned to the first person he saw. "Pack it up. Now! Let everyone know we are gone by nightfall."

The camp immediately jumped into action. Tents fell, were rolled up and stored. Caravans went from homey living quarters to tightly packed moving vans. It was a mere three candlemarks later when everyone stood before their caravan, vardo, trailer, or animal, ready for travel.

Part II

Chapter Eighteen
A NEW BEGINNING

The Blue Knight and Head Counselor sighed deeply and stretched languidly.

"I know I've said this before," Rupert turned toward Minerva lying beside him, "but I think you are the most magnificent woman in the world!" He placed a soft kiss on her cheek, rolling to his side to wrap an arm around her and snug himself up close.

Minerva smiled, keeping her eyes closed but taking in all that Rupert gave her with every other sense she had. His masculine smell, the deep rumble within his gentle tenor voice, the warmth of his lips and body, and the tenderness in his touch. Finally she spoke, the smile on her face reflected in her voice, "You do have a habit of repeating yourself," she chuckled softly and felt his arm pull her closer, "I hope I find that's your worst habit." She felt the puff of his breath against her neck, not sure if it was a snort or a laugh, then she sucked in her breath as his lips gently caressed and kissed her neck.

For several long, exquisite moments she let him linger there. "Love?"

"Hmm?" His ministrations unceasing.

"I'll add indefatigable to your habits list," she gasped as he sucked on a particularly tender spot, "but" she was having difficulty catching her breath, "I think that's redundant." Just as she managed to get out her last word Rupert took her mouth in his and proved, again, just how indefatigable he really was.

74

When they awoke again, it was to the sound of a clearing throat and the stamp of hoofbeats. "Head Counselor?"

Minerva nudged Rupert and whispered, "Wake up love."

"It's just me, Mud."

She raised her voice, "Yes Mud?" Nudging Rupert again she moved to sit up and groaned at all the new aches and sore muscles the movement flared into being.

"Are you alright ma'am?" Mud asked with great concern.

Hurriedly before the diminutive but mighty man rushed into the tent she answered him, "Yes Mud. Just feeling my age and the joy of sleeping on the ground."

Underneath his breath she heard him snort and mutter, "Yeah, a lot a sleeping was done."

Beside her, Rupert stirred and rose. She envied the way his body responded to his every command. Truth be told, she enjoyed the way his body responded to his and her every direction, immensely.

The Blue Knight pulled on his breeches and tunic and flipped open the flap. "Good morning Chief Engineer," he took a step out into the bright mid-day. "To what do we owe this," he couldn't keep the smile off his face, "interruption?"

The Chief Engineer snorted and stretched out his hands. The Blue Knight looked around and realized that they now were the only standing tent in what had been the encampment of four knights and their entourages that had covered several acres. Their horse and wagon stood hitched and loaded. Simon was stirring the fire and the final smoke from it was wafting away. The Blue Knight's horse turned toward him with a look that could only be understood as "Seriously, you're a knight, get it together".

"Ah." The Blue Knight rubbed his stubbled chin and said again, "Ah." Unfortunately the grin on his face and the continued relaxed nature of his pose only served to cause more irritation to the Chief Engineer.

"Are you two, newlyweds, ready to go?" Mud glared up at Rupert. Simon rose wordlessly and tossed the few remaining items into the back of the cart, crawled in, covered himself and tucked in for the trip home.

"Umm, yes," the Blue Knight looked over his shoulder at the tent, "Yes, umm just a few more minutes and we'll be ready." Ducking his head he slipped back into the tent only to find Minerva grinning at him like a kid who was caught red-handed with her hand in the sweets jar. As soon as he dropped down beside her, she let out an explosive laugh. He shook his head and shrugged his shoulders, smiling.

"I guess it's time to get moving. Mud has everything packed up, except us. And Simon, well, he's buried himself in the cart." He began gathering belongings and rolling up the bedding. Finally, he turned his eyes to Minerva. "Good morning, wife."

Smiling she replied, "Good morning, husband."

He leaned over and kissed her before taking her in his arms and carrying her out to the cart, setting her down next to the chief engineer on the front bench. He watched Mud hand Minerva a steaming mug and knew from the smell it was the potion the man with the aura of green had left for her. He nodded to Mud, returned to the tent, removed all its contents, tossed them into the cart, narrowly missing Simon, who only grunted.

He quickly dismantled the tent and slid it into its place in the cart. Moving over to his horse he stroked his neck fondly. Under his breath he said to his horse, "Did you ever think it would happen?" He looked over his shoulder at the backs of the Head

Counselor and Chief Engineer. "She is the most magnificent woman," at this his horse shook his head up and down and then lightly bumped the Blue Knight. "She likes you too, my loyal friend."

The Blue Knight finished harnessing his horse and led him to the cart slipping the reins over the rail once. He hopped in the back of the cart and took a seat behind the Head Counselor and beside the ensconced Simon. "Alright Chief Engineer, take us home."

Mud snapped the reins and the cart horse moved forward.

Chapter Nineteen
BLUE KNIGHT & HEAD COUNSELOR
RUPERT & MINERVA HEADING HOME

The cart rocked slightly and the Blue Knight moved with it, falling into a waking sleep, replaying what had happened just this past morning.

After the knights had gathered and formally asked those with them to join in saving the kingdom, each had returned to their camps to depart. The White Knight had followed him back to his camp, husband a respectful half step beside and behind her, until she reached out a hand, which he took and stood beside her.

"Rupert, Minerva," she nodded to both. "I made you an offer earlier this morning. I and my husband are here to accomplish that promise."

"Sir Knight, I don't think now is the right..." but Minerva was interrupted by Rupert.

"Why not my love? When will be the right time, if not now?" Rupert looked a bit desperately at Alexandra and her husband.

"Head Counselor Minerva, I understand your concerns," Alexandra, the White Knight said smoothly, "But I agree with Rupert, Sir Blue Knight. What more significant event than a marriage to start a new world. I think it is the perfect time." She squeezed her husband's hand. "Trust me, having a life mate is not something to wait for, or lose, when they are before you."

Ethan, the White Knight's husband, released her hand and slipped his arm around Alexandra's waist, then gave her a soft kiss on the cheek. "Trust her. She's a very smart knight." He squeezed her slightly, "And one amazing woman." The White Knight laughed and gave him a quick kiss before removing herself from his grasp.

"Chief Engineer Mud, will you stand as witness for the Head Counselor's family?" Mud nodded emphatically. "Rupert, will you allow my husband to stand in for your family?" The Blue Knight nodded just as emphatically. "Head Counselor Minerva of the Northern Mountains, will you take the Blue Knight, Rupert of Sapphire, as your husband?" She looked expectantly at the Head Counselor.

The Head Counselor looked from the Blue Knight to the White Knight, then at her Chief Engineer, and finally at the White Knight's husband. "Yes," it came out a whisper, so she tried again this time with the assurance and confidence of the head counselor, "YES!"

Things moved quickly then. It seemed like only a few words from the White Knight and they were hand fasted. A slap on the back from Ethan to Rupert, a few whispered words into Minerva's ear by Alexandra, and suddenly they were alone, well almost – Simon and Mud were still with them. But that hadn't stopped them.

Rupert thought they had done an admirable job consummating their marriage. He smiled a bit shyly thinking of what was ahead, both in and out of the marriage bed. The cart jolted sharply and the Blue Knight was knocked, literally, out of his reverie. He heard Simon groan and watched him roll over and tuck in more tightly.

"Easy there Mud." The Blue Knight picked himself up off the floor of the cart and retook his seat, checking quickly on his wife. He smiled as he said it in his head, *His wife.* Turning to her, he asked, "Are you alright love?"

Mud jumped in quickly with a falsetto voice, "Yes sweetie." The Blue Knight cuffed the back of his head. "Ouch" Mud mocked pain.

"You two are worse than brothers, I think." The Head Counselor shifted slightly and grimaced in pain. Thinking, *Making love to your husband,* she smiled at that "her husband" *and then taking a long trip does not wear well on this body of mine."* Turning her smile on the Blue Knight, her husband Rupert, she said, "Surviving as well as can be expected on a bumpy road." Which at that precise moment set them for another large jolt and caused one of the horses to stumble momentarily. She gasped and grabbed her seat holding on.

The Blue Knight reached out and laid a hand upon her, "How much longer before we can stop Mud?" His voice filled with concern. Into her ear he whispered, "Do you need the other pain leaf?" She shook her head no and stroked his cheek.

"Will you always take such good care of me? Or is this just a newlywed's attention?" She smiled knowingly.

"You wound me dear wife. I will gladly and always be your faithful servant, husband, lover, and knight until my life is taken from me." He leaned forward to give her a kiss, but they hit another bump and knocked heads instead.

"Ouww," they said in unison, then laughed. Mud looked at them with false disgust and muttered, "Newly-weds!"

Minerva looked into the back of the cart and indicated with her head the bump that was Simon beside her husband. "Is he okay?" she asked softly. The Blue Knight looked at the lump, gave it a nudge with his knee, and shrugged.

Fortunately for the three of them, it was not long before conversation began again and the time passed quickly. When they arrived at the place where the Chief Engineer had to depart, he left with promises of men, tools and materials to work on the road from the Blue Knight. The Chief Engineer made promises to relay everything that had happened to the ruling council and to tell them

80

that their Head Counselor would be returning soon with additional news. Just before he left the Blue Knight went down on one knee and offered his arm to the Chief Engineer who grasped it firmly. No words were spoken. The Chief Engineer looked to the Head Counselor and back to the Blue Knight, who nodded his understanding.

Mud crawled into the back of the cart, "Simon," he kicked what he thought was Simon's foot and heard a grunt. "See you soon." But all he received was another grunt.

The Blue Knight took his seat beside the Head Counselor, gathered up the reins and started them toward the final leg of their journey to his home. For many minutes they sat in companionable silence.

"I'm going to have to make some adjustments to my accommodations," he couldn't help but smile, "for my wife." He leaned into her slightly and she leaned into him. "My household has been a man's home for many years. I think even those few females who live within have given up on us."

"Oh, wonderful. I've given up my life of luxury and decadence for a bachelor's chaos." She tried to mimic haughtiness but the pleasure in her voice was too bright.

"I know. I know. I just wanted you to be prepared." He smiled, "I'm giving you no excuses to leave me and return to your mountains, at least, not without me by your side."

She wrapped her arms around one of his and squeezed him close to her. "How about I promise not to leave immediately," The Blue Knight started but she held onto his arm, "If you promise to let me add a few feminine touches to your home."

"Our home." He said immediately.

"Our home," she responded softly, "but remember I still have another home and responsibilities there."

He was quiet for several minutes. When he spoke it was with deep conviction. "I will give up my knighthood if you need to be in your mountains."

"Oh, my love," she squeezed his arm again, "I would not ask that of you." She contemplated carefully her next words. "I think neither of us will have much time at either home. If we are going to save your King and Kingdom..."

He interrupted her, "Our kingdom."

She paused, not wanting to say something she could not honor or follow in their future. "If we are going to make safe and remake the kingdom into a place companionable for all to live, we will have little time to make 'our' life and home together." He started to interrupt but stopped when she squeezed his arm. "If we succeed in making a new world . . . " This time he did interrupt, "When we succeed." She assented, "When we succeed, we will have lots of time to make our home and life together."

The Blue Knight slumped and hung his head for a moment, feeling the weight of all that was ahead, all that was unknown and all that he longed for now that he had found his soulmate. He lifted his head, straightened his shoulders and spoke in a voice more lighthearted than he felt, "Then we better get started, because I want to see what the male bastion of the Blue Knight can be with a *few* feminine touches." He flicked the reins lightly moving the horse from a walk to a canter. Looking into the sky he added, "I think it's best you see it in the dark, but I don't want to travel in the dark, so we better get moving." He gave her a kiss on the head and flicked the reins again.

She looked at the sky noticing the waning dusk, then at her husband, the Blue Knight. "Just how bad is this place?"

He winked, "Oh you'll see," looking ahead smiling, "you only have to wait another candlemark or so." He flicked the reins again, quickening the horse's pace.

The Head Counselor released the Blue Knight's arm and straightened herself, groaning between clenched teeth, hoping he hadn't heard her. She saw him reaching for the small pocket where the pain leaf was held. She laid a hand upon his, "Later, my love. When we are no longer moving, and I can actually recover a little." He let his hand drop and gave her a look of concern but acknowledged her request. She smiled and thought, *How did I get so lucky? To find a man of such character and accomplishments, who is thoughtful and attentive to my needs?* "I will definitely take a backrub too."

"Only with your tea."

"Ugh," she moaned, "can't we forget the tea just this time?"

He looked over to her as a parent would to a child, "No tea, no backrub." He winked, "But you can have the pain leaf because pain is written all over your face."

She sighed and raised her hands in surrender, "Leaf, tea, backrub."

He then gave her a look more lascivious and leaned closer to say huskily, "And if you're good, and feeling up to it, I'll make you feel even better."

She gasped and laughed. "What happened to the respectful knight I fell in love with?"

"You married him!" the Blue Knight laughed.

Meanwhile, buried in the cart's bed, Simon was stewing. He had been so angry when the White Knight married the Blue Knight and the Head Counselor. He respected the Head Counselor; it wasn't her fault that she was deformed. Just because he could tolerate being around *THEM,* he didn't want to have to live with them. His weeks of recovery in the mountains had pushed his tolerance to the limits. Sure, they had helped him heal, but they had cost him his leg. He still had pain in a leg that no longer held him up. The wooden leg worked alright, but now he was one of *THEM* too. He respected the Blue Knight, but this, this was too much.

Chapter Twenty
THE BLUE KNIGHT'S JOURNEY

As they rounded a long curve in the road the Blue Knight slowed the horse and then stopped. He stood up for a moment looking around and then dropped back to the bench they shared.

"Problem?" she asked.

"I guess it's late enough that everyone is in for the night." He said, puzzled.

"And?" she asked becoming more concerned.

"Well, I don't have sentries per se, but those who live at the edges of my protection usually keep watch and we should . . . " he stopped mid-sentence, stood up again, and waved. Returning to his seat smiling. "We should have been greeted, aah here they come now."

Two men galloped up and halted before them. "Sir Knight, welcome home."

"Greetings my lord."

Simon had slipped out of the cart and stood beside the horsemen.

"Matthus and . . . I'm sorry, I don't recognize you." The Blue Knight peered into the dark trying to identify the second man in the party.

"Pardons, my lord. We have not met. I am one of the soldiers who was supposed to be at the King's castle." He looked toward Simon who stared at him. "I have only recently escaped."

"Escaped?" The Blue Knight's tone was alert and harsher than he intended.

"Yes sir, I . . . "

The Blue Knight held up his hand. "Wait. We need to get to the stronghold and give my wife . . . " he hesitated and corrected, "get the Head Counselor a comfortable place to recover from our journey."

Simon started to ask a question, but a shake of the Blue Knight's head silenced him for the moment. Matthus extended Simon a hand and he mounted behind Matthus.

Matthus said, "They have prepared for your arrival Sir." He did not hesitate but started home expecting the others to follow, which the soldier did; the Blue Knight hesitated a moment more, then clicked his tongue and flicked the reins.

"It's already begun," the Head Counselor said. The Blue Knight nodded, and both were lost in their thoughts until they saw the Keep's gates and the throng of people gathered to greet them. The Blue Knight also wondered about Simon's odd behavior but set it aside for the moment.

Chapter Twenty-One
HOMECOMING

It was a warm greeting. The Blue Knight's people obviously thought highly of their knight and respected him as a person of value, as well as protector and knight. The Blue Knight made sure he acknowledged everyone gathered. Calling each by name and asking a question that was relevant and meaningful to each one specifically. But he did not linger. He had given Simon silent directions to get the Head Counselor's chair out of the cart and take it inside. When he saw that it was done, he interrupted the greetings and spoke formally.

"My friends, thank you. There is much to share and much to do. I have a very important person with me. She is the Head Counselor of the Mountain Folk we met during our quest for the man with the aura of green."

Everyone curiously turned toward her and she felt the weight of their appraisal. She gave them her best head counselor smile and acknowledged those who made eye contact.

"We have had several days of travel and discovery. I am a poor host if I do not offer succor and nourishment to her." He moved beside her and without looking down said under his breath, "Are you ready?" He received a slight nod. "Do I have your permission to carry you in?" Another nod. The Blue Knight extended his arms and lifted her gently. She worked hard to keep her moan of pain as quiet as possible and the smile on her face intact. Moving quickly he proceeded inside, setting her in her chair gingerly. Turning to address the crowd he gave a farewell for the moment and closed the doors to those outside and dispersing those within.

Immediately he was on his knees beside her with the pain leaf extended to her, which she took gratefully and chewed slowly, letting the relief wash over her. The Blue Knight's Head of House came and went while Rupert waited and watched his love anxiously. When Minerva finally opened her eyes, some of the pain had released her face and her eyes were clearer.

The Head of House returned with a concerned look and a porcelain teapot with steaming hot water and a porcelain teacup. She moved a small table beside the Head Counselor's chair and placed the pot and cup down. With a smile to the Head Counselor, she extended her hand in front of the Blue Knight and waited, motionless, until he produced the special tea mix. She started to prepare it when the Head Counselor stopped her with a gentle touch.

"Please, madam, I have been instructed to consume the tea leaves when I've finished drinking."

The woman nodded, departed, and returned quickly with a stout clay mug. She held it out for the Head Counselor's inspection. Receiving a smile and nod, she placed a portion of the tea in her hand holding it out for approval.

"A bit more," the Head Counselor shivered as she spoke, unable to remove the foul taste of the tea from her mind, yet approving the larger portion she was shown.

The Head of House placed the tea in the mug and poured the hot water into the mug. She turned to a sideboard and picked up a blanket which she opened and asked with her eyes and arms if she could cover the Head Counselor. Seeing a nod she laid it gently on Minerva's lap, tucking it smoothly around her withered legs and up under her arms. She picked up the mug and stirred it gently then set it aside, "Not ready yet," she said softly and left again.

Minerva turned to her Blue Knight who was smiling after the Head of House. "Rupert?" He turned his smile on her. "Does she have a name?"

He slapped his head and stood up. "I am so sorry. Sarah has been such an essential part of my life for so long, I just assume everyone knows her." He stepped aside hastily when Sarah hustled back in and gently pushed Minerva's shoulders forward slightly and slipped a warm sheepskin down her back.

Minerva sighed with pleasure. "Oh madam, thank you! That feels so good on this sore aching body." Minerva adjusted herself slightly and sighed again, more pain releasing her body.

The Blue Knight took the Head of House's hand and kissed it. She smiled and pulled away, smoothly. She checked the tea again, "Almost." Then she turned the full force of her personality and warmth on the two of them. She crossed her arms and waited.

"Sarah, I would like to introduce you to the Head Counselor of the Mountain Folk." The Blue Knight said with all formality and officiousness warranted by his knighthood.

Sarah gave her a small curtsy and said, "A pleasure." Her voice was rich and textured in a lower register, so her words felt like a warm caress. She looked at the mug again, stirred, and offered it to the Head Counselor, who took it gratefully.

The Blue Knight moved beside Sarah and wrapped an arm over her shoulders, leaned toward her, a silly grin on his face, and said, "And my wife."

Sarah pushed his arm off her shoulders and turned him to face her squarely, looking intensely at him. Rupert was nodding without ceasing, looking like a small child about to burst with pleasure. Suddenly she wrapped her arms around him, squeezing as she picked him up, forcing a grunt from him and then laughter.

"About time my boy, about time!" She turned to the Head Counselor looking her up and down, watching her sip and grimace as she drank the tea. "Healing tea, eh? They are always nasty. You would think something that makes you feel better should be pleasant with the taste of . . . of mint or?"

At the mention of mint, the Head Counselor jumped in, "Yes, mint, I asked the man with the aura of green why he couldn't use mint and he just huffed at me."

Sarah chuckled, "He is a reserved one about his potions, isn't he!"

"You know him?" Minerva was leaning forward slightly, most of her pain abated by the herbs and her excitement. Then as if the thought just hit her, "I'm sorry, I hope you didn't need his services."

"No dear," Sarah reached out and patted Minerva's arm tenderly. "Thankfully I was the caregiver, he was there when we needed him most." She had a far-off look and then came back to the present. "All survived and I learned a few more healing potions." Nodding with her head toward the mug, "Including that disgusting one, so I can make you more." She looked into the mug and saw that the liquid was gone, but the leaves were still present. Not unkindly she said, "Finish it."

Minerva grimaced, swiped her finger in the mug collecting the remaining leaves. She placed the finger in her mouth and shuddered. When she finished swallowing, she turned the mug toward Sarah for inspection and getting approval, set the mug down.

Sarah turned toward Rupert, "Did you learn the back rub?" He nodded positively and moved behind Minerva, rubbed his hands together, then began the massage, eliciting more sighs and moans of relief from Minerva.

"Good boy." Sarah cleared away the teapot, mug, and table. As the back rub was still in process she looked back over one shoulder. "I'm preparing a meal. When you're done take your wife to the dining room."

"Sarah, I much prefer the kitchen," the Head Counselor managed to get out between moans of relief.

"You're the Mistress of this house now, as you wish." She turned away and said to no one in particular, "I like her!"

Chapter Twenty-Two
RED KNIGHT – WALKING

The Red Knight and Hmway listened to their wives talk. Hmway hummed an uplifting tune softly. Every time the Red Knight turned toward Hmway to speak, his eyes were closed and the humming got just a little louder. After a few candlemarks the Red Knight could hold in his thoughts no longer.

"My friend, I fear we are about to go to war."

One of Hmway's brows went up but the humming continued.

"I don't want you or your people to be hurt."

Hmway nodded and continued humming.

"Hmway!" The Red Knight sounded angry, but he repented immediately, "Sorry, Hmway, I'm worried."

Hmway stopped and turned toward the Red Knight. "My friend, we **can not** change our paths, we can only make our way, with our eyes open."

"But ... "

Hmway placed his large, strong, gentle hands on the Red Knight's shoulders. "If we are not part of the solution, we will be part of the outcome, without any power to influence it." He dropped his hands and resumed walking.

Flustered, the Red Knight said, "Well at least we could be riding our horses!" He reached out to stroke his steed's neck and together horse and man pressed foreheads. "I hope you're enjoying this. My feet are killing me!" His horse shook his reins and stomped once, then pushed the Red Knight forward and followed Hmway.

The Red Knight knew that on horseback it took a day of hard riding or two traveling easy, to reach his Keep. On foot, the Red Knight and Hmway's party was on day three. Home was within reach today, but the Red Knight was getting uneasy. What little the sentries at the castle had told him, and that which he overheard as he lingered outside their quarters after dinner, had him worried.

General Mallory and Bear had agreed to go out into the country for the *protection* of the people. They each had left ten soldiers to guard the castle. But Mallory had returned and taken half of those he had left and all of Bear's men with him, leaving only the laziest and poorest trained. From what he could only infer from the crass comments: Bear's men had left under protest and perhaps even in restraints.

The Red Knight knew that the White Knight's group would be passing by General Bear's outpost. He was sure she would stop and check out the situation. He knew it would be a day's detour on foot to find Mallory's outpost, and he'd chosen to go to his Keep first. The Red Knight wasn't as confident as the White Knight about General Mallory's motivation.

He also did not feel safe. These two days of walking should have been an enjoyable trip. But the fields were empty and the people whom they met were reserved and even fearful. The Red Knight thought long and hard about the people's reactions. Did they know about the state of the King? Did they know that the man with the aura of green had taken the Princess? What was feeding their fear? What, or maybe more correctly, who are they afraid of?

The Red Knight also thought they had been watched. He couldn't point to anything specific, but the unease and paranoia had continued to build as they got closer to the turn-off to Mallory's outpost. Suddenly, he realized he was standing alone. He looked forward and saw that the women had joined Hmway and they were singing. The Red Knight listened carefully. The tune was unknown to him, but the three-part harmony was giving him a feeling of . . . ? He listened harder, closing his eyes and trying to feel the melody with his own body. *What is it?* He struggled to define the effect on his feelings. As the three came to a crescendo and ended, he knew it: Optimism, but cautious optimism.

So everyone had felt it. He put himself in motion, first catching up to his horse who snorted as he trotted by, "I know, I know," he said to his faithful steed. *I've got to get him an extra treat when we get home,* he thought. He was only slightly winded when he caught up to everyone. He slipped an arm around his wife and gave her a kiss.

"What was that song you were singing?" he asked the group.

His wife smiled broadly, "New song, we just made it up as we walked." She looked at Hmway and Allayu who now were also walking hand-in-hand.

Hmway's white smile lit his face and the love in his eyes spoke louder than any words, "My Allayu is quite the songstress. She always finds, or creates, the right song for the right time

Chapter Twenty-Three
FIRST CONFRONTATION WITH MALLORY / MALICIOUS

They walked for several more myles before being confronted by a mounted party of four. The soldiers (or bandits?) seemed to have some sort of uniform, but it was obviously hap and slap, made of leftover used cloth and other mis-matched uniforms.

"Halt!" The man in front pulled out his sword and pointed it at the Red Knight's wife. Immediately both the Red Knight and Hmway stepped in front of the women.

"Who addresses me thus," asked the Red Knight and knocked the sword aside. "On my own lands?"

One of the men further back said, "I told you it was the Red Knight!"

The first man replaced his sword but did not dismount nor show the proper respect due a knight.

"Name yourself." The Red Knight stood to his full height and seemed to swell in width as well. His voice held all the force and authority of a knight.

The first man faltered, while the other three dismounted, giving the Red Knight a slight bow of their heads. Finally, the first man dismounted, now significantly shorter than the Red Knight, but his defiance was still clear. He took a step forward. "I serve General Mallory. You are crossing territory that is under his protection."

The Red Knight crossed his arms across his chest which forced the man to take a step back. "Well, isn't that interesting." He looked around seeming curious. "Just exactly what are you protecting **MY LANDS** from?"

The man paled a bit but regained his courage and spit out an obviously memorized statement meant to cow those he met. "The knights are on a quest for the King. In order to secure the safety of the kingdom General Mallory and General Bear have set up outposts to protect our kingdom until they return."

"Aah," the Red Knight nodded his head. "Well, as you can see. I have returned." He uncrossed his arms and casually placed one hand on his sword. "Tell General Mallory all the knights have returned to their homes and protectorates. If he would like to join me in two days' time, we can discuss the future of his outpost."

The man started to bluster, "You don't command General Mallory . . . Who do you think you are? . . . We are in charge here."

Quietly, Hmway took one step forward silencing the man immediately and backing up the other three. Hmway smiled slightly and said, "I also look forward to meeting your general in two days." That said, he took his wife's hand and walked through the men and horses who parted for him.

The Red Knight looked the men over slowly, gauging each, finding the three in the back wanting in substance, he turned to the front man. Stepping close enough to the man that his breath moved the soldier's hair when he spoke, the Red Knight leaned down over him. In a soft but threatening voice he warned, "If I find any of General Mallory's men on *my lands* they will be imprisoned."

The little man tried to back up but the Red Knight matched him step for step. His voice rose slightly, "If any of General Mallory's men are found committing a crime - *of any kind* - they will receive the harshest punishment under the kingdom's law."

The little man tried to object. He was sweating profusely and looking around nervously for an exit. "Y-y-you, don't command the General or his men," he stammered.

The Red Knight laughed, causing the man to stumble backward. The Red Knight reached out one hand and grabbed the man's shoulder, none too gently, preventing him from falling, then slowly pulled him in close. "Son, your General," he paused, deciding he didn't want to reveal too much of what was going on with the king, "your General has *my permission* to visit me in two days." He released the man who stumbled again because the Red Knight had been holding him up on his toes.

The man started to speak then thought better of it. He scrambled on his horse and hurried to catch up to the other three, looking over his shoulder frequently, as if he expected the Red Knight to pursue or shoot him in the back.

The Red Knight wiped his hands on his breeches in disgust. "Aaarr, the man is filthy and stinks!" He wiped his hands in the dirt preferring the dirt to the man filth. He saw his horse had paced him, stayed just behind, and now moved beside him. "I think we have trouble." The horse snorted his assent. The Red Knight mounted and sighed. "Did you miss me? I sure missed you!" He clicked his heels and his horse pranced forward. Anyone looking would have thought the horse was just as pleased as the man to be reunited ey because his cantor looked like prancing.

Horse and rider quickly caught up to the walkers, then only slowed enough to say, "I'm going ahead to let them know we're almost here. I want you to get a better greeting than the one we just got!" He raised a hand as he galloped off.

Allayu leaned into her husband and said softly, "You really should have let him ride." She nodded to the departing knight. "I think the horse missed him as much as he missed the horse these past three days." She laughed her beautiful, lyrical laugh.

"I know my love. But he's so much fun to tease," Hmway purred. "He's so willing to please. This is an easy lesson for him." The two women looked quizzically at him. "Soon he'll realize he doesn't have to give up his horse to meet us halfway. It will help him better negotiate with others in the future."

Beatrice, the Red Knight's wife, let out a guffaw. "I knew it! Serves him right. Sometimes I think he loves that horse more than me."

Allayu turned a serious face to her, "Oh no, no!"

"It's all right my friend," Beatrice reassured her, "I knew how much he loved his animals before I married him." She winked, "It was part of his charm and helped me fall in love with him." She looked lovingly after her husband. "Besides, anything that makes him a better man and knight is worth a few blisters, I think."

Allayu gave another lyrical laugh, relieved. She linked her arms with both husband and "sister", and they finished the walk to the Red Knight's Keep.

Chapter Twenty-Four
MALLORY - INTERRUPTED

General Mallory stormed around the outpost, kicking at anyone or thing, that came too close to him. He backhanded the soldier he had sent to intimidate the Red Knight, drawing blood from the cut lip he created.

"FOOL!" Mallory looked for something else to hit or break, and found a small cask of whiskey his men had stolen from an innkeeper. He flung it against the wall, shattering the cask and spraying the remaining liquid across himself and the soldier lying in the dirt beside him, to whom he delivered a sharp kick in the gut.

Then just as suddenly as the storm had started, it stopped. Mallory stood in the middle of the yard, straightened his shoulders, clasped his hands behind his back, then dropped them, unclenching his white-knuckled fists. His dark harsh eyes scanned the yard, noting the men who were scuttling out of view and those who had arms drawn, waiting for a fight.

"Men, we have an invitation from the Red Knight." He surveyed the men slowly, letting the full force of his ire scorch them if they dared to meet his eyes. "Recall everyone. Tomorrow, we make our introductions in full force."

From his position on the ground, the soldier with the split lip and more guts than intelligence spoke up, "The invitation was for two days hence, Sir."

Mallory turned swiftly and kicked the man in the head, ending his life. The death was not intentional, but with a perverse sense of pleasure, he savored what his action had done.

He took a deep breath, then spoke, almost calmly, "My time for a visit is tomorrow." Again he fixed those still able to make eye contact, "We leave at dawn." Having made his pronouncement he turned and strode into his office, grabbing the door just before it slammed. "Calm, calm," he said to himself, pushing the door closed gently. With an evil vehemence he whispered, "You have no idea who you are dealing with Sir Red Knight." He picked up the bell on his desk and contemplated throwing it, but instead rang it once and ordered a bath when his knave appeared. "Must look good for the knight," he said to the knave and smiled. His smile could only be called wicked and ugly. No one could mistake that his intentions were anything but evil. The knave hurried to do his bidding.

Chapter Twenty-Five
THE MAN WITH THE AURA OF GREEN & GENERAL MALICIOUS

The man with the aura of green moved as stealthily as he had ever done. It was his practice to appear without announcement, attend those in need and then leave without thanks. Even though many thought he appeared 'magically,' his arrival was welcomed. For the first time since he began healing, he was not sure he'd be appreciated here. In General Mallory's compound the air reeked of desperation and despair. Violence permeated the area like a heavy dense fog.

He found the first man slumped against a building. Blood covered his head and it was immediately evident he was dead. *No attempt to even bury their dead.* He thought, *This is worse than I feared.* He moved on and found another attempting to crawl, having only one arm functioning and moving with his hips more than his legs. The man with the aura of green laid a hand upon the man's head easing him to sleep, then dragged him as gently as possible into the closest building. He splinted one leg, immobilized one foot, applied salve to bruises and cuts, and slowly dripped a painkilling drink into the unconscious man's mouth. When he had done all that he could he moved on.

He found three more men in similar states of damage which he likewise attended. The fourth was in a drunken stupor. The man with the aura of green added an herb to the bottle he held and smiled when a few moments later the man took another sip and began to vomit. *Hopefully a different cure.* He thought without regret.

The fifth man was another issue. As soon as he saw the man with the aura of green approaching he began to shout: "Who are you? What do you want? To arms!" The man with the aura of green stood calmly hoping the man would quiet, but when it was evident that he wasn't going to calm, he moved quickly behind a building to avoiding an ever-growing number of Mallory's soldiers.

During this hide 'n seek, he treated a horse's whip injuries, put a dying chicken out of its misery, freed a stuck pig from a hole, but saw no others who needed or wanted his healing ministrations. It was with a heavy heart that he slipped out of the compound and went on to those who did need and want him.

Chapter Twenty-Six
RED KNIGHT MEETS GENERAL MALLORY

The Red Knight gloried in the ride home on his horse. He truly had missed the noble steed, not just because of his sore feet, but the power and speed of the beast, and the quiet, strong equine wisdom that he felt when they traveled together. He spurred his steed on faster and faster, as if both of them needed to work out the kinks of the three-day walk. The horse galloped and pranced and even reared up on his back legs to show off.

When the Red Knight approached his gates, he slid off his mount and rushed to those working in the courtyard garden. "Sound the alarm. We need every able-bodied man and woman to be armed and ready as soon as possible." He looked around to find what he called his "captain of the guard," even though he kept no soldiers within his lands. When he finally saw Malcolm coming toward him, he raised a hand and drew him close. "General Mallory is going to storm the Keep, probably tomorrow. We need to meet him with full force and show him he can't intimidate or control us."

"But Sir Knight, he has been running roughshod over your lands for many weeks now, very shortly after we left for the King's Quest." Malcolm, the captain of the guard, had traveled with the Red Knight and now he was looking beyond him searching for Beatrice, Hmway and Allayu, anxiously.

The Red Knight realized who he was looking for and put his fears to rest. "They follow close behind. We met four of Mallory's soldiers, and I use that term loosely." He gave Malcolm a slap on the back. "We must anticipate and outplay the viper in the grass my friend."

Malcolm smiled and said, "Then I have just the men you need to meet!"

The Red Knight stopped and looked at Malcolm, clearly puzzled.

"We have four of General Mallory's soldiers, or I should say General Bear's soldiers, who escaped from Malicious." The revulsion was plain on his face. "What Malloy – NO Malicious - did to these men . . . " he shook his head, unable to go on.

Now the Red Knight laid a consoling hand on Malcolm, "Take me to them." The two turned as one and strode toward the infirmary area of the Keep. "Are they alive?" the Red Knight's concern evident.

"Yes sir, but just." Malcolm spat in frustration, "broken bones, whippings, starvation." Malcolm gulped in his loathing for those who could do such things to another human being.

The Red Knight's hand squeezed Malcolm's shoulder gently. He had left it there as they walked knowing his friend needed a kind touch. "How did they come here?"

Malcolm looked at his knight and friend, thinking carefully before speaking, "Bartholomew, I'd rather not say." He looked down and then back to the Red Knight, "I think they did what they had to, to survive."

The Red Knight waited, he knew another's death must be involved, and he too didn't want to punish men for surviving.

"Let's see them Malcolm. First, we attend their bodies, then their spirits. Hopefully they will be able to tell me something I need to give me the upper hand over Mallory."

Malcolm nodded and before opening the door, placed a hand on the Red Knight's chest slowing him down. "It isn't pleasant." The Red Knight leaned forward, "Control your rage at the injustice. They need safety and people they can trust." Malcolm waited until he was sure the Red Knight had heard and understood him.

The Red Knight nodded and stood upright. He visibly calmed himself and replaced his worry over Mallory with concern for these men. He closed his eyes one final time and nodded to Malcolm who proceeded him in.

Malcolm cleared his throat and looked around the room before speaking, making sure the men were awake and put to rights as best they could. "Gentlemen, I want to introduce you to the Red Knight, man of honor and a friend."

The Red Knight approached each man and extended a hand. If one wasn't available to shake, he laid a comforting hand upon the body part that seemed the least damaged. Two men could only acknowledge him with their eyes and very small sounds of greeting. When the Red Knight had made the rounds, he turned his back to the men facing Malcolm and let his horror show. It took a few moments before he could regain his calm demeanor.

"Gentlemen, I need your help." He took a chair from the wall and placed it where all could see him. The two more mobile men shifted to see him clearly, and the other two turned their heads toward him. "I think Mallory plans on storming the Keep tomorrow."

The fear and misery were immediately visible in all four men. Two groaned and one said, "I thought we were safe."

"You are safe." The Red Knight gave them a reassuring smile. "I will not let such a vile man have any more power over me or mine. And you are now mine." He met each man's eyes giving each his silent promise of protection. "I need your help." He looked from man to man. "Tell me what you know of Mallory and his . . . method of governing soldiers."

The man who was most damaged snorted beneath bandages and got out one word. "Torture!"

The Red Knight nodded, "I see that. To everyone?"

The most fit man spoke, "No, only to those who objected to his brutality and to the way he treated those he was supposed to be protecting."

The Red Knight faced him squarely. "Did many of the . . . soldiers object?"

"No, only those of us who came from General Bear's forces. We were supposed to stay at the castle and protect the king. But Malicious came back and drove us like cattle out of the castle and left four, I don't know, people he found on the road," he said with disgust, "as "sentries" with four of his men." He looked at his fellow sufferers. "We started as ten. Four here, I think two or three got to the Blue Knight's Keep, the others . . . " he shook his head sadly unable to go on.

A sob came from one of the bedridden men, "My brother."

"Stand fast Ceril, we don't know who escaped and who didn't."

The man in the bed continued to cry, a tear escaping his uncovered eye and running down his bandaged face.

The Red Knight moved his chair and sat beside the man. "If he is alive, we will find and free him. If he is dead, we will avenge him."

The man searched the Red Knight's face, tears still flowing, and finally nodded, "Thank you."

"I need to know Mallory's weaknesses. I need to know anything we can use against him. I need anything you think will help me show him that I," he tapped his chest, "am smarter and stronger than he."

"You're already bigger Sir," the fourth man said. "I think he whipped or beat anyone taller than he just on general principle – which was pretty much everyone." He looked over at the other three, "Bit of a little man's complex I think, barely five foot tall he is."

The Red Knight nodded. "Go on please."

The man who had been crying spoke softly, "He is evil."

No one contradicted him. The Red Knight waited.

"He doesn't like to be contradicted. If he thinks you're stronger or have the upper hand, he'll twist your words or present himself as the superior one so that you find yourself agreeing with him. He is clever that way. Wickedly clever."

Several more of Mallory's habits and behaviors were offered. The Red Knight listened intently, offering encouragement and comforting touches. By the time he left, he had even gotten a smile or two from most of them. He and Malcolm exited the room and as soon as the door closed, he bent at the waist, hands on his knees, grasping them tightly, taking deep breaths.

"Monster." He rasped.

"Yes Sir." Malcolm had already experienced this horror and was slightly less disturbed than the Red Knight, but his stomach churned also. "Sir?"

"A moment more Malcolm." The Red Knight continued to breathe heavily, bent over. When he felt he could move forward without anger, he straightened, pasted a look of confidence on his face and went out to the courtyard with Malcolm at his side.

The courtyard was bustling with activity, close to a hundred men stood in the yard, straightening the jerkins that represented the Red Knight's protectorate. All were armed, some with swords, some with spears, some only with knives or staffs. The Red Knight went from man to man, shaking hands, straightening, offering encouragement and acknowledging those gathered. When he had spoken to everyone, he stepped up on a bench beside the outer wall.

In a loud clear voice he began, "The Princess is alive, but the King is ill. All knights have returned home and are preparing for what is ahead." He watched the men still and concern rise. "I won't deceive you. All is not right in the kingdom."

The murmuring and muttering began.

"I know many of you have already had a confrontation with General Mallory's men."

There were shouts of anger and frustration from many.

"Mallory no longer serves the King, but his own agenda."

More shouts rose up, in support of their king.

"We must prepare. I believe Mallory intends to storm the Keep tomorrow."

Now the conversations ranged from rage to shock, to fear, to determination.

"We must present an armed, united front. We must look as if we are an army, prepared to fight and destroy him, if necessary."

Now shouts of victory and encouragement rang out, hands, tools, and weapons raised in the air.

The Red Knight looked at Malcolm who nodded. He had gathered ten reliable men around him. They would help direct the gathered throng: sentries, gatekeepers, arms men, mounted soldiers. There were almost as many women ready to defend their homes as men. In truth, the women would be useful in more ways than the men. The only question was: Would they have time to make all the preparations needed before Mallory and his men appeared?

The Red Knight surveyed those gathered again and noticed that his wife, Hmway and Allayu had arrived. They stood barely inside the gates against the wall, away from the activity and unnoticed.

The Red Knight raised his voice one more time, "For King and the lands of the Red Knight and the people of the kingdom!" Cheers went up from the crowd. Then Malcolm's team set to work.

The Red Knight crossed to the three waiting for him. He wrapped his wife in his arms and held her tightly for a long time. When he finally released her, she held onto him, looking deeply into his eyes. "Is it that bad?" she asked. He nodded. "What can we do?" The look of determination on her face steeled him.

"We prepare to greet . . . our guest, with force, power and," he kissed her hand, "grace." He turned to Hmway and Allayu. "My friends, I will take any strategic advice and help you can offer, but for now I think you need to remain out of the public eye."

Hmway nodded, then slapped his hands once, rubbing them together. "Let's get started."

Beatrice took Allayu by the arm, "You're with me. We have a banquet to prepare."

Darkness fell, but activity did not cease and by dawn the Red Knight's Keep looked like an armed fortress. Everyone was armed, sentries posted, diversions created to fend off any large force attacking en masse. The stables were empty and prepared to billet Mallory's men and lock them away. Food had been prepared that would strengthen the Keep and encourage lethargy in their guests. Plenty of spirits were available, not to make one intoxicated, only to make one sleep. Behind every tapestry and doorway stood armed persons ready to protect and defend the Red Knight.

The women had been particularly busy, setting up alarms so the Keep would know from where and when Mallory approached. They had set up traps they could trigger when needed. The women had worked independently, knowing that if brute force failed, something more subtle and more damaging would be needed, and they had prepared just the thing.

As dawn broke, everyone was settled into their places and knew their assignments. They rested for the moment and ate, hoping they had time to actually recover from their night's activities. Unfortunately, but not unexpectedly, Mallory made his appearance only two hours after dawn. He marched boldly down the road toward the Keep.

Chapter Twenty-Seven
MALLORY'S "SURPRISE" VISIT

Mallory was the only person mounted. He was surrounded by twenty men with spikes and knives who marched like protectors of Mallory and his horse. His haughty demeanor and arrogant countenance could be read from a myle away. The bulk of his army marched behind, a rag-tag group of dirty, disgruntled men.

Those in the Keep knew he was coming more than two myles away and had set up roadblocks. These blocks stopped what Mallory believed would be his unimpeded march and surprise attack, taking several strategic moves away from him, instead giving the surprise and control to the side of the Red Knight.

The first roadblock was a temporary gate, just a bar closed across the road with two lone sentries on either side asking for identity and purpose of visit. When Mallory tried to push his way through by having his horse step over the gate, twenty men came out of the trees with spears and spikes pointed directly at Mallory and his protectors. Mallory and his troop of almost two hundred could have easily overtaken them. But they had caught him by surprise and in his arrogance, he was not yet prepared for a fight. So he answered the questions, identifying himself – General Mallory of the King's Army here by invitation of the Red Knight. He was allowed to pass with only a little pushing and shoving between his protectors and the road guards.

The next roadblock was a half myle down the road, still a myle from the Keep. This time Mallory saw the gate and was determined to pass without pausing. He sent his phalanx of twenty protector guards ahead, marching double time, only to watch them fall into a ditch and be covered immediately by large wooden doors with men moving to stand upon them. Mallory then ordered half his troops to move forward to overtake the gate and sentries.

As Mallory's line of ten men moved forward, large spikes and flaming posts fell at an angle on either side of the road forcing the line to only four men wide. The men hurriedly reformed their ranks, trying to avoid being burned or skewered. As they came out of the narrow pathway, they were grabbed and thrown into large cages that waited on either side of the road just as they exited the spiked road.

Another fifty or more were caught before Mallory raised a hand and stopped all movement around him. Mallory had just seen almost half his men be captured. His rage was so rife within him that he could barely speak. He wanted to draw his sword and strike someone dead or pull out his whip and give many a lashing they would not recover from. He sat frozen, unable to do anything. His troop had been decimated by half with no violence or force and he hadn't even reached the Red Knight's Keep. He let his hand drop. He had to think. His men mulled around him uncertainly, aimless without his directions. They listened to the captured men swear, scream, and eventually quiet.

After many long minutes, he finally moved forward alone and approached the gate guards alone, announced himself and stated he had an invitation from the Red Knight.

Respectfully but firmly one of the guards responded, "I believe that invitation was for tomorrow."

It was all Mallory could do not to pull his blade and run the guard through. But he stilled his hand and when he had his voice under control he said, "But I am here now."

The guards put their heads together and spent several minutes talking, watching Mallory get more and more angry. Eventually, the guard came back and spoke to Mallory. "We will send a runner to the Keep and see if the Red Knight wishes to receive you today." He looked over his shoulder at a man on a horse headed to the Keep.

"Fine," Mallory said with all the control he could muster. After a few minutes of watching the rider leisurely move toward the Keep, he looked around at the caged men and down where the muffled cries of his protectorate guard came from the covered ditch. Again his first instinct was to reach for his sword or whip, but instead he asked, "Do you intend to detain my men?" he said with gritted teeth.

The guard looked him up and down as if he were slow, or stupid. "That depends on what the Red Knight says." The man then turned his back on Mallory and began speaking casually to the other guard.

Now don't be fooled, knowing who Mallory was, there was nothing casual about the guard. Every move and action was carefully scripted to incite Mallory. The guard looked casual, but every nerve was so tightly strung he was about to explode. Many eyes watched Mallory and his men from the woods beside the road. Three archers had their arrows trained on Mallory. Again, they were still outnumbered five to one, but they had the element of surprise and Mallory's fury which caused him to act irrationally. They hoped it would be enough if they had to act and protect the Keep.

Mallory was furious! His face was red. He was slapping his leg with his riding crop and blood had begun to seep through the fabric where he struck himself over and over. Finally, he spun his horse around and cantered back through his ranks, slapping heads with his crop and kicking others. His men parted for him, leaving him a clear path, but he intentionally drove his horse into their midst, determined to vent his frustration with violence on the men.

It was perhaps a full candlemark before the rider returned. He eyed Mallory, now in the middle of his phalanx striking his men, he went to the guard and spoke to him softly. The guard nodded and looked over his shoulder at Mallory and nodded more, then he waved for Mallory to approach. The guard had to wait until Mallory's men could get his attention and point him toward the guard. Again the guard motioned him to come forward. Mallory hesitated, not willing to be ordered around by a mere roadside guard, but relented and moved toward the man, only to be stopped by a line of men pointing spears at him.

The guard stepped up and stood between two of the armed guards. "Sir Red Knight says he is willing to welcome you. Since you have chosen to arrive at such an early hour he will prepare a midday meal for you. You may proceed." He motioned for the armed guards to move aside and the other guard lifted the single bar gate, opening the roadway. Those standing on the covering of the ditch moved aside enough to let Mallory's horse pass with only two men abreast on foot.

Mallory stopped on the boards covering his men. "What about my men?" Mallory seethed and his horse stamped on the wood. The Red Knight's men standing on the boards suppressed smiles because they could hear Malloy's men swearing at him as the horse stomped and showered them with dirt and even struck those on the head and shoulder who weren't leaning over low enough.

"Ah, yes." The spokesman tucked his thumbs in his belt, looking very pleased with the situation. "As my knight informed your lackey yesterday anyone who breaks any of the kingdom's laws will be met with the most severe punishment."

"My men have done nothing." Mallory ground his teeth barely getting the words out legibly.

"Trespassing, armed trespassing, threatening people of the Red Knight's Keep." The guard ticked them off with his fingers. "That's thirty days in the stockade. For a start."

Mallory stood in his saddle and drew his sword, pointing it at the guard who had been speaking.

Now you must give the man credit, he did not step back, nor even flinch when Mallory's sword touched his chest. He pushed the sword to one side and said quietly, "If you don't go now, I'll assume you are declining the Red Knight's invitation." He took a casual step back and to the side, so he was out of Mallory's reach. Stretching out his arm first back the way Mallory had come, then toward the Keep. "You can either go home or go on."

The look on the guard's face displayed boredom and tediousness. He could not have demeaned Mallory's threat more if he'd knocked him off his horse, grabbed him by the neck, and shook him as if he was a spoiled, misbehaving child.

Mallory's horse backed up a few steps and he kicked the horse much harder than necessary in an attempt to move forward. The horse reared on its hind legs. Mallory held on and struck the horse across his nose with the crop. The horse cried out in pain and went back to all four hooves.

This action moved the guard more than anything that had happened so far. He spoke softly but clearly, fury making his voice tremble, "You strike your horse like that again and I'll kill you myself."

Malicious stilled. The explosion all present expected did not come. The guard watched the shift in the General. In Mallory's mind he had just won this exchange. He thought he now had something over on the guard: hit the dumb beast below himself and he could take the power away from the guard. He stared at the guard and then let out a short bark of laughter. "Forward men, we have a Red Knight to welcome home."

Mallory's troops moved forward shuffling through the narrowed passages and looking at the comrades in cages. All the men were bedraggled, filthy, and many had the same empty look of vileness in their eyes as their General Malicious. When they had finally all passed, the men in the ditch were disarmed and moved to the cages and the cages were covered with tarps.

When all appeared secure, the guard who had acted as spokesman let out a long breath. "Kings and knights! I'm glad that's done."

His fellow guard slapped him on the back. "I never knew you could keep so calm under pressure like that. I was ready to soil my breeches."

Before the spokesman guard could get out another word a woman came running out of the woods and threw herself into his arms. The two hugged and kissed and murmured to one another. Finally she released him, placing her small hands upon his cheeks.

"I am so proud of you." She let her hands drop, "But so scared. Next time have him," she indicated to the other guard with her thumb, "do the talking."

"Hey, what did I do to offend you?" the other guard cried.

"My love, if I am married to one of the chief strategists of the Red Knight," the spokesman looked to the ditch and the still burning spike poles that narrowed the path and the bow slung across her back, "I should be able to carry on a few minutes conversation with an evil general."

She slapped his chest playfully and then kissed him again. Getting serious she looked around the woods and the road, "I just hope Mallory hasn't out-tricked us and still has the majority of his men waiting elsewhere." She unslung her bow and nocked an arrow.

He looked at her with concern. "But none of your traps or early warning trips have alerted have they?"

"No," she shook her head, "but I don't trust that man. Evil oozes out of his very being."

They both turned and looked down the road at Mallory and his men.

"I certainly understand why he's called Malicious!"

"I just hope we've done enough. We only cut down the troop by half. I feel like this is just the beginning. Even if we've won this move, the game has just begun." She took her husband by the arm and turned him back to the gathering of the men and women, seen and unseen, who had protected the road.

Chapter Twenty-Eight
GENERAL MALLORY SURPRISED

Surprisingly, Mallory was feeling quite pleased with himself. One blow and he had raised the man's ire and taken his control away – or so it seemed to him. *These animal-loving fools,* he thought, *"nothing but beasts of burden to be used and disposed of. Why waste time and energy on them*! He slapped the crop on the horse's rump harder than necessary again and it sidestepped. Malicious smiled. *So easy, so easy.*

But his mood darkened as he approached the Keep. He could see sentinels posted about half a mile around and outside the Keep. Fires burning and flags waiting to be hoisted to relay messages. Sentries were posted at each corner of the Keep. Large stones filled the road in front of the gate, barring a frontal attack from a large force. Guards patrolled the walls and the perimeter of the Red Knight's Keep. The gates were closed.

Malicious had been using and abusing the Red Knight's lands for most of the time he had been on the quest for the man with the aura of green. Although he had avoided the Keep itself, he was familiar with its layout. These fortifications were new. Or had he been misinformed about the Red Knight's ability to mount armed forces? *Someone will pay,* he thought.

From a smaller entry door at one side of the gates, a woman exited with her arms wrapped around a full basket looking distracted. After she moved around the stones in front of the gates she looked up in surprise.

"Oh my," she looked Mallory up and down and then at his army of men. She tsked, "Was the Red Knight expecting you?" acting as if an army showed up at the Keep every day, but how rude to do so without an invitation.

Mallory's face flared red and he snapped out, "Of course!"

She nodded, "Oh, well just in case, let me tell him you're here." Without waiting for a response she turned her back on him and went back into the Keep leaving Mallory and his men, unannounced and unwelcomed. Malicious fumed and stewed vowing to make the Red Knight and this particular woman pay for this indignity, but he did not move forward.

When the gates did open an obvious underling came out. "The Red Knight is in conference and not available to meet with you. Allow me to offer his hospitality and see that your men have a place to rest and food." The gates behind him opened wider and about forty armed men stood waiting to escort Mallory's men to the stables for temporary housing and dining. Thus, further dividing Mallory's troops and putting them in buildings that could be locked down on a moment's notice. The underling reached for Mallory's reins, noticed the crop mark on the horse's nose, glared briefly at Mallory but said smoothly, "Sir, if you will allow me, I will tend to your horse and the Captain of the Guard will escort you to the banquet hall where you will meet the Red Knight at his convenience."

Malicious watched the man carefully, studying him, trying to find a weakness, before dismounting. Then General Mallory pointedly ignored the man and turned to Malcolm, who indicated the way they were to go.

The man holding Mallory's horse stifled the chuckle that had nearly escaped when he had dismounted. Mallory was short and dumpy. He stroked the horse's cheek and whispered in his ear, "We'll get some salve on that wound and some water and grain for you." He took the horse away, not to the stables, which for now were temporary holding cells, but to the verdant pasture behind the Keep where the rest of the animals were grazing.

Malcolm strode across the yard, intentionally lengthening and quickening his stride, forcing Mallory to trot to keep up. Which he did for several steps before realizing he was chasing after the Captain of the Guard like a puppy. Suddenly Mallory stopped dead. He spread his legs apart and placed his arms akimbo, looking around the yard like he was a chief inspector. He didn't like what he was seeing.

First, there was no livestock. He had no way of assessing what the Red Knight had for horses, cattle and other animals. Second, he saw groups of women preparing food. *Servants*, he thought. The women were spaced evenly around the yard, and as he looked more closely, he noticed each group had readily available weapons. When one group finished preparing the food, they passed the food on to others who bore it away, while they picked up the weapons and sharpened or repaired them. *Armed servants?* He was puzzled and slowly realized he was in an armed fortress – alone. Trying to look casual, he turned slowly in a circle, confirming that he had been isolated from the rest of his men.

Malcolm stood at the doorway and called across the yard, "General Mallory, the Red Knight has other commitments today. If you'd like to see him, now is the time. Or you can come back for your *scheduled* appointment tomorrow." He leaned nonchalantly against the doorframe, arms crossed with a look of casual disregard, treating Mallory as if he was nothing more than a common peasant come to voice a complaint.

Mallory stood for a moment longer, debating whether to take a stand and demand the respect he thought he deserved. He contemplated but realized that, for the moment, he didn't have enough force to make a demand, so he took a step toward Malcolm, then started strutting as if he owned the Keep until he was forced to stop because Malcolm had not moved from the doorway.

120

Standing upright, Malcolm looked down at Mallory, shrugged, stepped in front of Mallory and moved slowly down the corridor, forcing Mallory to stutter step behind him so as not to step on his heels or bump into him. Malcolm worked very hard to wipe the smile off his face before he had to face Malicious again. He knocked on the appropriate door, three times, and waited and waited and waited.

"Is he here or not!" Malicious exclaimed, his frustration building.

Malcolm turned slowly, "I told you, *you* were not expected until tomorrow. You should be grateful to be given the opportunity to meet the Red Knight at all, today." He spoke in a calm tone, as if addressing a small child or individual with limited intelligence.

Malicious reached for his sword and was surprised when he was immediately flanked by two armed soldiers. He looked from one to the other and then to Malcolm, slowly he lowered his hand, then lifted both hands facing the Captain of the Guard.

"No harm," Mallory looked at the soldiers again, "just anxious to meet your knight."

Behind Malcolm the door opened, a maiden whispered to him, then shut the door. Malcolm nodded and asked one of the soldiers, "Will you find a chair for General Mallory please. It appears there may be a bit of a wait."

Malicious began to rage, shouting and swearing at the soldiers, pushing over the offered chair. He started banging on the door, failing to realize that the two soldiers and Malcolm were standing back watching him with amused expressions, letting him have his tantrum. When the door did open, Malicious jumped back almost falling on his rear, then the men laughed out loud.

"What is going on out here?" The Red Knight opened the door and filled it fully. He was easily twice the size in height and width of Mallory. He looked down at Mallory and extended his large hand, "You must be Mallory. I've got time to see you now." He turned and looked over his shoulder, withdrawing his hand before Mallory could grasp it, and said, "Come in, we're about to eat."

Malcolm stepped up behind Mallory leaving him no option but to follow the Red Knight. Inside the room, it looked like a war council, armed soldiers lined the walls. Four men and one woman sat at the table serving themselves from the platters of aromatic but simple foods in the center of the table. (Fresh bread, fruit, a heavy meat stew) A pitcher of water was passed around the table. There were only two empty chairs, one beside the woman which the Red Knight took, and one further down the table on one side.

Waving his hand to the empty chair, "Join us," the Red Knight said.

Malicious was barely containing his fury. His face was red, he was physically shaking, he clenched and unclenched his fists, trying to rein in his rage. Slowly he moved toward the empty chair. As he sat, the man next to him pushed an empty plate in front of him and with his knife indicated he should help himself. Malicious sat unmoving.

The Red Knight took a large bite of the stew, then looked at Mallory. "The invitation I gave was for tomorrow." He did not allow Mallory to speak but moved on casually, "I have recently returned from my quest and my officers tell me there have been roving bands of thieves and criminals causing harm and mischief on my lands." He took another large bite without breaking eye contact. "They also tell me you've set up an outpost on land protected by both the Red and Blue Knights, to *protect* the people." The Red Knight slowly placed his spoon beside his bowl and leaned back, eyes never wavering from Mallory. Just as Mallory was rising and about to speak, the Red Knight continued, "So why are you here, today, uninvited?"

Mallory slowly sank back down into his chair. Everyone in the room stared at him. All could clearly see the dawning understanding on Mallory's face. His attempt to surprise the Red Knight and gain a strategic superiority with his armed force descending upon the Keep had failed, miserably.

He was sitting alone in a room filled with the Red Knight's armed soldiers. The Red Knight already knew what Mallory and his soldiers had been doing. And now he was indirectly accusing Mallory and his troops of criminal activities and daring him to deny it. Mallory looked around the room, where all eyes were on him. All present waited. The Red Knight raised one of his eyebrows, clearly saying "Well?"

Mallory sat very still, his look of arrogance and haughtiness gone, but his belief in himself was not yet shaken. He had lots of practice outwitting those he had intimidated, but here he had no power, no threat, nothing to give him the upper hand. He took a deep breath.

"Sir Red Knight. Obviously, I was given the wrong message. I was honored to get your invitation and came immediately."

No one in the room moved, no expression changed. Silence pervaded the room.

Mallory rose slowly, "I can see I have arrived at an inconvenient time. I am willing to return tomorrow." He started to move around the table, but everyone seated at the table pushed their chairs back, making it impossible for Mallory to pass. He went to stand behind his chair but realized the back was taller than him, so he was forced to sit down again. "Lord Knight," he said and was interrupted before he could continue.

"I am not a Lord. I am the Red Knight of the Kingdom."

Malicious paused, his temper barely in check because he was unaccustomed to being interrupted or corrected. He ground his teeth and managed to growl out. "Sir Knight."

Those at the table had turned toward the Red Knight when he spoke. Now everyone in the room turned toward Mallory. It was unsettling, eerie, and Malicious felt the threat increase.

"Sir Knight," he started again,63 all haughtiness in his tone gone, "General Bear and I felt it important to protect the kingdom during the quests of our knights."

Everyone leaned toward Mallory, visibly doubting his claim.

He looked around the room, uncertainty rising and showing on his demeanor. "I am unaware of the incidents of which you speak but will make certain to address . . . "

The Red Knight stood up, again interrupting Mallory. "There is nothing to address because the knights are home and expect all lands to be restored."

Mallory started to respond, but everyone at the table rose and faced the Red Knight, ignoring Mallory completely. The Red Knight nodded once, received a nod from those present, and watched them leave the room. Mallory started to follow but the armed soldiers standing against the wall on either side of his chair dropped their swords onto the table, halting any movement. Malicious gave the soldiers a glare, that had no effect, then started to sit down.

The Red Knight sat down slowly, "Don't sit," the Red Knight said in a normal voice, "I'll have someone escort you back to your horse." He paused to take another spoonful of soup, savoring it, making Mallory wait. "I'll expect you and your remaining men to vacate the lands you commandeered within the next five days."

Malicious couldn't help himself, he blurted out, "Remaining?" Then "FIVE DAYS?"

The Red Knight was surprised at how quickly Mallory had realized he'd lost a large portion of his troop. He set the spoon down and stood up, towering over Mallory even from the other end of the table. "We have been very clear that all violators of the kingdom's law will be punished to the fullest extent." He placed both hands on the table and leaned forward slightly. "I already have a list of crimes committed and harm caused to my people and lands by your men." He leaned further forward on the table, lowering his voice, "In addition to those who attacked my road sentries."

"We attacked no one!" Malicious stood and shouted. "If anything we were att . . . "

As if Mallory had never spoken or raised his voice, the Red Knight continued speaking in a strong but quiet voice, "There have already been a few incidents here at my Keep since you arrived." He shook his head as if scolding an unruly child. "Honestly, what sort are these men? Definitely not soldiers of the Kingdom."

The dismissal and inference of incompetent leadership slapped Mallory harder than if the Red Knight had physically struck him. He dropped into the chair.

"Guardsmen." The soldiers beside Mallory snapped their swords up in a salute. "See that General Mallory finds his horse and make sure he and his men depart the Keep immediately." He gave Mallory a stern look. "I will be checking the condition of my lands six days from now." He turned and left Mallory alone in the room.

The guardsman on his right indicated with his sword that Mallory should leave. Malicious moved forward, confused and angry. He tried to huff and bluster but only received a shove with the hilt of the guardsman's sword. Armed soldiers lined the hallway Mallory was forced to exit. As soon as he was past the doors, he saw his horse and then his men in two lines stretching out through the front gate and along the road, with one of the Red Knight's soldiers in between each holding their weapons.

He mounted his horse so angry he didn't notice the healing salve on the horse's nose. He jabbed his heels in cruelly, turned the horse quickly, trying to hurt someone who might be in the way, but only succeeded in knocking down his own soldier who stood closest to him. The horse reared up, but could not fight against the bit and reins and was forced to move forward at a trot, forcing the soldiers to fall in behind and run to keep up.

As the last soldier was handed his weapon and chased after the small, disheveled crowd following General Mallory, only a quarter of what had arrived, the Red Knight's people fell back into the Keep. When Mallory and his men were far enough down the road to no longer be seen, everyone in the Keep took a collective breath. The Red Knight stood in the center of the yard watching out the gate. After several long, quiet moments he said, "Does anyone else feel like they've just been swimming in a pond of vile waste?"

Chapter Twenty-Nine
THE MAN WITH THE AURA OF GREEN
VISITS THE RED KNIGHT'S INFIRMARY

This released everyone and conversations began discussing Mallory and his men.

The stable master approached, "Sir? We need to clean out the stables before bringing the livestock back in. Those men were filthy and vermin-ridden!"

The Red Knight shook his head sadly, "Please do so, bring all the livestock into the yard. I don't trust Mallory or his men."

The stable master nodded in agreement and called out the people he needed to herd the animals and clean the stables. The Red Knight gave the sign for the gates to be closed. Then he seemed to deflate.

Hmway approached and laid his large, gentle hand upon the Red Knight's shoulder. "Come, my friend. Evil is exhausting. Let me help refresh you." He turned the Red Knight and drew him into a warm room where their wives waited. As soon as the door opened he heard his wife and Allayu humming. He saw the cozy fire and four chairs drawn around it. The women looked up and smiled. His wife reached out her hand to her husband, while Hmway sat down by his wife.

The Red Knight kissed his wife's hand. "My love I have one more thing to do before I can rest." He walked slowly toward the infirmary and took time to sit with the men Malicious had so badly abused. While he relayed the day's events, he smiled and laughed with the men until one started gasping for breath and crying out in pain.

The nurses came to attend him and while they were trying to help, the door of the infirmary opened. The man with the aura of green entered striding quickly over to the panicked, suffering man. He crushed the herbs he held in his hands directly under the nose and mouth of the man who was struggling to breathe. Within mere moments, the man began to breathe easier, taking deep inhales and slowly letting out his breath.

Turning away from the patient, the man with the aura of green handed the crushed herbs to one of the nurses and said "Tea." The nurse rushed away to complete his directive. The man with the aura of green pulled another wrapped packet out of his vest pocket, unwrapped it carefully and extracted one single leaf. Opening his own mouth, lifting his tongue, he mimed placing the leaf under the tongue. The man in the bed immediately opened his mouth and lifted his tongue, under which the leaf was placed. "No chewing. Wait." The man with the aura of green watched the man for a few minutes making sure he wasn't chewing, had no ill side effects and that his pain was being relieved. Then he moved to the man's legs.

When the man with the aura of green gently began to remove the blanket, everyone in the room could see and smell the infection in the most badly damaged leg.

The Red Knight asked, "Who is responsible for this?" But the man with the aura of green shook his head once and with a look told the Red Knight to be still.

Then the man with the aura of green turned to the Red Knight, "Water, clean cloths." Without hesitation the Red Knight found the requested items. While he was away, the man with the aura of green created a paste. When the Red Knight set down the bucket and cloths, the man with the aura of green took a cloth, dunked it in the water and began cleaning the leg.

"May I help?" The Red Knight asked.

The man with the aura of green nodded and the two worked silently side-by-side until the leg was clean. This removed rotted skin, infected fluids, and previous treatments so that the infection was exposed. Then the man with the aura of green took a clean cloth and wiped a generous amount of the paste on it and laid it upon the infected area. He repeated this until all areas on the leg were covered, then he wrapped the whole leg with more clean cloth.

The Red Knight watched as the man with the aura of green made more of the healing paste. He observed the injured man carefully. The man was breathing easier and more deeply. The extreme distress that had painted his face with a mask of pain had eased. After the man with the aura of green finished the paste, he inspected the rest of the man. His other wounds were healing properly and he nodded approval. When he had finished his inspection, he wiped the man's face with a cool cloth and laid it upon his forehead.

The man opened his eyes. "Thank you." It was barely a whisper, but it bore no pain and the extreme suffering was gone from his eyes.

The man with the aura of green nodded and smiled. The smile totally transformed his face but in too short a moment it was gone. "If you need me, I'll be back." He rose and took the tea with which the nurse had just returned. He raised three fingers and said, "A day." The nurse nodded his head. The man with the aura of green gave the nurse more herbs for the patient. "Crush under nose, mouth, if he struggles to breathe again." The nurse nodded. Lifting the paste and pointing to the leg and clean wrap. "Daily, or as healing needs." The nurse looked at the leg, concern and uncertainty crossing his face. The man with the aura of green reached out a hand and laid it gently upon the nurse's shoulder, with a slight smile he said, "You'll do well." He held the nurse's eyes until the nurse let a small smile appear. He nodded again and turned to leave.

The Red Knight Bartholomew, being just a little more alert than most, fell in step with the man with the aura of green. "Sir, can I offer you sustenance or lodging?"

The man with the aura of green shook his head no, never ceasing his steps.

"You're help is always appreciated." The Red Knight hesitated, knowing he was losing his chance to ask the question that lay so heavily on his heart and mind. He took a deep breath and said softly, "The Princess?"

The man with the aura of green stopped and turned to face the Red Knight. Not unkindly he said, "She will be ready to return home when the time is right." Then he laid a hand upon the Red Knight's heart. "Rest, brave knight." He kept his hand there until the Red Knight's shoulders relaxed and he sighed deeply. Bartholomew, the man, closed his eyes and the man with the aura of green was gone.

Bartholomew ambled back to the small gathering room, finding only his wife Beatrice waiting. She rose and stroked his face. "My love, you look weary and" she hesitated, looking at him more closely. "I was going to say overburdened, but I see something else now."

Bartholomew took her hand and placed it upon his heart. "*He* touched me here." He patted her hand upon his heart. Together they stood quietly. Beatrice leaned her forehead upon their hands and took in a deep breath.

The door opened and Hmway and Allayu returned with warm drinks. While the Red Knight's Keep put itself in order and reset its watches, the knight accepted the wisdom and wise words, consoling songs and smiles, and a few moments of peace with those who surrounded him with love and support. He went to bed with thoughts of the man with the aura of green instead of General Malicious.

Chapter Thirty
THE BLUE KNIGHT'S KEEP'S NEW MISTRESS

Sarah stirred up the best comfort food she could bring to the table quickly. The bread was just out of the oven and would still be warm if she served it tonight. She had made a heavy meat and vegetable stew and considered only a moment before deciding the new mistress of the castle would appreciate it. *There will be another time to impress her with culinary skills*, she thought. She smiled broadly as she pulled the mixed berry pie out of the oven and took a deep sniff. "This is the ultimate test." She checked the pie and set it on a sideboard to cool. "If she doesn't like my pie, I'll just have to send her home," she said with a chuckle.

"Send who home?" Simon asked as he entered the kitchen.

Sarah jumped and chuckled again, "Anyone who doesn't like my pie, Simon."

Simon leaned over the pie and took a deep breath. "Anyone who doesn't like your pie is sick in the head or just plain tasteless." He started to stick a finger in the pie but Sarah slapped it away none too gently.

"You do that boy, and you will never get another bite of my pies."

Simon tucked his head, grabbed a handful of the leftover berries, and moved over to the table about to sit down.

"What is your problem child?" Sarah gave him a glare. "Set the table. Are you eating with us?"

Simon moved toward the dishes and stopped, "Us?"

"Yes, us. If you are eating with us, we need four bowls and cups."

Slowly Simon pulled out the bowls and set them on the table, as he reached for the cups he tried to sound casual, "Whose eating in the kitchen with us?"

"Rupert and his bride," Sarah said, barely noticing Simon.

"You mean the Head Counselor?" Simon put the mugs on the table.

"Yes, you know her, right?" Sarah was finishing her preparations and giving Simon a very small portion of her attention.

"Yes, I think she is a very good leader of *her* people but I'm not sure she should be here." He finished setting the bowls and mugs around, laying spoons by each. When he turned to face Sarah she stood staring at him. He froze. She looked at him quizzically, waiting. Finally, he shrugged and said, "What?"

Sarah continued to look at Simon, hoping that if she stared long enough, she could see into his soul and understand fully what he had just said. Slowly she repeated, "She is a good leader, but shouldn't be here?" Simon remained frozen. "Because she belongs in the mountains or . . . " Simon took a step back. "Simon?"

Simon turned and fled the kitchen. He heard Sarah call his name one more time, "Simon?"

He was breathing heavily and barely avoided running into one of the housemaids. He got to his room and slipped inside, slamming the door and leaning against it. "Why, why, why!" He moved over to his bed, removed the wooden leg and rubbed his nub. "Why didn't I just die!" He reached for his crutches and moved over to the wash basin, splashing his face with water. Grasping the table, head bowed, he groaned. "I'll never be able to get away from *them* now!" He splashed more water succeeding only in covering the front of himself. He sighed and moved back to the bed, eased

133

himself down, drew a blanket over himself, and almost immediately fell asleep.

Back in the kitchen Sarah was still looking at the door Simon had exited. She was good and truly confused. Usually, she thought herself clever enough to understand the people around her but she was totally baffled by Simon's behavior. She was sure it wasn't really about the Head Counselor, but it was definitely something having to do with the Head Counselor.

As they say, "Speak of the devil and it will appear." As she stood staring after Simon, Rupert and Minerva entered the kitchen from a different door and stopped to observe her, waiting until she realized they were there. Sarah didn't turn however, so Rupert cleared his throat.

Sarah spun toward him and smiled. "Perfect timing, everything's ready." She pulled the chair away from the side of the table making room for Minerva's wheeled chair. She moved around the table, removed the fourth setting, and replaced it with the pie.

"Ohhh my!" Minerva took in a deep breath. "Sarah, if that pie tastes half as good as it smells, I may never leave your kitchen!"

Sarah laughed, coming back to her usual good humor. "Life is short Mistress, want a small piece now?" She was already cutting a piece.

"Please Sarah, it looks as wonderful as it smells," she leaned closer to the pie and reached out to take the offered piece. Turning toward Rupert she offered him the first bite.

"No, my love, I have had Sarah's pie all my life. I want to see your first bite. Then we can share the addiction together." He encouraged her to take the first bite.

"Hmmmmm." Minerva took another bite, sighing with pleasure. She looked at Sarah and started to say something but took another bite instead. She continued to make sounds of pleasure and finished the piece, barely resisting using a finger to clean up the plate. She looked from empty plate to Sarah, who burst out laughing. "I have no words," Minerva looked at the rest of the pie, "that was probably the best pie, no, the best food I have ever tasted!"

Sarah moved the pie off the table and brought the pot of meat stew to the table. "Well my dear, you'll have to wait until you've eaten dinner before you get a second piece." She dished up three hearty portions of stew and set the warm bread between them before taking her seat.

For awhile all that could be heard was the sounds of chewing and delight. After Sarah had served Rupert a second serving of stew, she finally asked. "How bad is it?"

Minerva looked at Sarah, "You don't mince words do you?" It was said with a smile and perhaps, thought Sarah, some admiration.

"Honey, I'm too old and have seen too much to waste my words or time." Sarah smiled, then added a bit sadly, "It's also written all over your faces, so tell all."

The Blue Knight and Head Counselor took turns talking: about the King, the man with the aura of green taking the Princess, the knights' decision to take proactive action, and the fact that the Green Knight was staying with the King. Sarah in turn, told tales about General Mallory and his marauding men. They sat for a long time in the kitchen, eating almost all the pie. Sarah made sure that Minerva had a pot of hot water for her healing tea.

As they were leaving the kitchen Minerva turned to Sarah and took her hand, "I believe you can tell a lot about a man by the people he surrounds himself with," she looked lovingly at Rupert who stood behind her chair, "if you represent those around the

Blue Knight Rupert, I am a very lucky woman and hope I will be welcomed by all as I have been by you."

Sarah leaned down and gave Minerva a warm but gentle hug and whispered in her ear, "You're my daughter now, you can always come to me." She stood up and shooed them out of the kitchen. She watched as the Blue Knight wheeled his new bride down the hallway. Under her breath she said, "I think we are the lucky ones, Head Counselor."

Chapter Thirty-One
BLUE KNIGHT & HEAD COUNSELOR PREPARE

In the morning the Blue Knight's Keep was filled with those who wanted to welcome him home, meet his wife and tell him what had happened in his absence. The Blue Knight and the Head Counselor sat side by side at a table and received all comers. Sarah served food and made sure the Head Counselor had her healing tea every four candlemarks. It was dark when the Blue Knight finally closed his door and sat with his guardsmen and local craft and trade spokespeople.

"My friends," the Blue Knight rose and took time to survey everyone in the room. "Our Kingdom is at a point where we can move either forward or fall into decay." He moved from behind the table, walking among those gathered. "I believe that General Mallory is a sign of what could happen if we don't come together and make a better world." He saw everyone nod and saw fear on a few faces. "It won't be easy," he paused, "and it will probably mean great changes for all of us."

He answered questions from those gathered and tried to respond as candidly as possible. When he felt that everyone's questions and concerns had been addressed, as best he could for now, he looked to the Head Counselor who nodded slightly to him, giving him permission to proceed. "I know most of you have met my wife. Now I'd like to introduce you to the Head Counselor of the Mountain Folk.

Several people in the room smiled at the Blue Knight's wife. Some looked around the room for another person. Some looked at the Head Counselor curiously, others with skepticism. "Will you join me here Head Counselor?"

She backed away from the table and rolled around the end of the table. As soon as she started moving her chair, several in the room gasped, a few rose and started backing away. She stopped beside the Blue Knight and said in her most comforting and authoritative voice.

"Hello good people. I am the Head Counselor of the Mountain Folk. It is an elected position. I have served for ten years. Soon I will need to decide whether to put myself up for the position again or step aside for another." Hearing more gasps from some present, she said gently and with good humor, "Or perhaps I should say wheel myself aside for another. I was born with withered legs. I was left in the mountains and saved by the people who live there, most of whom had been abandoned themselves." She waited, but everyone sat or stood immobile, unsure what to do or say. "I met the Blue Knight when he came on the King's quest to find the man with the aura of green to heal the Princess. Many of you came and helped us build a road upon which people without able limbs could travel and we thank you."

The Blue Knight stepped closer and laid a hand on her shoulder. "It is time, for *all* the people of the kingdom, to be part of the kingdom." He removed his hand. "I have found the Head Counselor to be an able and wise leader. First, I came to respect her for the way she took care of her people, then I became awed by her insight and intelligence. I found her ability to comprehend information and analyze situations inspirational." He looked at her, trying to look as knightly as possible and not let his total love and adoration show, too much. "If the kingdom had counselors like her, we would not be in this crisis now."

Then they waited. The Blue Knight watched those present process the information. The Head Counselor saw some take the expected turn toward disgust and dismissal of her, but it appeared to be a very small minority. Many were befuddled by all the information about the kingdom and having to deal with *those* people they had thrown away like so much trash. As the room quieted, people started to look curious, wanting to know more but hesitant to ask. Reading the group expertly the Head Counselor spoke up.

"I'll be happy to answer any questions." She hesitated and smiled before adding, "About the kingdom or the Mountain Folk."

The Blue Knight called on one of the tradespeople and asked him if he had anything he'd like to share about his time with the Mountain Folk. The Blue Knight had chosen well, the man stood up and started talking first about the road, then about the machinery the Mountain Folk had created, then about how they worked together to do anything he could do and often much better.

It wasn't long before everyone was asking questions and getting honest responses from the Head Counselor, no matter how personal or unintentionally hurtful. She answered with candor, sometimes sharing the pain, sometimes using humor to assuage discomfort, and declining only one request - to look at her legs, but even that she handled with grace.

Then Sarah brought in pie! Everyone had a piece, some tried to get two, but Sarah kept a watchful eye on the pie, ensuring everyone got a piece, before taking away the few scraps that remained. She winked at the Head Counselor as she walked by with the last bit letting her know it would be there for her later.

With everyone sated with pie, the Blue Knight finally brought up the topic that everyone had avoided: General Mallory, or Malicious as he is known by his army and those who've suffered under him. "I think he is the embodiment of evil. He is the tangible force of a hidden undercurrent of evil that has been growing since the Queen died." He pushed back his hair and sighed. "I have chosen not to have an armed knighthood. Instead I promote trades and skills. My priority was to make sure our farms and livestock thrived. That everyone had a roof over their head, food, a job, treatment when injured, and a basic education." Everyone nodded and smiled, each one here represented the success and prosperity of the Blue Knight's stewardship and guiding philosophy. "But I fear we need to arm ourselves and prepare for the worst before things get better." He spent a few more minutes explaining briefly what he had in mind and sent everyone home with the promise of a community gathering on the morrow. He also let them know that he was open to all suggestions.

The Blue Knight and the Head Counselor took positions beside the door and shook everyone's hand, if offered, and accepted congratulations and welcoming to the Head Counselor as it was given. It was a minority who avoided the Head Counselor, but none refused to shake the Blue Knight's hand. When they were finally alone, the Blue Knight sat on the floor beside the Head Counselor and put his head in her lap. For several minutes they sat together in silence, consoling and giving each other comfort.

Reluctantly, the Blue Knight rose and pushed the Head Counselor into the kitchen. Sarah rose as they entered and offered Minerva her healing tea. She placed a warmed sheepskin along her back and slid the last bits of pie in front of her. Minerva finished her tea quickly. Rupert warmed his hands and began her massage. She divided the remaining pie into three bites. She offered one to Rupert who leaned over, took the bite of pie, and gave her a sticky kiss on the cheek. Minerva slowly savored her bite and then scrapped the plate clean making a final bite on the fork and offered it to Sarah. Sarah's first instinct was to decline but she leaned forward and took the final bite, realizing this meant more than just a bite of pie.

Chapter Thirty-Two
EVIL ACTS

Unfortunately for the Blue Knight, he was unaware of what happened at the Red Knight's Keep – Mallory's humiliation. While the Blue Knight gathered his community together the next day, it left his lands unprotected. As an angry and frustrated Malicious ran his soldiers toward the illegally usurped land of his outpost, he realized there were no people on the Blue Knight's land immediately around the outpost. He ordered his soldiers to steal everything they could find and burn the rest.

General Mallory entered his outpost. He commanded the gates shut. Then Malicious went on a rampage. Staying on his horse, he kicked, whipped, and struck out at anyone not quick enough to get out of his way. While General Malicious Mallory extinguished his flames of rage on those around him, outside the fires burned and Malicious's ill intent consumed the landscape. The damages that were done went far beyond the mere physical. They would have far-reaching consequences for General Mallory, the Blue Knight, and the Red Knight.

Chapter Thirty-Three
TRUE SEEING & KITTENS

The Blue Knight was a very happy man. He had always had a good life. Coming from a well-connected and wealthy family he had received the education and training needed not only to run a successful Keep but also to assume the role of the Blue Knight. The previous Blue Knight had only daughters and none of them wanted the responsibility of knight or keeper of lands. Those who had challenged for the position had more gumption than skill and more desire than physical prowess. Fortunately, there had been no fights to the death, Instead, Rupert as the new Blue Knight had secured some new allies because of the way he handled himself during the challenges. After the challenges were complete, he had pursued the challengers to discover their true talents, skills, assets and then to repair or build new relationships.

For example, now the farmers who grew the unique flower used to make the dye for blue silk had strong trade agreements and alliances with the farmers who grew food for human and animal consumption. No one got rich at the expense of another's hunger or lack.

The sapphire mines had always been productive. They were overseen by a collective of families who had both their own and others' best interests at heart. An uprising within the mines a few years ago happened because the miners thought they were not getting a fair wage for their work. Citing the White Knight's profit-sharing diamond mine agreement, they demanded such equality of share. The Blue Knight and White Knight spent many nights at the table discussing the pros and cons of various options before the Blue Knight went back to his own people and negotiated better wages and a few other safeguards for his own mines. Some of the workers took note that the Blue Knight's shares had not increased, nor his share of the profits. His reward was far greater with the respect and loyalty he earned.

The Blue Knight's lands had been blessed with a preponderance of builders: road builders, bridge builders, building builders, tunnel builders. If you can imagine it, children sat in the schools on the Blue Knight's lands, building their own miniature creation of what was to come. Hence, the Blue Knight's roads were the best constructed and maintained. No bridges were swept away by flooding or collapsed under the weight of neglect. Some of the most elegant buildings in the whole kingdom existed as the homes and businesses of those living in the Blue Knight protectorate.

People were constantly improving the tools needed to build. When they designed their next build, it always included something new and creative. When the Mountain Folk had asked for help building a road, it was a challenge they accepted gladly. When they found that the engineers and builders of the Mountain Folk had designed tools and machines they had never imagined, it was, how do you say? "A marriage made in heaven."

Let me tell you honestly that for most people, but not all, the physical appearance of the people on the mountain was off-putting for only as long as it took to get to know them. Most Mountain Folk were intelligent, resourceful and witty. Having chosen a sense of humor instead of doom and misery as their mantle. If they were unable to accomplish a task on their own, they paired with another, or created a new tool, or were humble enough and self-assured enough to ask for help. Since the Blue Knight's quest had ended, many of those who had volunteered to help build the road had returned to the mountains to continue the friendships they had forged. They continued to learn more from one another, and for a few, try to find the family members who were lost long ago.

I remind you of these things only to help you understand why there was such a large number of Mountain Folk who journeyed to the Blue Knight's lands. When Mud returned home to the mountains and gathered the people together in his official capacity as Chief Engineer, there had been great concern. But when he told them of their Head Counselor's marriage to the Blue Knight, immediately a party formed to travel to the Blue Knight's lands to celebrate the union. There still happened to be a group of Blue Knight builders who had continued to work on road improvements for the Mountain Folk during his absence. All seemed ready for returning home so it became a great caravan of people who headed to the Blue Knight's Keep when they came upon the burning lands and destroyed properties.

The journey turned from merriment and excitement to fear and worry, then action. The caravan set about putting out fires, collecting the remains of tools, bracing some buildings, removing smoking timbers in others, and filling gaps. The wells and waterways were cleared of some of the detritus. Had this group not been moving through the land shortly after Malicious' people had done their damage, the fires would have continued to rage, destroying all the flowers used for silk dying, and the mulberry fields upon which the silkworms fed and made their cocoons. Also at risk were other areas that were cultivating different forms of silk creators for sericulture (the production of making silk).

Most of us think silk can only be made by the larvae of insects undergoing complete metamorphosis, but the clever silk farmers were also working on the silk of arachnids – web spinners, who spin all their lives and during Hymenoptera of bees, wasps, and ants. This quest to create silk without destroying their co-creator was a desire deeply embedded within the silk farmers and something they were very close to succeeding at. (To produce 2.2lb of silk, 29lbs of mulberry leaves must be eaten by 3000 silkworms.) Nearby stood the warehouses where the reeling of silk occurred, then the processing and dying. Some buildings were already ablaze, some but for chance or luck, were still standing. The whole silk industry could have been destroyed. Some of the travelers started asking questions about the silk, when the Chief Engineer called for quiet.

Standing close to a nearly destroyed building were two of the Mountain Folk. Each had his and her head cocked with looks of intense concentration on their faces. They heard something and were trying to find its exact location. Everyone stilled - a portrait of attention by all.

The man was the first to move, tapping his stick gently before him as he made his way through the debris. The woman waited, occasionally directing the man further to the left or right. Finally the man stopped and raised his voice to call others over. "Here, she's here!"

The Chief Engineer moved to assist the two blind seekers away from the now frantic search under the fallen building, murmuring, "Well done, well found," softly to both.

"Found her!" one man shouted.

"We need a ladder to get to her," another said, turning to find the ladder.

"She's just a young child," signed the deaf mountain man who had, with amazing strength, moved large debris to uncover her.

After being uncovered, a young girl holding three young kittens in her arms was quickly extracted from the pile of rubble that had once been her home. A blanket was wrapped around her. She would not release the kittens. Turning aside all needs for herself, she begged for some milk for the kittens. In the field, a cow could be heard mooing in great distress. Soon she was handed a cloth teat someone created that was filled with fresh milk from the heifer who now contentedly chewed its cud.

As the kittens nursed, the child calmed. She said softly, "Momma cat was bringing her kittens in from the fire." A soft sob left her as she nuzzled the kittens. "Then she didn't come back. I heard men shouting so I grabbed the kittens and hid." It took her several moments before she could speak again. "The house fell in on me. I thought . . . " she stopped again, unable to go on.

The Chief Engineer brought the two who had heard the girl and directed others over to save her. Gently he said, "Little Miss, these are the people who found you."

The girl looked into the kind face of the Chief Engineer who stood only three tall with a stubble of a beard. She reached with her free hand and touched his face. "Are you a child, like me?"

Mud smiled, "No Little Miss, I'm old enough to be your father." She seemed to accept that without question and looked at the two people standing beside him. "This is Mary and Joseph. They can not see you but they hear very well. They heard you crying and found you."

Mary and Joseph smiled down at the girl. Mary asked, "What kind of kittens do you have?"

The girl held up one. When Mary did not move to take it or look at the kitten she said, "This is a black one with a bent ear." Then Mud guided Mary's hand to the kitten and the girl released the kitten into Mary's hand. Turning toward Joseph she said, "This is a grey one, I think she'll be a good barn cat 'cuz she already loves to hunt." She held up the kitten to the man who seemed to be looking at her but made no move to take it. She looked puzzled, then asked, "Do you not like kittens?"

Joseph reached out both hands, "I love kittens I just didn't see you offer her to me." Again Mud guided his hands so the girl could place a kitten in them.

146

The girl cuddled the final kitten. "This one is mine. I think she got a little burned and has hair that goes all different ways but I love her."

For several moments the three caressed and nuzzled the purring kittens. Then Mud cleared his throat. "Little Miss where are your parents?"

She bent her head and said almost so softly no one heard, "Don't have any, just like kitty."

"Who do you live with then?" asked Mud, almost as softly.

"Farmer lets me work in the barn. They don't know my ma and da are gone and that I sleep in the barn too." Suddenly she looked afraid and sat more upright. "I didn't do this; it was the men, the men who play soldiers at the fort over there," she waved an arm across the field. "Please don't make the farmer send me away."

"Shh, shh, now Little Miss." Mud looked at Mary and Joseph who had their heads together and were whispering. Turning back to the young girl, "Well now, it seems we have a puzzle to solve, a farmer to find and some cat caretaking to sort out," he sighed.

Mary leaned forward, "Chief Engineer do you think this young girl would be willing to let us help care for the kittens? We would very much like to keep them but think the three should not be separated."

The young girl looked up hopefully, then confusion crossed her face. She looked intently at their blank sightless eyes. "How did you find me if you can't see me?" she asked with complete innocence.

Mary leaned forward, smiled, and said, "Just like I can tell you're sitting by a lilac bush and there is a running creek behind you."

The girl turned from side to side, first spying the lilac bush, then turning to find the creek. "That's magic!" she exclaimed.

"No," said Joseph. "That's what happens when you lose one sense, but have enough sense to keep going on and use your other senses." He spoke earnestly but his smile was warm.

The little girl rose and nodded, then realized they couldn't see her so she spoke earnestly, "I would like very much to have your help take care of my kittens."

Mary reached out her free arm and the girl tucked herself under it. "What shall we call you Little Miss?"

The girl hesitated. "I don't like my name."

Mary chuckled and gave her a quick one arm hug. "Alright then, you pick a name that you like and that's what you will always be for us."

The girl thought and thought and finally said, "I like the name Mary."

Mary smiled, "That is a great compliment. But since we are going to be together for a while, don't you think that would confuse people?"

The girl nodded, stopped nodding, and said out loud, "Uh-huh," and looked very serious and thoughtful.

Mary also looked thoughtful. "What did you feel when we found you and they brought you out safely?"

The girl was still, pensive, then she smiled and said, "Joy."

Mary smiled and asked, "May we call you Joy?"

"Yes, oh yes!" The girl bounced and hugged her kitten. "Joy. Yes, I like that name."

Mud got Mary and Joseph settled back into their cart, with Joy between and kittens in the hands of all three. Joseph took the reins of the pony and let it pull their cart back into the caravan. The three began a conversation that would last a lifetime.

~~~

Chief Engineer Mud approached the foreman of the Blue Knight's lands and motioned for him to step away from the clean-up for a bit more privacy. "What happened here?"

The foreman shook his head, "Evil has moved in, I fear."

"What?" the Chief Engineer said a bit angrily. "I thought you were supposed to live in the good land of peace and prosperity!"

The foreman shook his head again, "My friend, a kingdom is not always what it appears to be. While our knight was looking for the man with the aura of green in your mountains, the King's two generals left the palace and set up outposts."

"But that should be a good thing," Mud asked, "they did it for safety or . . . "

The foreman interrupted him, "Perhaps General Bear did it for the welfare of the people, but I think General Malic . . . Mallory," he pointed a thumb over one shoulder, "did it to make his own kingdom."

The Chief Engineer took a step to the side and peered around the foreman, trying to see what he had pointed to. "What am I supposed to see?"

The foreman turned around and looked more carefully, spotting his target. Lifting his arm he pointed to what appeared to be a poorly fenced yard. "That," he turned his point to a clenched fist, "is General Malicious' outpost."

Mud stepped up onto a stack of stones and wood and peered across the field. He pulled a scope out of his pocket that he used for sighting measurements in the field. He squinted and tried to see more clearly but gave up. "Huh, if that's an outpost for protection, you're all in trouble, it's a mess."

"More trouble than you know my friend, more trouble than you know," the foreman said sadly and shook his head. "Let's get to Blue Knight's Keep and I'll tell you everything I know on the way."

Chapter Thirty-Four
A KNIGHT'S WEDDING PARTY

At the Blue Knight's Keep people had gathered and an impromptu wedding party was being held for the Blue Knight Rupert and the Head Counselor Minerva. The courtyard had been cleared of animals, stalls and tools, and filled with tables, chairs and a place to dance. All the gates open. A small band played gay music, people were dancing, clapping and singing along. Seemingly out of nowhere, Sarah had produced a feast with assorted meats, breads, vegetables, and OH, don't forget the pies! How she had managed to bake almost fifty pies of different flavors Minerva could not imagine. Every time she rolled by the table, a different scent caught her and she could not resist taking another small piece of pie.

Rupert danced up behind his bride and stole the last bite of pie off her fork. "Oh, how could you!" Minerva tried to sound angry but the laughter in her eyes reached her voice before she even spoke. "Thank you! I think if I took one more bite, I would explode!"

He leaned down and stole a kiss licking a bit of berry off her lips. Smiling he extended his arms. "Dance with me." She set her plate aside and extended her arms. He pulled her onto the hard, smooth courtyard for a formal court dance, using her wheeled chair to turn her back and forth, eliciting a joyous laugh from his bride.

When the band finished, he bowed deeply and she responded with a dip of her head and doff of her hand. Applause broke out. The two dancers looked from each other's eyes to see everyone gathered around, surrounding their dance floor, cheering and applauding. Then the clapping became rhythmic and a chant began: "Kiss, kiss, kiss, kiss."

The Head Counselor blushed just a little, as she was not uncomfortable being the focus of attention, just a little shy about being asked to give such a public display of her affections. She tipped her head up and hesitated, seeing the twinkle in Rupert's eyes. She raised an eyebrow asking the question, *"What's happening?"* Rupert leaned forward and brushed both cheeks with his lips and in her ear said, "All the male residents of the Keep want to kiss the bride." He gave her a soft kiss on the lips and winked at her. Standing up straight, he raised his voice and said, "Gentlemen, my bride is yours." He moved to her side and watched the procession begin.

The men who knew the Head Counselor were first in line. They leaned in and kissed her on one or both cheeks. Many winked, some added a congratulations. Then came those who dwelt and served in the Keep. Most of these men kissed her hand but a few of the younger males were bold enough to give her a peck on one cheek. As each man approached, the Blue Knight said his name and greeted him.

He faltered only once. The young man smiled broadly and said, "I didn't think you'd remember I was just a wee lad," with his hand he indicated a smaller size child, "the last time we met. Thank you Sir Knight." He shook the Head Counselor's hand and bowed, "My Lady."

The greeting and descriptions got longer as the general population gave the bride "kisses". The Blue Knight always said the name first, then his position or role, and if the man had a special talent or skill, he mentioned that too.

Finally, the last and youngest male approached. Across the courtyard Minerva could see his mother encouraging him. She watched the boy to determine the best way to greet him. When he finally stood before her, he was shorter than she, even seated as she was. He looked tentatively up at her. She smiled and extended her hand. As he reached out, she grasped his hand and pulled him close, up onto her lap, and offered him her cheek. He giggled and blushed and leaned in quickly to kiss her, then slid off her lap and scampered away. He got halfway back to his mother before he remembered; turning quickly, he ran back and bowed before the Head Counselor and the Blue Knight, then waved and ran to his mother.

"Music," the Blue Knight directed. More softly he said to Minerva, "How are you my dear?"

"Charmed," she said wistfully. She looked around the courtyard at the collection of people talking, dancing, laughing, eating, and enjoying the companionship of Blue Knight's Keep.

He leaned closer, a look of concern crossing his face, "And?"

She reached up and stroked his cheek, as was now her habit, and something that made him feel loved. "Never in my wildest dreams did I imagine I would be the bride in a knight's keep with his people celebrating us." She felt him smile beneath her hand. "I just wish some of my people were here to share the festivities."

As if it were the command they had been waiting for, the caravan from the mountains rolled in through the open gates. The Foreman and Chief Engineer dismounted their wagon and approached the Blue Knight and the Head Counselor.

Mud looked past them at the table of food. "Ah good, we're not too late, I'm starving." He nodded to them, thus having greeted his Head Counselor sufficiently in his mind, he moved to the table and began filling a plate.

The Foreman watched him for a moment before giving the Blue Knight a nod, "Sir Knight." He turned to the Head Counselor and took her hand kissing it for a bit longer than most, "My Lady." When he released her hand the Blue Knight grasped his arm and shook it firmly once.

Chapter Thirty-Five
A NEW FAMILY OUT OF THE ASHES

Looking at the laden caravan the Blue Knight asked, "What have you brought to our celebration Foreman?"

"Sir," the Foreman hesitated, "Originally we were a party of thirty, twenty from your mountains My Lady, and the ten of us who had been there working on the road."

The Head Counselor asked with excitement, "How goes the road?"

He smiled, "Well, the Chief Engineer and I will give you a full report soon." Looking from her to the Blue Knight he went on, "When the Chief Engineer returned and told us of your nuptials, we knew we had to return posthaste to celebrate with you." He looked over his shoulder and indicated with his head the people now entering the Keep. "But our number has increased by five: three of them seriously injured, one orphaned, and one who hasn't spoken since we found him."

The Blue Knight and the Head Counselor were immediately alert, finding the five and observing them thoughtfully.

The Foreman continued, "Someone has burned almost all the lands around General Mallory's outpost." The Blue Knight's head snapped back to the Foreman. "They destroyed everything they could; buildings, wagons, tools," he sighed deeply. "If we hadn't been passing by, the fires would still be burning, and by the time this celebration is over, everything would have been destroyed and we could have been in flames ourselves."

One of the Blue Knight's hands went to the Head Counselor's shoulder, he clutched it, then relaxed, leaving it lying there. "General Mallory's outpost?"

"Yes. It looks like his mob just went crazy trying to do as much damage as possible without purpose." The Foreman looked over his shoulder spotting the little girl with the kitten. "See that child?" The Blue Knight and the Head Counselor nodded their heads in unison. "Mary and Joseph heard her and the kittens crying under a pile of burned and burning timber. I don't know how they survived because most of the house was destroyed." The Blue Knight's hand clenched the Head Counselor's shoulder and released.

The Blue Knight spoke calmly but the tension in his body was so tight he felt he might break. "Please introduce us to everyone and make sure everyone has something to eat then I would like to talk to the five you rescued."

The Foreman gave a nod and turned to gather the caravan and survivors. Mud walked up with a plate piled with food and a full mouth. "You've got big problems Blue Knight. That General Malicious sounds like trouble." He took another bite and before fully swallowing spoke, "Looking good Head Counselor, marriage suits you. I just hope you get a chance to enjoy it."

She cast a speculative glance at the Chief Engineer. "Thank you," more a question than a statement. Then she was drawn to greeting her people and the Blue Knight's travelers. She accepted congratulations on her union and postponed questions about her return to the mountains. She encouraged her people to join in the celebrations. She turned to Mary, Joseph, and the little girl with the kittens.

"Mary, Joseph. I see you have some new additions to the family." She reached out and touched Mary's hand before giving the kitten a stroke.

"We hope so Head Counselor but it's really up to Joy. They are her kittens," Mary said.

"Joy, what a beautiful name! A name for a person filled with love I think," the Head Counselor said sincerely.

Joy beamed and held out her kitten for the Head Counselor to pet. Then remembering herself and who she was speaking to, she bobbed a little curtsy and stepped back. "Ma'am. I think Mary and Joseph will take good care of my kittens. But when they go home, I don't think I want the kittens to go." She looked very grave now.

The Head Counselor looked from Mary to Joseph who were trying very hard to communicate something to her without speaking, then she looked at Joy. "I understand your home was destroyed. Where will you go when Mary and Joseph return to the mountains?"

Joy's head drooped, her shoulders slumped, she mumbled, "Don't know."

"We've been discussing the possibility of Joy coming home with us." Joseph turned toward Joy and smiled. Joy returned his smile even though he couldn't see it, but he seemed to know she had. He went on, "Three kittens are a lot to care for alone, but one kitten each we could manage. If Joy would be willing to let us keep them and come with us to help take care of them, we could do it together."

The Head Counselor looked compassionately at Joy. Speaking kindly, "Taking care of another creature is a great responsibility. I know Mary and Joseph. They are very good people." She looked up at them and then leaned closer to Joy and whispered, "But I don't know how they'd be to live with."

Mary burst out, flustered, "Head Counselor you know we are mild-mannered people. We'd be very easy to live with." She wanted to go on, but Joseph laid a hand upon her arm. "Hush Mary,

I think Head Counselor is pulling our leg." Mary stopped puffing and stilled.

The Head Counselor and Joy were smiling watching Mary and Joseph. The Head Counselor nudged Joy, "What do you think? You think you can keep them in order and help them with the kittens?"

Joy looked very happy but stilled and became thoughtful. She said seriously, "I've never lived anywhere but the farm." She looked at Mary and Joseph and then spoke to the Head Counselor, "And your Mountain Folk are different than anybody I've ever known." She stopped, dipping her head slightly, waiting for a rebuke or maybe even a blow.

"Do you have a problem with different?" The Head Counselor asked in a neutral tone.

Joy took her time before answering for she was a thoughtful girl. "I don't think so. People have called me different," she tapped her head. "Will they accept me because I'm different?" She was very intent now.

The Head Counselor stifled the smile that was growing. "You are not the first person to ask that question." Joy looked at her surprised. "I asked the same question when I came here." She tapped her wheels with her palms. "I wasn't sure people would accept my difference here, but they did." She crooked a finger so Joy would lean closer. "Mary and Joseph are very wise and understand different. I believe they would help and protect you if you agreed to help them." They both leaned back and looked appraisingly at Mary and Joseph.

After several silent seconds Mary leaned toward Joseph whispering, "What's happening? I don't hear anything."

Joseph smiled and said, "Be patient dear."

157

Joy leaned toward the Head Counselor and asked conspiratorially, "Can they cook? I'm awful bad at cooking."

It was all Minerva could do not to let out a little giggle, but as Head Counselor she managed to hold it in, barely. "Don't know. What do you say we check with the head cook around here, see if she will let them in her kitchen and we can find out what they can do? If they are really bad, maybe you can all have some cooking lessons before you go home."

The Blue Knight took that moment to hand Joy a piece of pie. "If you're lucky maybe the cook will even teach you how to make pie." Nodding his head and pushing the pie forward, "Go on, take a bite."

Joy took a tentative taste, then a bigger bite and a big smile crossed her face. She took another bite which was much too large, but she managed to get it all in and chewed. Then she did something that surprised everyone. She went over to Mary and Joseph and offered them each a bite. As if she had been with them all her life, she put their hand upon hers so they could guide the bite safely to their mouth. When everyone was done chewing she asked. "Do you think we can learn how to bake pies like this?"

Mary said, one tear sliding down her beaming face, "We will give it our best try my girl."

The Foreman took Mary by the arm, which brought Joseph, and he reached out a hand to Joy which she took. "Come, eat. There's more pie!" Then he took them to the banquet table.

Chapter Thirty-Six
BLUE KNIGHT REALIZES THE TRUE DANGER

The Blue Knight summoned three of his couriers. He gave instructions for one to go inspect the lands around General Mallory's outpost and be circumspect. He asked the other to set a watch and let the Keep know immediately if General Mallory or any of his men approached the Keep. He sent the third courier off to the Red Knight with a summary of the events and asked for any information the Red Knight could share. He ordered the third courier to return as quickly as possible.

Next, he found several of his farm and building leaders and arranged a meeting when the day's celebrations were done. Finally, he found a few Keep laborers who had not imbibed too much and upon whom he could rely to keep watch. He asked them to take shifts around the Keep while enjoying the festivities in moderation. The Blue Knight wanted some warning if General Malicious moved on him.

The Head Counselor had sat quietly while the Blue Knight had taken action. When he finally returned to her, she asked pensively, "Where are your military arms?"

A bit distracted he said, "Probably locked up. We use them rarely and usually only for ceremony."

"I would suggest you bring them to a location easy for your people to access should we get an unwanted visitor."

He looked down at her. "You are brilliant." He leaned down for a kiss, lingering but not igniting passion. Looking into her eyes he whispered, "How did I ever get so lucky to find you?" She reached up and placed both hands on his cheeks and pulled him back into another kiss.

"Go," she whispered. "We've still got celebrating to do before we go to war." She released his cheeks and shooed him away to attend to his knightly duties.

After the celebration, the Blue Knight's leaders joined together to discuss General Mallory's actions. The Blue Knight and the Head Counselor sat in stunned silence as the list of horror stories of General Malicious' "protection" grew. The Head Counselor had started taking notes so she could remember people's names and made a list of the reparations that would need to be made. What horrified her most was the senseless violence. These "soldiers" seemed to have no sense of honor or humanity. She was becoming deeply worried. These were the kind of people you couldn't reason with because they had no reason. These were people hard to fight, because they had nothing to lose, they often enjoyed the killing, and had no fear of dying.

While they were gathered, the courier arrived back from Red Knight Keep. He gave a summary of how the Red Knight's people divided General Mallory's forces, imprisoning about half within his Keep. How they had humiliated Mallory. They had not expected him to act out senseless revenge. The Red Knight sent a written apology for the burning of lands and property and offered to help restore things to rights. Privately, the courier extended a personal message to the Blue Knight and the Head Counselor, which chilled them both.

They all worked through the night to establish a system of observation and alerts. Each property owner was connected to at least five others who would respond at the first sign of danger and notify the Blue Knight. They all worried about the most effective and quickest way to communicate, discussing options, when the Head Counselor asked if they would be willing to learn a new language. Most responded with an affirmation, but a few were skeptical and hesitant to commit. The Head Counselor thanked them all and said she would talk with her language "experts" and share if they had an appropriate option. This left most highly puzzled, some confused, and the reluctant, even more skeptical.

As dawn broke and everyone was departing the Keep the Blue Knight asked them to pause. Taking the Head Counselor's hand, he stood before them. "My friends and neighbors, the world we know has changed. Our kingdom is at risk. We can bow to the evil that has been moving in our kingdom or take a stand. Now is the time to decide what our world will be." He looked down at the Head Counselor, shook her hand once. "Together we can make a better world. Now is the time to think differently, speak boldly, and not be afraid to act for the good of all." His voice had been growing in strength as he spoke. The Blue Knight's presence emanated sincerity and intensity. He gazed at them all, searching, hoping, expecting, and then suddenly, all his energy and strength drained away, and he seemed to wilt before them.

The Head Counselor took up his call without hesitation. "Sleep now my friends, soon we will have to face the unthinkable. *We will* survive and then have something new to celebrate. Go home in peace, let us hear from you soon."

Silently, everyone left, leaving an exhausted Blue Knight, Head Counselor, and Keep residents. The celebration of joy - almost forgotten. The weight of an uncertain future bore heavily upon them. Rupert roused himself, "To bed everyone. We all need our rest and strength." He wheeled Minerva to their sleeping chamber. After setting her gently in bed and tucking her under the covers he fell in beside her and was instantly asleep. Minerva smoothed his hair off his face and kissed his cheek softly.

"Good night, my brave knight." She nuzzled up beside him and was soon breathing deeply too.

Chapter Thirty-Seven
A NEW SONG

The Red Knight Bartholomew awoke slowly. Bad dreams and restlessness had troubled him all night. Malicious would not be put aside. Sighing, he reached across the bed to find it empty. *She must be up already,* he thought, rolling over to look out the window where dawn was just breaking. *Hmm, I wonder why so early?* He stretched and made ready for his day, taking his time, then headed down to the kitchen, thinking it was too early for many to be up.

As he neared the kitchen, he heard singing. Soft, with many harmonies, not really words, except now and then, but an uplifting tune. He stopped outside the door listening. He heard Beatrice, Hmway, Alleyu, and was surprised to note that there were also several other voices: the cook and cooking maid, his captain of the guard, and another male voice he didn't recognize. They made a marvelous choir. He closed his eyes and let himself get lost in their melody. When the music stopped, it took a few moments for him to come back to himself and realize there was silence.

"Are you going to join us?" Hmway softly asked from his place in the kitchen.

Bartholomew entered the kitchen, surprised to see all the activity and brightness therein. "I didn't want to interrupt." He looked around the kitchen acknowledging all present. "You sounded so good. But isn't it early for music?"

"Frankly, Sir, I can't think of a better time for it!" the cook said, still working with her hands to make the morning fast break. "It was right dark and gloomy in here this morning - like that evil general left some of his darkness behind." She shivered. "Til we started singing."

"I am an early riser," Alleyu said softly in her musical voice, "and I always sing in the morning." The cook smiled warmly at her.

"I heard them singing and came in from the stables," Malcolm said. "There is an awful chill out this morning and the kitchen seemed to glow with warmth and goodness." Then he blushed.

The Red Knight mused, he had never before seen his captain of the guard blush. *Was it the admission of wanting the warmth or the goodness of someone* **in** *the kitchen?* he thought and a corner of his mouth curved up into a smile.

The others in the kitchen nodded assent. Bartholomew's wife came over and put an arm around him. "Music always makes things better." She sat him at the table next to Hmway and placed a basket of apples in front of him. "Peel." She sat down next to him and did just that. After the first apple was done she said, "I've been thinking." Bartholomew picked up a knife and began peeling, waiting for her to go on. "We need a song."

"Like a battle song?" he asked.

"**No!** Not a song of war. A song of hope. Something to lift us up when things get tough. Something to take us out of despair. Something to combat the evil without shedding blood." She had already peeled three apples to the Red Knight's one – still only half done.

"An anthem," Hmway intoned.

"YES, exactly! An anthem that we can teach everyone." Beatrice took the basket of apples from Bartholomew. "Dear just eat the apple before you cut a finger off."

The Red Knight looked at the mess he'd made of the apple and cut off a piece, offering it first to his wife, then finishing off the bite. "An anthem," he mused.

Hmway and Alleyu started humming the tune he had heard earlier and soon everyone in the room had joined in. It was a simple tune anyone could remember and repeat. It was uplifting and the more voices added, the brighter and more hopeful it sounded.

"We need words, don't we?" the Red Knight asked.

"I'm working on those," Beatrice said quietly, "but I needed inspiration." She looked at Alleyu. "I'm afraid I was letting the darkness overtake me too."

Alleyu took the last peeled apple and cut it expertly into eight pieces, offering everyone present a piece. She raised her piece up and the others followed. "To the anthem of joy, success, overcoming, and peace."

"Joy, success, overcoming, and peace," everyone said together and bit into their apple.

The day seemed to have a much different feel after a fast break with music. The ill feeling that the Red Knight had woken up with wasn't gone, because the problem wasn't solved yet. But the possibility of - joy, success, overcoming, and peace - gave him hope. His step was lighter. He walked in time to the rhythm of the tune which would be the anthem that led them all to a new day, a new kingdom.

RISE UP!

Chorus: x3
> Rise Up. A new day's begun
> Rise Up. So much to be done
> Rise Up. To meet our fate

> RISE UP! RISE UP!

Verse 1:
> Never a day too dark or gloomy
> Never a struggle too hard or looming
> Our spirits will prevail over darkness

> RISE UP! RISE UP! RISE UP! RISE UP!

Chorus: x1 Rise Up! Rise Up!

Verse 2:
> Gathered we strive and gathered we overcome
> Rise Up, Rise Up, in hope we will succeed
> We will conquer all with harmony and grace

INTERLUDE

Chorus: x1 Rise Up! Rise Up!

Verse 3:
> The time will come when challenges won
> Evil, pain, and grief will be undone
> Voices in the heav'ns will all cry REJOICE

Final Chorus:
> REJOICE, a new day's begun
> REJOICE, so much to be done
> REJOICE, to live our fate.
> RISE UP!

Chapter Thirty-Eight
LIFE WITH A SPOUSE –
BLUE KNIGHT RUPERT & HEAD COUNSELOR MINERVA

Rupert and Minerva snuggled into their bedding. Rupert pulled the top comforter over their heads.

"Hiding?" Minerva asked without moving.

"Yes," he said softly. Together they lay in each other's arms, warm in the semi-darkness of their comforter.

Minerva sighed, "I feel like a small child. Safe and protected in my bed." She sighed again. "I wish that safety was a truth, not just a feeling."

Rupert pulled her a little closer and flipped the comforter off their heads. "It may take a day or two . . . " he kissed the top of her head, "but your safety *WILL* be a reality." Several moments passed then Rupert moved suddenly, throwing the covers off and hopping out of the bed.

"HEY!" Minerva reached for the covers, pulling them back up to her shoulders. Then she started giggling. "Ummmm." More giggles. She pulled the covers over her mouth and nose, peering over them with just her eyes, her giggling unabated.

At the end of the bed stood the Blue Knight, naked, posing, flexing his muscles. He posing as a fighter, a speaker, then in more and more ridiculous positions. When he finally fell over and remained on the floor laughing, Minerva crawled to the end of the bed and peered down at him, her giggles now full-blown laughter.

Gasping for breath, "Wh-wh-wh-a-t are ... you... doing?" She tried to regain her aplomb, but watching Rupert, now writhing and squirming on the floor, only increased her laughter.

Finally, when both were exhausted, and Rupert had stopped squirming, a soft voice was heard from the floor. "When I was single, I did this every morning you know." Minerva rose on her arms and looked over the edge of the bed at the now still, but panting Rupert.

"Oh really?" She tried not to smile but he was being just too silly. Finally, she was able to raise one eyebrow and look a bit more serious. She watched as he nodded solemnly. "Clothing always optional?" she said as seriously as possible, but her smirk betrayed her.

Rupert jumped up covering his private parts with his hands. "Why didn't you tell me I was naked?" He looked aghast. It took only three more seconds before he bent and dropped his hands to his knees, laughing. When he could speak again, he said, not at all seriously, "Clothing is always optional." He leaned down to give Minerva a quick kiss and strutted off to attend to his morning ablutions, shaking his backside a bit more than was necessary.

Minerva watched him, appreciating the view, smiling at his ability to be silly. She marveled at how this man, this Blue Knight, never forgot a person's name or details, had uncanny insight, embodied all the qualities of a knight, could be tender and loving, yet had the capacity for silliness and unbridled joy. She shook her head and took a minute to gaze around the room, her bedroom. *How did I come to be here?* she thought. She closed her eyes and spoke briefly to the Power, giving her thanks and then making a request for wisdom in the challenge ahead. Then she put herself to rights, straightened the bed covers and wheeled herself to the kitchen. She had things to do this morning, other than laugh at her silly husband.

When she entered the kitchen, Cook was serving two bedraggled men. She recognized one as the man the Blue Knight had sent to watch General Mallory's activities, the other was a

Mountain Folk. She stopped in the doorway and watched quietly. The Blue Knight's watcher tapped the table softly between the two men and the other man turned to watch his hands. The watcher was making specific movements with his hands – obviously communicating with the other. The second man replied in kind with hand language and returned to eating. The first man looked up at Sarah and asked, "Do you have pie?" He looked a bit embarrassed, but when Sarah placed a whole, steaming, fresh out of the oven, berry pie on the table before him, he smiled widely and nudged the man next to him, who was already leaning toward the pie, sniffing appreciatively.

The Head Counselor wheeled the rest of the way in. "Sarah's pies are the best in the world, aren't they?" The first man started and turned to her. The second man whose eyes were closed so he could take in all the pie's wonderful aromas, did not react to her spoken words.

The first man stood up. "Ma'am." She waved him to sit down. "Yes, Ma'am. Sarah's pies are the best!" He sank back into his chair and smiled at Sarah warmly.

"Just back?" the Head Counselor asked.

"Yes Ma'am." Involuntarily he shivered. "That man is a monster," he said under his breath. Aloud he said, "I was told to report to Sir Blue Knight as soon as I arrived. Is he available?" While speaking, he nudged the other man, tapped the table once, and pointed with one finger to the Head Counselor.

The second man turned his head quickly, saw the Head Counselor, rose, nodded his head to the Head Counselor and raised his hands to give her a greeting in hand language. She responded in kind. Then both speaking and using her hands she said, "I DIDN'T KNOW YOU TWO KNEW EACH OTHER."

The second man nodded. "WE MET SCOUTING OUT THE GENERAL," he said in his hand language.

The first man agreed both speaking and using hand language, **"I WAS ALMOST AMBUSHED BY SOME OF MALICIOUS' SOLDIERS AND KIRK SAVED MY HIDE!"**

The second man, Kirk, laughed soundlessly. Speaking with his hands he said, "ALL I DID WAS TELL HIM TO DUCK!" He gave the first man, Doug, a punch on the shoulder.

"YEAH, BUT YOU HAD TO STAND UP AND EXPOSE YOURSELF TO TELL ME. LUCKILY, I UNDERSTAND HAND LANGUAGE." Doug said punching Kirk back.

The Head Counselor watched the two, then told them to sit and finish eating. Turning to Doug she asked, "How did you learn hand language Doug?"

He hesitated a moment then looked at her wheelchair and the warm smile on her face, "My father." He paused again, knowing that in his world those who could not speak or hear were outcasts. He watched her look become puzzled and decided that truth was the best course. "He had done some trading with the Mountain Folk and learned the hand language." He took a bite of food, giving himself time to decide how much he should reveal. He observed the Head Counselor carefully. All he saw was acceptance and understanding. Swallowing his food, he continued, "As he got older he started losing his hearing, so he taught us the hand language so we could tell him what customers were saying to him so they wouldn't know he couldn't hear them." He watched her reaction to his words.

The Head Counselor tapped the table getting Kirk's attention. Using hand language and speaking she asked him, **"DID YOU KNOW DOUG'S FATHER?"** Both Kirk and Doug shook their heads no. **"SO HOW DID YOU KNOW DOUG WOULD UNDERSTAND YOU?"** Kirk shrugged.

The Head Counselor looked at Doug who also shrugged and added, "Just lucky I guess."

Sarah set a plate in front of Minerva. "Eat Mistress. You've got a busy day."

Minerva looked up at Sarah and laid a hand on her arm. "Thank you." She released her with a soft squeeze. Sarah ducked her head blushing and bustled away to her tasks. Minerva dug in, hungrier than she had thought and savoring every bite.

Silence fell among them. Only the clack of a utensil on a plate, or a swallow and pleased sigh could be heard. Then the Blue Knight entered.

"Good Morning!" Rupert said much too loudly. "How are my favorite ladies?" He stopped mid-step and altered his entrance and turned to the two men at the table. He stopped between them laying a hand on each shoulder. "News?" he asked with concern.

Doug started to stand up, but the Blue Knight gently pushed him back to his seat. "Sir, not good. General Mallory is a monster." He took a deep breath. "Frankly, I don't know how long we have before he takes his rage out on everyone and everything around him." His whole body drooped and he hung his head. Quickly he became more formal. "I have an official report for you." He tapped the table getting Kirk's attention. "THIS IS THE BLUE KNIGHT." He said.

Kirk gave Doug an exasperated look and said, "OF COURSE! YOU THINK I'M AN IDIOT?" He rose, bowed to the Blue Knight, then sat back down. "IS IT TIME TO GIVE YOUR REPORT?" He asked before digging back into his food.

170

The Blue Knight watched the hand language and looked to the Head Counselor who was smiling, obviously following the conversation. Over their heads, he mouthed silently, "One of yours?" indicating Kirk. She nodded. The Blue Knight watched a moment more before interrupting.

"Let me eat my meal, then we'll have your formal report with all those involved." He moved around the table and sat next to the Head Counselor. "Eat." He said and his man dug in again. As Sarah placed his plate before him, he said brightly, "Thanks dear."

Sarah lightly slapped the back of his head. "Respect Sir."

Rupert chuckled and said, "Thank you Madam Cook." For which he received another swat and a smile from Sarah. But when Sarah cut the warm pie and served the three others at the table a piece, he looked downright mournful. "No pie for me?" he asked soulfully.

"Finish your meal, then pie," Sarah said sweeping the remaining pie off the table and out of his reach.

The Blue Knight's good mood could not be muffled by having to wait for his pie. He hummed a tune and wolfed down his food.

Minerva touched his arm, "Slow down dear. The pie will be there when you're done. If you haven't choked yourself to death."

Rupert gave her a food-filled smile and slowed down, actually chewing and swallowing his food. As he took his last bite, he noticed that Minerva held out her fork with her last bite of pie to him. "Noooooo, I'm not falling for that. I want a whole piece."

Minerva smiled, shrugged, and took the final bite.

Rupert looked surprised, then disappointed, until his empty plate was replaced by a smaller plate with a large piece of pie. Before he could raise the first bite to his mouth Minerva said. "If

171

you don't savor that pie in the manner appropriate, I will ask Sarah to cut you off till you learn how to enjoy her cooking properly."

He held a fork-full just outside his open, gaping mouth. Slowly he set down his fork, pie untouched. He stood up, went over to Sarah, and gave her a kiss on the cheek. "Thank you Sarah, for all the pies you've baked and will bake for me." He returned to his seat, took up his bite and chewed slowly. When the others turned their attention away from him he quickly shoveled the rest of the pie in his mouth in four huge bites, berry juice escaping down the sides of his mouth and running down his chin.

The two men looked aghast. The two women looked displeased. The Blue Knight chewed and smiled, with teeth full of pie. Once everyone else was finished, they all moved to the large hall where others had been gathering.

Chapter Thirty-Nine
A NEW WAY TO COMMUNICATE

The Blue Knight and the Head Counselor moved toward the small dais, greeting those gathered and accepting the acknowledgments given. Internally, the Head Counselor practiced the names and professions of each person who spoke to her and, especially those who avoided her. Before they stepped onto the dais, she had Kirk face her and spoke to him alone. "WILL YOU TEACH THE BLUE KNIGHT'S PEOPLE YOUR LANGUAGE? I THINK WE CAN USE IT TO MAKE COMMUNICATION MORE SPECIFIC AND SECRETIVE."

Kirk watched her carefully, then searched her face, using hand language said only one word, "WHY?"

Minerva gave him her most authoritative Head Counselor look and deliberately spoke out loud to tell him. **"TO SAVE OUR WORLD AND DEFEAT GENERAL MALICIOUS."** Long moments passed as they examined each other for unspoken information. Then Kirk nodded his assent. The Head Counselor responded in kind. The Blue Knight and another man lifted the Head Counselor's wheelchair onto the dais and the Blue Knight and Head Counselor turned to face the gathered throng.

Silence fell quickly in a wave moving from the front to the back of the hall. The Blue Knight waited until all eyes were on him.

"I will not mince words. We have a great battle ahead of us. Some of it will be physical. I'm hoping most of it will be a war of minds and that we will come up with clever solutions to defeat unpleasant situations and people. But we must be armed and ready to fight." The Blue Knight waited while murmurs worked through those gathered and quiet returned. "While I was away on a quest to find the man with the aura of green for the King and Princess, General Mallory has spread harm and chaos. He is the first challenge we must face."

Several in the crowd whispered, "First?" "What other challenges?" "What is he implying?" "Are we going to war?" "What happened to the King?" There were many more questions along the same lines.

The Blue Knight waited until voices calmed. "The second challenge is creating a new kingdom."

This brought cries from those gathered: "Is the King dead?" "Have we been invaded?" "Why do we need a new kingdom?" As before, there were many more queries along similar and dis-similar lines.

Again the Blue Knight waited, but calm did not return, so he was forced to raise his voice and speak over the voices in the crowd. "We all have many questions, and not all can be answered now." Again there was an uproar in the crowd. "But first we must handle the problem of General Mallory."

The Blue Knight turned to the two men, Kirk and Doug, and motioned them to join him up front. "These two men have scouted out the General's compound." He pointed to Doug, who had gone to the Red Knight's Keep, and motioned him to join them. As Doug stepped up on the dais, he spoke out loudly again, "Here is the report from the Red Knight's lands." Slowly most stilled and turned their attention to the additional man on the dais. The Blue Knight looked at Doug and nodded encouragingly to him. "Please give your report."

Doug stepped forward, paling a bit as he looked over the large crowd. He cleared his throat once and stopped; then he felt a gentle squeeze on his fingers and realized that the Head Counselor was beside him. He cleared his throat again and began to tell the tale of destruction and violence produced by General Mallory in just the past two days. His voice broke slightly as he mentioned the men he found beaten and dying, cast casually aside along the road or in the fields. His voice hardened as he spoke about the burned lands and senseless destruction of equipment, buildings, and anything that could have a productive purpose. When he got to the killed and injured animals, anger and frustration were rolling off him. He took a deep breath and bent his head, looking out of the corner of his eyes at the Head Counselor. She nodded solemnly, agreeing and supporting him.

Loudly he said, "But most serious of all," he paused waiting for silence, "General Malicious is whipping up his soldiers with the intent of murdering us all."

At first there was dead quiet, then the hall erupted into chaos: some were shouting, others trying to leave, others so stunned they stood dumbfounded. The Blue Knight tried to quiet the crowd without success, he turned with a look of helplessness to the Head Counselor. She lifted one finger, "Wait." She spoke to Kirk in hand language. He disappeared returning quickly with four long spears borrowed from some of the guardsmen along the walls. The Head Counselor instructed him to give each person on the dais a spear and join them. She took the flat end of the spear and pounded on the dais twice. She looked at the others and said, "Follow me." Thump Thump pause. Thump Thump pause. Soon all four were in sync. The drumming had the dais shaking and was LOUD.

Those gathered took up the rhythm by clapping. Clap Clap pause. Clap Clap pause. In a very short time, the whole hall was drumming out in unison, with hands and feet. Pound Pound pause. Pound Pound pause. All eyes were on the dais. The Head Counselor lifted the spear high and let a piercing whistle end the drumming. A few stray claps and embarrassed chuckles went through the crowd before all stilled.

The Head Counselor looked at Doug. She nodded and Doug told how the Red Knight's people had reduced the General's soldiers by almost half, imprisoning them in and around the Keep. When he told of the General's meeting with the Red Knight, many were elated at the treatment he received. He raised his voice and said slowly. "The Red Knight believes that we are in great danger. He believes he may only made matters worse and he apologizes."

A stunned silence settled over the room.

Doug continued, "The Red Knight has promised to help restore our lands and properties. He is waiting for us to join him in the destruction of General Malicious."

Murmuring filled the room. The Blue Knight asked Doug if there was anything else and received a negative shake of his head. Forcefully the Blue Knight said, "We have already begun to take up this challenge. I've spoken with several of you about protection strategies, alert systems, arms training, and more talks are in process."

The Blue Knight looked around the room, pointedly making eye contact with several people. "We need your wisdom and expertise. We need your creativity. The Red Knight's people did some amazing things in a very short period of time, but it's only the beginning. There is so much more to do."

The Blue Knight looked to the Head Counselor unsure where to go. She brought him closer and whispered in his ear. His smile widened and he straightened. Addressing the crowd again, "Will the twenty leaders I met with last night please come forward." As the men and women came to stand in front of the dais the Blue Knight continued. "If you have an idea, information, or a concern, tell one of these people. Your suggestion may be the one that saves a life or tips the tides in our favor."

"Will those who gathered with me to discuss a warning system come forward." The Blue Knight looked at this gathering of people, "It is my hope that we can create a safety line between farms and neighbors, byways and highways, the towns and my Keep and our neighboring knights." He studied those gathered, seeing if they were comprehending his new notion for communication in his lands. I would like you meet with the Head Counselor after our gathering, she has a very specific solution for communications."

The Blue Knight turned a final time to everyone gathered in the hall. "My friends, my neighbors, I do not know exactly what is ahead, but together we can overcome any challenge, defeat any evil, and build a better world for all of us."

The Head Counselor took up the spear again and started the drumming: thump thump pause, thump thump pause. Within seconds the whole hall thundered together: pound pound pause, pound pound pause. The back doors of the hall were opened and the crowd spilled out into the courtyard still drumming: pound pound pause, pound pound pause until they reached their homes. The drumming reverberated in their hearts and bodies.

Chapter Forty
A NEW LANGUAGE

The Safety and Warning team gathered around the Head Counselor in the front corner of the hall. Every face had a renewed sense of hope and vigor, and an eagerness to get things in motion.

"Thank you for joining me. I'm anxious to hear your ideas. I have something I would like to offer you first. I welcome your thoughts and reactions. Nothing is off limits if it is said with an open mind and willing heart."

Those surrounding her nodded.

Reaching out to Kirk and drawing him to her side, she began, "This is Kirk, one of the Mountain Folk. He *speaks* with his hands. It is a silent language. It can communicate across a crowded, noisy room or over greater distances than a voice can. When silence is paramount for safety." She turned to Kirk and spoke only with her hands to him, "I'M TELLING THEM THE VALUE OF HAND LANGUAGE. I THINK IT COULD HELP BUILD UP OUR SAFETY. AGAIN, I ASK, WILL YOU TEACH THESE PEOPLE?" Kirk looked around the circle of people who leaned toward him expectantly. He saw no hostility or rejection.

Kirk looked at Doug who nodded and took that moment to speak up with voice and hands. **"THIS MAN SAVED MY LIFE. HE ROSE OUT OF HIS HIDING PLACE AND SIGNALED TO ME, WITH HIS HANDS, THAT GENERAL MALICIOUS' SOLDIERS WERE ABOUT TO AMBUSH ME."** He looked at Kirk with great respect. **"HE PUT HIS OWN LIFE IN DANGER TO SAVE ME."**

Now everyone in the group looked from Doug, to Kirk, to the Head Counselor. No one spoke either with voice or hand. With great exasperation, someone spoke up, "Well, do we have to beg? Are you going to teach us?" Silence, then laughter.

The Head Counselor smiled and in her conciliatory counselor voice said, "My apologies. Kirk has agreed to teach us the language of hands. I think we can learn the basics needed and adapt it to communicate quickly and across distances."

Someone spoke up sarcastically, "My eyesight isn't that good. I can barely see him from here."

Unruffled, the Head Counselor went on, "If we add drumming, we can add distance."

The group quieted and became thoughtful till someone asked, "Like what we were just doing?" She demonstrated: clap clap pause, clap clap pause.

"After a fashion." The Head Counselor turned to the table and tapped out a sequence, then she repeated it slowly. "Tap tap pause means Danger. Tapity, tapity say Attack. Tap and an uplift arm means North."

Several in the group nodded and smiled in understanding. Then the sarcastic one spoke again, "So how does this hand language and drumming come together?"

The Head Counselor slowly turned her chair toward the voice and smiled shrewdly, saying, "That's the fun part."

It was like a door opening and those within spilled out from sheer excitement alone. Everyone started talking at once. Several were tapping on the table. Others crowded around Kirk watching his hands. The Head Counselor let the chaos continue for several minutes before letting out another piercing whistle.

"Go home and enjoy your midday meal. Think of the words we will need most to communicate quickly and effectively. We will gather at two bells to work out our safety warning language. Bring the words you believe will allow us to communicate like the wind sweeping across an open grassland."

Several spoke to the Head Counselor before departing. Virtually all left with another speaking animatedly about the task ahead. When only Doug, Kirk and the Head Counselor remained. The room was calm and still when the Blue Knight appeared.

Clapping his hands together he said, "Midday meal time!" He looked at Minerva, "Push or roll?"

"Push please," she said softly.

He stepped behind her and started moving. "Come on you two. We need to keep up our strength, much to do, much to do!" Without waiting to see if they followed Rupert pushed Minerva briskly through the courtyard to the Keep's kitchen.

Chapter Forty-One
SAY WHAT?

The community hall was abuzz with activity. On one side of the room several people discussed words: words of importance needed for communications. Unfortunately, progress was slow because the scribe spent almost as much time crossing out as writing or re-writing words for the list. The discussion was heated but good-natured with more agreements than disagreements. When a word was agreed to by all, they turned to Kirk or Doug and asked if there was a hand sign for the word. Which of course there was! After the sixth, or tenth time Kirk was asked that question, he said to Doug, "TELL THEM I HAVE EVERY WORD THEY HAVE! AND MAYBE A FEW MORE!" He demonstrated but Doug told him he wasn't sharing that!

The list was growing longer but the debate did not wane. Some insisted only terms used in warfare should be included. Others demanded that every day words were needed for effective communication. The scribe took it upon herself to divide them into two lists. With words whose category could be questioned shown between the two.

WAR	DIRECTIONS	DAILY
Danger	North	Attention
Fire	South	Water
Help	East	Gather
Need	West	Want
Numbers	Questions	
	What, Why, When, How	
Look		
Coming	(The list continued.)	

On the other side of the room, there was constant drumming and discussion. "Is one beat enough? How will anyone know that it's a signal?" "Do we need a sound to let people know to listen? This is important!" In frustration one of the men slapped his hand on the wall, silencing all. "That's what we need," he said with frustration. "A loud single noise unlike anything else." Silence lingered.

After several moments one of the shepherds pulled out his whistle and held it up. "I use this to call my dogs when they and the sheep are too far away for me to see." The group waited until he put it to his lips and blew. SSSSSSSSSSSSSSSS. The whole hall fell into silence.

From across the room someone from the word gathering group called out, "Did you want something? I'm not a dog, but I get your message." This broke the tension and chuckles circled the room. The shepherd responded, "I wanted your attention. I think I got it!" More laughter broke out before both groups returned to their tasks.

Off in another corner, away from either group, but within eye and earshot of both, Minerva and Rupert sat with heads together, pointing and whispering.

"Now we're going to need whistles," Rupert said.

"That's an easy solution to an important issue," Minerva answered. "Your people are very ingenious. If I didn't know better, I'd think they were my folk."

Rupert turned loving eyes on her and said in all sincerity, "Thank you. I take that as a great compliment." He raised a hand to stop her response. "I know, I know. A few months ago that is something I never would have said or thought, but now it is true." And to convince her of his conviction he kissed her.

Chapter Forty-Two
THE RED AND BLUE KNIGHT BEGIN TO COME TOGETHER

The Red Knight checked frequently on the wounded under his care. The man with the aura of green had stopped appearing daily so he considered that a good sign of the care they were being given. Slowly, more stories of General Mallory's (now almost exclusively called Malicious) activities were told. The Red Knight was perplexed. Malicious gathered around him the lowest, cruelest, most disreputable people. The few soldiers he stole from the King's castle guard had all deserted or died. Malicious seemed intent upon wanton destruction, without purpose or provocation. Malicious' army appeared to be accomplishing little except creating chaos and harm. Even within Malicious' self-proclaimed "Fort", the conditions were deplorable. Food was scarce. Drink was plenty. Neither animals nor people were kept in any hygienic or safe condition.

The confrontation with the Red Knight served to let Malicious know that he could not continue his activities unchecked, at least not within the Red Knight's lands. The underlying insidious threat Malicious posed undermined everyone's well being. The unsettled feeling of never ever being safe was slowly invading everyone's mind and heart.

"How's the song coming?" Bartholomew asked Beatrice softly, as they lounged around the evening fire.

Hmway and Alleyu sat across from them asleep, for there was no humming or music of any kind coming from either of them. He nodded his head toward the sleeping pair and smiled. In a whisper he asked, "How has it come to be that they are already family and I can not picture life without them here?"

Beatrice stroked her husband's arm and took his hand, kissing his palm before setting their joined hands in her lap.

"Because our souls sing the same tune, my love," she replied quietly.

He nodded an affirmation, then sighed heavily. "But I fear they must leave us too soon." He continued sadly, "If we go to war with our own people, they shouldn't be involved. They need to go home and be with their people of the desert."

"You are our people." Hmway's deep, sonorous voice filled the room completely, even though he spoke so softly that Bartholomew wasn't sure he hadn't imagined it.

"I agree," Alleyu said in her beautiful, lilting tone.

"I'm sorry. I thought you were asleep," Bartholomew breathed out.

"We were at peace, my friend. But you are not," Hmway stated.

"I admit I am at odds, dear friend," Bartholomew sighed. "I can't figure out Malicious' motivation for the destruction he is causing." He shook himself. "It's unsettling!"

Beatrice stroked his arm again with her free hand. "Unfortunately, I think Malicious is just a symptom of some greater evil." She shivered and placed her husband's arm around her shoulder, snuggling close. "We need to find the underlying cause!"

They were all silent for several moments. The fire crackled. Then there was a soft knock on the door.

"Enter!" The Red Knight turned toward the opening door, "Malcolm, what . . . ?" Seeing concern on his Captain of the Guard's face, he stood and faced him. "Speak man, speak."

Malcolm took a moment to compose himself. "The Blue Knight has sent a messenger."

Puzzled the Red Knight replied, "Good, send him in."

184

Malcolm shook his head negatively. "Sir, he . . . was ambushed on the way. I, I don't know how he got as far as he did before one of our new watch guards found him and brought him in."

The Red Knight began to move around Malcolm to head to the infirmary, but Malcolm put up a hand to stop him. "The man with the aura of green arrived shortly after the injured messenger." Malcolm's face lightened a bit, with a weak smile he continued, "He should live, but the man with the aura of green asked that we not bother him for at least the turning of night to morn."

Under his breath the Red Knight mumbled, "Give him time to heal a bit, of course, of course." Directly to Malcolm he asked, "Any other news?"

Malcolm held out his hand and handed the Red Knight a missive from the Blue Knight. He bowed his head once and started to leave, then turned back. "I'm going to check on our new alert system. Make sure everyone is at least in pairs." He didn't wait for the Red Knight's response.

It may have seemed like disrespect but the Red Knight knew better. Malcolm's priorities were in the right place: safety first, protocol when needed. He turned back to the now standing group before the fire. "I need better light. You're all welcome to join me. I'm sure we're all curious to know what the Blue Knight has to say." He reached out and took his wife's hand, turned and exited the sitting room with Hmway and Alleyu close behind.

Chapter Forty-Three
THE MAN WITH THE AURA OF GREEN FINDS AN ASSISTANT

In the infirmary the man with the aura of green worked quickly. The man's injuries were very serious. He marveled at how the messenger could have continued as far as he had. His injuries had been inflicted with great intent to do the most damage possible. Senseless violence. Senseless pain. Senseless evil.

A woman returned with the splints he had requested to set and secure the man's broken foot and leg. He nodded his thanks and handed her the cloth he had been using to wipe blood from the man's shattered face and missing eye. She took the cloth without hesitation and continued cleaning the man's face. Another nod of thanks. He never failed to acknowledge those who were willing and able to help and did!

More and more, he was finding hesitation or reluctance both with those who needed help and those who could help. It puzzled him but did not distract him from his work.

The foot and leg were efficiently set and secured. He moved to the long slash in the other leg's thigh. It had already been cleaned and needed only to be stitched, which he did like a master tailor.

His helper whistled as he tied off his work. "Nicely done healer," she said with admiration and added with a bit of humor, "If you ever decide to give up being a healer my husband's business always needs good stitchers." She continued cleaning, her admiration and comments not ceasing her labors.

The man with the aura of green actually let a chuff of laughter escape. He moved along the man's torso assessing damages, finding only bruising from deep wounds that only time would heal, he stood beside the woman. Smiling, he said softly, "I may seriously consider your offer."

Then he was back to work. First administering more pain and sedation medication to the injured man. He stopped her cleaning and looked carefully at the man's eye socket and cheek. He asked, "Is there a plaster, something that will set firmly and quickly here?"

The woman rose immediately and left the room. The man with the aura of green finished applying a healing salve to the numerous scrapes and minor cuts. Under his breath he murmured, "They must have drawn him behind a horse. I'm going to need to turn him over."

The woman dropped down beside him with a bucket that appeared to be a plaster. "I can help turn him." She shook her head. "Poor lad, who would do such evil?"

The man with the aura of green shook his head, "I don't know," he sighed. Realizing that there was nothing more he could do to heal the man's cheek and eye, he decided to make a mask to hold the bones in place and minimize movement. He finished the mask. "We need to let that set before we turn him." Looking at the woman he asked, "Is there anyone else I can help while we wait?"

The woman rose and held out her hand. The man with the aura of green hesitated only a moment before taking her hand. He was not used to such familiarity. He knew people appreciated him, but never did they touch him and only rarely did they converse with him, much less in a humorous, companionly way. His thoughts briefly wandered to the Princess' three handmaids currently occupying his home and Sophie, who might just be a healer also.

"You need to see the soldier you took care of a few days ago." She smiled, again with a bit of humor and went on, "The Red

Knight tries his best and he's getting better at changing bandages," she paused and winked, "But he is no man with the aura of green."

The woman dropped his hand and leaned down to speak softly in a man's ear who was covered head to toe with bandages. Only one hand was free of cloth. "Now Seth, the man with the aura of green has come to check on you. No tales out of school now! But if you need something or if we can do something better, let him know." She squeezed his one free hand and stepped away.

"How's your pain?" the man with the aura of green asked as he inspected bandages. When he got to the leg injury that had been so badly infected, he was pleased to see a fresh bandage with the healing salve thickly applied.

"Less," a mere whisper, "I think they are afraid to give me too much medicine." His chest lifted and fell indicating that those spoken words had taken great effort.

The man with the aura of green placed a small leaf under the man's tongue. "Let it melt away. It will help the pain. I will instruct them again on your pain medication."

"Thank you" the words faded away as the man fell asleep.

The man with the aura of green made his way around the infirmary, checking wounds and bindings. Offering a word of encouragement or a smile here and there. As he finished, the woman appeared waving him back to their first patient.

The plaster had set well. Half of the man's face, from chin to forehead, front of ear to side of nose was covered, including the empty eye socket. He nodded his approval. He pulled out an herb, crushed it, using a spoon he mixed the leaf pieces and a drop or two of water. He very carefully dripped it into the man's mouth. When all of the mixture was in the mouth, the man with the aura of green very gently stroked the man's throat so he swallowed.

The woman was watching his every move intently, nodding at his method of administering to an unconscious person. When he moved to rearrange the bedding so they could turn him over, she stayed out of the way until he showed her what he wanted her to do. She was surprised by the way they turned the injured man. The man with the aura of green fastened the bottom and top sheet together to hold the man tightly between. They lifted him up, turned him in the air, then set him down. He was a slight lad, so they could do it easily together. With only mild groans of pain the man was turned, the sheets untied, and the wounds on his backside attended to.

Thankfully there were no open, gaping wounds. Lots of abrasions, confirming that he had been drug on his back. A large quantity of salve was applied with thick bandages and then they turned him again. Instructions were given for pain medication and changes of bandages. The face mask was to remain untouched till he returned.

The woman bent to tuck in the sheet and blanket. When she finished and she turned to the man with the aura of green, he was gone. Putting her hands and arms akimbo, shaking her head disappointedly, looking where she assumed the man with the aura of green had departed, she breathed out, "That man. Such a lonely life."

The man with the aura of green was still within earshot and his step faltered only slightly faltered as he made his departure.

Chapter Forty-Four
RED & BLUE KNIGHTS UNITE

On the other side of the Keep, the Red Knight, Beatrice, Hmway and Alleyu gathered around the kitchen to read over the Blue Knight's message. The Red Knight spread it out on the table, pulled a candle closer and began to read.

"Sir Red Knight,

Greetings from all within the Blue Knight's lands. We hope you and yours are faring well. We wish all We have just celebrated the joyous union of our beloved Blue Knight and the Mountain Folk's Head Counselor. There will be another gathering for all the Kingdom when the current unrest has ceased, our good King restored, and the Kingdom's fate settled.

It is about this unrest that I write with great dispatch and urgency for my Knight. We find the threat presented by General Mallory and his militia to be of great distress. It compels us to respond with haste. It is our understanding that you do not have a standing battalion ready for military action. Neither do we. Nor do we wish to take up arms or change our people into soldiers. But we cannot stand by. Action must be taken.

To wit, the Blue Knight and the Head Counselor have formed groups with the intent to create new forms of communication. A new language, perhaps, to handle immediate needs and greater distances with stealth and accuracy. We wish to share this with you and your people. We hope you have no less than six persons who can attend us here, to learn the new signaling method and teach it to your people, so we can establish a system of communication between our lands.

In addition, we request your assistance in preparing our people for defense. We have heard with great satisfaction about your successful confrontation with the General and his militia. It is understood you decreased its numbers by more than half and perhaps also the General's haughtiness by similar measure. We need your assistance to prepare in like kind.

We dare not concede to the evil moving within our lands. It is our hope that by sharing communications and military skills we can overcome and move toward a new kingdom unified not by a ruler, but by its people. Undoing what has been done. Removing the evil that moves within. We desire peace, joy, and a successful overcoming of what our Kingdom has become.

Respectfully, Scribe of Sir Blue Knight.

Bart, Well done. We have much to share. Stay safe. Send word quickly. Evil is on the move. R.

A silence fell over the group. Then Alleyu began humming their new tune. Beatrice whispered "Peace, Joy, Overcoming, Success." Hmway laid a warm hand upon Bartholomew's shoulder giving it a single gentle shake. "It is time."

The Red Knight knew what lay ahead could not be avoided, now he knew it would be shared, at least with the Blue Knight. The evil uncovered, the powers of the evil divided, and (offering up a prayer to the Power) evil defeated.

Looking searchingly at Hmway the Red Knight asked, "Dare I ask you and Alleyu to go to the Blue Knight? You can share our song and learn, with ease I'm sure, this new language they have to share."

Hmway took Alleyu's hand. They continued to hum the new tune for more moments than the Red Knight could bear.

"I'm sorry! It was too much to ask. I . . . "

Hmway interrupted the knight. "Bartholomew, we are family. You can always ask." He paused and looked at Alleyu who nodded an affirmation. "How will we be received by those who ask?"

Relief overtook the Red Knight. He had only been thinking of the evil forces moving. Hmway and Alleyu were now family. He hadn't even considered their differences to be a threat to them. Breathing out a large sigh of that relief, he replied, "As we have. The Head Counselor is of the Mountain Folk." Seeing no recognition on either of their faces he explained. "It is not a proud explanation I offer but one of great shame. The Mountain Folk come from those who have been cast out, thought to be damaged, less than enough. The Blue Knight's people have come to know and respect them. You have met the Head Counselor. Lack of working legs has not affected her mind, reason or spirit. The Blue Knight is well-met in his match to her."

Hmway nodded. Alleyu nodded and in her lyrical voice said, "So many new adventures. How full is our life!"

So it was settled, on the morrow Hmway, Alleyu and ten militarily inclined individuals would head to the Blue Knight. All alert for dangers on this short journey, but anxious to discover what potential was ahead.

Chapter Forty-Five
EVIL WITHIN (BLUE KNIGHT)

She leaned closer and returned the kiss, with just a little heat, then touched his cheek gently. "How did I ever get so lucky to find you?"

He turned his lips into her hand and kissed it. "It is I who am lucky, my love."

"You two need to get back to your rooms! You're either making us sick from all the sweetness or jealous!" One of the men from the Safety and Warning Team stopped before them, giving a shake of his head. He waited for their response, but getting none but smiles from both, continued. "An ill wind blows my Knight."

The Blue Knight stood and was immediately attentive only to him.

"Our messenger was attacked and nearly killed on the way to the Red Knight."

The Head Counselor rolled forward and also gave her full attention to him.

"Fortunately, he was found and taken to the Red Knight's Keep with the man with the aura of green in almost immediate attendance. We assume he survived."

The Blue Knight leaned closer and with great solemnity asked, "Have *his* people been told and taken care of?"

The Head Counselor looked up at her husband and smiled. His first concern is always for his people, she thought. She turned to the man and asked, "How do you come by this information so quickly?"

He turned to her, "We have started setting up the network of signalers who discovered him. We don't know how Malicious' people knew, but they attacked him between two stations. He managed to get to the next one and the signalers took care of him." He paused, a look of concern covering his open face. "We must have a spy in our midst."

Both Knight and Counselor took in a breath and in unison said, "How?"

The man hesitated, then asked, "May I speak freely?" Both nodded. "There are some in our Keep who are not, um, I mean to say, they don't . . . "

"Oh for heaven's sake man, spit it out, there's no danger to truth!" The Blue Knight almost shouted.

The Head Counselor reached up and laid her hand upon the Blue Knight's. He took a deep breath and continued much more calmly. "Sorry. Please. Tell us what you know."

The man bowed his head, then looked them both squarely in the eyes. "There are people who do not think you should have married the Head Counselor and that the Mountain Folk should go." His eyes did not waver from theirs, but he wrung his hands.

The Blue Knight reached out and laid a hand upon his hands, stilling them. "Thank you for your candor. I was not unaware of this fact but did not think it would lead someone to sabotage our efforts or put one of their own people in danger." He sighed heavily, looking around the room, realizing that all present were now quiet and listening. He shook the man's hands once more and released them. He touched the Head Counselor's shoulder before moving to the middle of the room.

"I have sad news to share." He looked around but already knew he had everyone's attention. "The messenger we sent to the Red Knight was attacked." There was a collective gasp in the room. "Someone is already undermining our efforts. Our sentry post locations, only just established, have been given to our enemy

194

General Malicious and his soldiers." His voice was calm, but he spoke through clenched teeth.

An uproar began. "How could that be!" "Why would anyone do that?" "That can't be true!" "It was just chance for him to be caught out of sight." The questioning and outrage went on for several moments.

The Blue Knight waited as the ire and frustration worked its way through the room and calmed. "I can not express how disappointed I am at this turn in our plans." He looked solemnly around the room. "It not only puts our friends and families in danger but compromises our neighbors and our kingdom." He paused again to look around the room, watching for any turned eyes, or challenging expressions. "I now formally request that if anyone knows anything about this to please let me know. I will keep your confidence, but we **can not** let the seed of evil be planted within our own hearts and homes."

The Head Counselor rolled up beside him. Without looking at her he continued. "I also ask that you come to me honestly and with immunity, to share your thoughts about the Mountain Folk." He reached out his hand and she took it. "I will not sacrifice my soulmate or her people. It would break my heart to abdicate my knighthood, but if we," he lifted their joined hands, "are not considered your people, I will make my home elsewhere."

The silence, like a death pall, covered the room. They looked at each other, shocked and deeply troubled by the knight's pronouncement. The Blue Knight and Head Counselor waited, quietly hoping that their life together had not come this quickly into tribulation.

After several moments, the Blue Knight looked down at the Head Counselor and was about to speak, when the man who had brought the troubling news stepped forward. "I stand with my Knight and Counselor."

Quickly several others stood up and repeated, "I stand with my Knight and Counselor." However, not all stood.

"Thank you," the Blue Knight said placing a hand on his heart. "For those of you who did not speak, I hope you will come talk to me personally." He started to turn, but stopped, "Let's take a candlemark break, for refreshments of mind and body. I will be in my study if anyone would like to talk." In unison, he and the Head Counselor turned and exited the hall. She pushed herself and he walked beside her until they entered his study.

After the door shut, Rupert almost collapsed before Minerva's chair, releasing what sounded to her like a sob. She reached out and drew him close, almost bringing him into her lap. They remained that way, slowly finding the calm within that they could share with the other.

Minerva was the first to speak, "Rupert." She spoke softly but with authority. He straightened, found a chair, and pulled it close to her. When he had settled, she spoke again. "My love," shaking her head so he did not interrupt her. "You are my soulmate. But I can not ask you to give up your life here for me."

He jumped in quickly, speaking passionately, "You didn't ask. I made that decision the first time I met you. I go where you go." He remained seated, but it took all his will to do so.

"At another time, perhaps we could exist as one, but now is not that time." Although every fiber of her being wanted to reach out to him, she resisted.

After only a brief hesitation, he asked, "If not now, when?"

"I . . . " she stopped, truly not knowing what to say.

"Now is the only time. Our kingdom is changing. Who knows if the King will regain sanity or the Princess return. Evil grows throughout our land. Malicious is one of the representatives of that evil. As is the betrayer of our people today." He paused, regained his perspective, and continued softly, "If not now, will change ever come? If not now, will our time ever come?" He leaned close but did not touch her.

Softly, so softly he almost didn't hear her, she said, "Is it not selfishness to want you so much?" An uncharacteristic tear escaped one eye, "Your people need you now more than ever. Would I not be another tool used in evil's plan to take you away from them?"

He almost leapt from his chair to embrace her. As he began to encircle her in his arms, there was a soft knock on the door. He stopped and stood, looking first at her, then the door. "Come in," he said with more confidence than he felt.

A woman the Head Counselor did not recognize entered timidly. She hesitated when she saw them both present. "Sir," she bobbed to the Blue Knight, "Ma'am" she bobbed to the Head Counselor. "I, um, I . . . " She looked back at the still partially opened door and shut it softly. She turned back around and bobbed to them again.

"Margaret," the Blue Knight indicated a chair, "come sit with me. You have my full attention." The Head Counselor noticed that the chair he selected placed her off to the one side slightly, allowing the woman to sit and focus directly on him. The woman was still hesitating.

"Perhaps I should go, so you can speak freely." Minerva started to push herself away but Margaret startled.

"No, no ma'am. No, you need to hear this too." She shuffled to the chair and sat. The Head Counselor remained where she was and the Blue Knight took the seat across from Margaret. "Sir, you know my son, Simon." The Blue Knight nodded. "He went on your quest." Again the knight nodded. "They fixed him up right when he lost his leg. He can do almost ever'thing as good as a fore." She looked down and wrapped her hands in the shawl she wore. "He tain't been the same since he returned. It's, it's, like a little bit of that evil goin 'round got into him." The Blue Knight remained still not wanting to interrupt. "I thinks it was him who told about the sentries." Tears rolled slowly down her cheeks. So quietly they barely heard her, she said, "He used to be such a good boy."

The Blue Knight reached out one hand and laid his fingers very gently upon the woman's twisting hands. She stilled immediately. Slowly she looked up and into his face - his compassionate, caring face. The tears fell more quickly. She gulped out between sobs, "I locked him in his room when he got home last night." Her sobs grew.

The Head Counselor wheeled out of the room. She found a man who knew Simon and asked him to bring Simon back to the Blue Knight. She directed him to be cautious and not be surprised by anything Simon said or did. Thinking further, she asked him to take at least one other man with him, because she told him, Simon might resist.

This gained a raised eyebrow from the man and then a nod. She watched him as he left her, stopped to gather another man and then a third. She stayed in the hallway for several moments. Eventually, Margaret departed. She stopped to acknowledge the Head Counselor and gave her a smile. Softly she said, "We're glad you're here." Looking over her shoulder she nodded to the Blue Knight. "As good a knight as he is, he's better with you." Before Minerva could respond the woman was gone.

She rolled back slowly into the study. Rupert was standing by the fire, but he moved quickly to her, lifted her out of her chair and embraced her tightly. There were no words spoken.

Chapter Forty-Six
EVIL RISES

Simon paced back and forth. It was an unusual pace. He had not put on his wooden leg so he needed support in order to move forward. A hand on the dresser, then his stump on the bed, another hand on the dresser, then a shoulder against the wall to pivot on his whole leg, then back across with only the assistance of the dresser. Pivot, repeat.

Simon mumbled as he paced. "I'm only doing what is right. Only trying to take care of my knight." Pivot. "Only taking care of my knight. Foolish, thoughtless, knight." Pivot. "Why did he have to marry her! We were fine. We don't need them here! Now they are everywhere!" Pivot.

"Knock, Knock," the guard called out to Simon through the door, unlocking it and entering. "Simon, the Blue Knight wishes your presence." He halted at the doorway. "Simon? Are you all right?" He spoke softly, taken aback at the state of the man before him.

"Sir?" One of the men who accompanied the guard stuck his head around the door and froze. The man looked stunned. He sucked in his breath, completely shocked at the state of Simon. He backed out of the room.

The guard spoke again, quietly, in a reassuring tone. "Simon, my boy." He looked around the room, its state of disorder, the smell of unwashed body and illness. "Simon, are you ill? Shall I fetch the healer?"

Simon continued to pace and mumble.

"Lad, where's your leg? Let's get you dressed and off to the healer." When Simon's path crossed in front of him he reached out his hand, stopping his movement, but not his mumbling.

"Got to tell him. Got to warn him. Got to go."

The guard blanched at Simon's smell, grabbed a blanket off the bed and wrapped him up. "Here we go lad, off to see the healer and a bath." The guard called out to his companions and together they escorted Simon, first to the bathing room, then to the healer.

Back in the study, the Blue Knight paced. Arms behind his back he crossed in front of the fire, then tapped the mantel twice as he moved past, two more strides, a touch to the back of a chair where he pivoted and crossed before the fire, tapping the mantel, and coming to his wife, whom he tapped on the shoulder, and pivoted to begin again.

"Rupert."

Pace, tap, pivot. Pace tap, touch, pivot.

"Rupert, love."

Pace, tap, pivot. Pace, tap, touch, pivot.

This time she took his hand when he touched her. "Rupert, please, sit here with me."

The Blue Knight hesitated and with a heavy exhale dropped into a chair beside her.

"Speak your mind, my love."

He let out a heavy sigh. "Here in my own home. A betrayer. An evil seed." His next words came out almost in a growl. "Someone I considered family, a friend." He seemed to gain his aplomb and continued, "I should have been more aware. Noticed the changes in his character after he lost his leg. His withdrawal when we returned home." His clearly spoken words dropped into a mumble,

"I should have taken note. I should have attempted to find out why. I should have ... "

Minerva again reached out and took his hand. Her touch brought him back to the present.

Rupert brought his wife's hand up to his lips and kissed it softly. "Sorry, love." He sighed. "I know there is evil afoot, but to have its roots here in our home," he paused and took another deep breath. "I must act decisively." He rose. "I need to confront him face-to-face." He started to turn when there was a knock. "COME."

The guard entered, alone. He dipped his head to the Head Counselor, "Ma'am, the boy is ill."

Minerva replied, "Is he with the healer?" She looked toward Rupert and continued, "And with a guard?"

The guard nodded and then hesitated. "He is with the healer, but he seemed so ill, I, I, I didn't think we need to set a watch over him."

The Head Counselor spoke with authority, "Return immediately. All near him are in danger as well as himself."

The guard bowed and backed out of the room.

"Ummmmmm," the Blue Knight looked from the door to the Head Counselor. "I, aaaaaaaaa?"

The Head Counselor smiled slightly, "Sir Knight, while you spoke to Margaret I asked a guard to bring Simon here," she cocked her head and continued, "under guard."

The Blue Knight snapped into focus, finally alert and attentive to the events surrounding him.

"I hope I did not overstep, or presume ... "

He stopped her, "Your actions were correct and forethinking." He took a deep breath, "Both as Head Counselor, my equal in authority, and my wife, Mistress of this home." He started to pace but stopped after two steps. "What do we do?" Turning to the Head Counselor with a questioning look.

She was pensive and after several moments spoke, "We gather together those whom you know you can trust. We contact the Red Knight and call a gathering, here or there. Again, only with the most trusted."

"Yes, yes." The Blue Knight knelt down before her. "What are we confronting? What evil is this?"

She reached out and touched his cheek gently. "The evil that dwells in all men." She started to pull her hand away, but he held it there. "The evil I have lived with all my life." She looked deeply into his eyes.

He squeezed her hand softly.

"An evil that now has an army and a general possessed with evil himself."

~~~

They were still for several moments, each lost in their own thoughts and emotions. Then, as if prompted by a silent command, they both moved. The Blue Knight rose as the Head Counselor rolled toward the door.

"Sarah," they said in unison.

"It must be well past for the even' meal." He clapped, then rubbed his hands together. "Shall we?"

The Head Counselor rolled forward shaking her head and trying to repress a smile. "I was thinking that Sarah is the heart of your home; if anything is astray, she would probably know."

"Aahhh, of course, of course. As always you are wise and intuitive." He began to push her. "A perfect place to uncover intrigue and fill our bodies with fuel for the search."

"You're hopeless," she laughed. "You do know that don't you?" She looked up and over her shoulder at him and he took that moment to steal a kiss. She laughed again. "Hopeless."

"That's why you're here my love. To show me and our world there is always hope!" He sniffed the air and added lustily, "And Sarah's pies!"

They entered the kitchen much more jovially than they had left the study.

"Ahh, the children have come singing for their supper!" Sarah said and continued to stir a pot of soup. "Mistress, you really should start insisting on eating in the dining room."

"But Sarah," Minerva cajoled, "the kitchen is always warm, there is always food. It saves you time and energy if we . . . "

"Tut, tut, tut, Mistress." Sarah shook the spoon at the Blue Knight. "And him! He's been under my feet since he was a wee lad. It would be good to have him act like the knight he is now and then when taking a meal."

The Blue Knight tried to look contrite but failed miserably.

They had gathered and sat around the table as the conversation had progressed. Sarah served Minerva, then Rupert and then herself. After all had enjoyed several delicious sips of soup and bites of the bread baked that morning Sarah finally asked, "So why are you really in the kitchen at this time of day?"

Silence fell.

Minerva took the initiative. "You know Simon well?"

"Indeed. He grew up here. Why?"

203

"And his mother? A good woman?" Minerva asked. Rupert shifted beside her.

"Indeed. She cleans here in the Keep. Hard worker. Always a kind word. Margaret loves her Simon." Sarah glanced from Minerva to Rupert. "What aren't you saying to me?"

Minerva sighed, "Has Simon seemed different since he returned?" She paused and corrected herself. "Since he lost his leg?"

Sarah rose and took her bowl to the washing tub. She glanced at Rupert and quickly away while she asked, "More?"

Rupert rose and filled his bowl, set it on the table, then took Sarah gently by the elbow moving her back to the table. Leaning close, he said calmly, "Speak truth Sarah." He returned to his seat and took a sip. "It is all for the good." He set his spoon down and gave her his full attention.

Sarah looked from one to the other. "Simon's a good boy."

"No one is disputing that Sarah."

Sarah stared hard at her Blue Knight. At this moment, he was not the boy she helped raise. He was all knight, all authority, yet she could still see concern and compassion in his eyes. She gave a small sniff and rose from her chair.

"Sarah." The Blue Knight's tone was firm.

"Pie," was all she said. She took an apple pie out of the oven and placed it on the cooling rock. She proceeded to make a pot of hot water and set out mugs for tea. She looked at the Head Counselor silently asking, "Do you need your healing tea?" Minerva shook her head. Once tea was made and they all sat at the table again, Sarah took a long sip and began her tale.

"It was long before the Mountain Folk came that Simon began to change. It was little things at first. A bird flew into netting, and instead of freeing it like he'd always done before, he broke its neck and threw it away. Not something I really noticed the first time it happened. Birds get caught and a quick death is a mercy. But it happened again and again, the birds Simon killed, they could have flown away.

As time went on it was the way he handled an animal or treated others. He acted like he was your son instead of one of the workers in the Keep." She held out a palm to the Blue Knight. "Sir you treat all of us like family, but we know our place." She lowered her hand and continued. "We thought it was good fortune when you took him on the quest." She rested her head in her hands. "Then the poor boy lost his leg. I have to admit that, for just a moment I considered that Fate was trying to teach him a lesson. Forgive me, I know I shouldn't have put that out into the world. When you got back, he was more withdrawn and seemed, I don't know how to describe it . . . seemed covered in darkness. Especially around the Mistress." Again she held out a palm, this time toward the Head Counselor, Minerva reached out and took it in her own. Changing the gesture from a warning off to a gathering in. Sarah smiled and said, "I am happy you're here. I think your differences make our lives richer." She dropped the Head Counselor's hand. "But I can not spare ye . . . not all think so. And dear Simon is one of them."

~~~

The conversation with Sarah left the Blue Knight and the Head Counselor in pensive moods. Their thoughts strayed toward their own people, their own lands.

Rupert could not imagine how the insidious evil had come to undermine Simon. Was it more prevalent than he knew? He needed to pay more attention to his own Keep, focus on his people.

Then his thoughts of his people turned. But what of my love? Minerva, Head Counselor to her people, many of whom are here now because of me. Have I somehow, because of my need for her love, put them in danger? Were the Mountain Folk touched by this evil before they arrived here? Did they infect my people? Or have mine infected them?

Minerva was mentally counting the folk who had come to the Blue Knight's Keep. How many were at risk being here? Should she send them home? Was it even safe to go back to the mountains? How could she leave Rupert? She had never expected to find love, much less one so all-consuming of her soul and body. A whole man, a knight no less, in love with her. How could that have happened? Was Fate playing cruel tricks on them? Giving them love only to have it stolen away in such a short time?

But she had to set him aside. She shook herself and told herself to focus. Her whole life had been spent believing that the King and Kingdom were anathema, to be avoided and ignored if at all possible. Now they were part of her world and she had put her folk at risk by bringing them here. She needed to gather them together. Find out what they knew, had seen, or had reasoned out, about the evil moving within people. She also needed to be a keen observer, making sure none of them had been infected or carried this evil within them. Only when she knew her own folk were safe could she help the Blue Knight take care of his people.

~~~

"Love?" They spoke at the same time.

"Yes?" Again in unison.

Both paused, waiting for the other to speak. Once more they both spoke saying, "I have to go."

Silence, then chuckles from both. She looked up for a kiss and he leaned down to kiss her.

This time he spoke first. "I'll see you at the even' meal. I think it should be something a little more formal tonight, with a few invited guests. Let Sarah know how many you will be including." He turned to go, already distracted by the task ahead.

"Have a care, Sir Knight. See you tonight." She rolled out of the room her own plans building in her head.

Chapter Forty-Seven
HEADING TO THE BLUE KNIGHT'S KEEP

The Red Knight stood in the courtyard helping those departing making final preparations for the journey to the Blue Knight's Keep. It was an easy four-day trip across the most direct paths. Unfortunately, the straightest route was also the most dangerous. Even more so now that General Malicious had set up camp between the Red and Blue Knights' lands.

So after much discussion, heavily swayed by the firm conviction held by Alleyu that horses were NOT meant to be beasts of burden or to carry those who could walk, the longer, more well-traveled, and protected route was agreed upon.

Malcolm, the Red Knight's Captain of the Guard, sat astride his horse. His face was set with a stoney conviction – he would ride! There were mounts for all there. They had selected horses that could be used, in rotation, to pull the two carts as well as riders. A few, very few to Malcom's disgust, were just for riding, again in rotation.

Malcolm would lead on horseback, scouting out ahead and returning with reports. One cart would lead the walking party, and the other would follow. The intention was to give his people some protection if they were set upon. No matter how the Red Knight and Malcolm had pondered and discussed the issue, there was no way to disguise Hmway and Alleyu. They literally stood head and shoulders among even the tallest of the Red Knight's people.

Additionally, they refused to don only garments of the realm. They had integrated layers for warmth, but their orange robes were a beacon for all to see. Although all who had come to know them and fallen under the spell of the constant undertones of music and the peace it brought, none could dispute that it too called out to all. It had been decided that the parade order was as follows: scout, horse and cart, walkers with two horses on each side between the first cart and the last cart and horse. This arrangement would only succeed on the larger routes that were well-travelled, further helping to negate any argument about which way to go.

The Red Knight moved through the crowd, stroking the neck of a horse here, tightening a buckle there. He offered a pat on the back to a person preparing or a handshake to helpers and to family members watching their loved ones ready themselves. He stopped beside Malcolm. He rubbed his horse's neck and whispered in her ear. The horse listened and then twitched an ear and stomped a front foot. "Thank you." He turned to look up at Malcom. "Don't say I didn't warn you when you're walking. She's a hard woman to resist." He looked fondly over to Alleyu who was talking to Beatrice.

"They both are Sir," Malcom said with no little fondness in his voice.

"Indeed! To the issue at hand. Make as much haste as possible. I know walking will slow you down, but Hmway and Alleyu will not. Match the pace they set. We've discussed it at length and they know the urgency here." He stroked the horse's rump as it shifted restlessly. "I know girl, that's why I'm counting on you." The horse stilled, then slowly turned its head to give the Red Knight a gentle snort. He laughed in response and kissed her muzzle. He extended his hand to Malcolm who grasped it firmly. "Travel safely, quickly, and come home with good news to share." He said it solemnly, hopefully, confidently, then let his hand drop. "Off with you all, we have work to be done!"

As a well-rehearsed caravan would do, everyone fell into their places quickly and it was mere moments before the courtyard was empty. Beatrice moved beside her husband and said softly, "They will be all right. The Power goes with them."

The Red Knight stood staring a moment more he placed an arm around her and turned her to go inside. He was still unable to express his fears of what really lay ahead of them - the evil they were just discovering and uncovering.

Chapter Forty-Eight
MORE EVIL DISCOVERED

Malcolm was surprised by how quickly their group moved. The stops to rotate horses gave them an opportunity to eat a bit, take their relief, and share any thoughts or sights they had. They had even arrived at the first waystation several candlemarks earlier than expected. Malcolm dismounted and waited until all had gathered round.

"We have traveled well today and are set for a good even' meal and a rest under a roof." He listened to the murmur of agreements. "We need to move with the sun and be on the road as it rises." He waited for disagreements, but hearing none continued, "If we can continue at this pace, I think we can cut a day off our travel." Words of appreciation were spoken by those in the party. Solemnly Malcolm continued, "Forget not that evil travels with us." Silence blanketed them all. "Soon we should begin to see the Blue Knight's watchers. We also are passing through land Malicious has been tormenting. Be on guard." He spoke very firmly, hoping his tone imbued the situation with the seriousness needed.

They settled their horses in the stable and unpacked the carts before entering the waystation which, to their surprise, was almost empty of patrons. When Malcolm approached the tavern keeper, he noted his trepidation. "Good fellow. We are a band of eight. Have you accommodations and food for us for a night?"

The man looked him up and down before answering. "What be ye business here sir?"

Malcolm decided to take a light tone with him. "Ah, we are traveling from the Red to the Blue Knight's keep. No serious business." He smiled affably.

"Ye be Red Knight's folk?" the tavern keeper asked quite anxiously.

"Yes." Malcolm started to say more then he paused and looked around the tavern again, seeing only one table with four drunken men. "Is there trouble?" He looked at the man directly, leaning a little closer to him. "Can we be of assistance?"

The man shook his head no, then nodded slightly yes. "I'm sorry but the inn is full." He gulped nervously. "Ye'll have to speak to the new owner, sir." With his head, he indicated the drunken men. "I can spare ye a round of ale, but my larder is empty."

Malcolm turned back to his party and waved his hand indicating where to sit, which was on either side of the drunks. "We can't stay, but they can spare us one drink before we go." He knew his people and that they had already perceived a problem here. Unfortunately, they could not have anticipated the response to Hmway and Alleyu as they took their seats.

One of the drunken men rose from the table and pulled out his sword swinging it dangerously. "Demons! Demons!" He screamed to Hmway and Alleyu, advancing more quickly than anyone expected from his drunken state.

Hmway rose and disarmed him so easily that those present started to chuckle. Hmway handed the sword to one of the Red Knight's people. This only served as fuel for another man to stand, draw his sword and advance. Hmway stepped to one side and let the new threat trip over his compatriot lying on the floor, while taking the sword out of his hand as he fell. Again, Hmway handed the sword to one of his party.

On the floor the first man still mumbled, "Demon, demon." The second man appeared to be unconscious. When Malcolm toed him to see if he was alive, he rolled off the first man, snoring. The other two men at the table stood but did not draw arms.

"You have assaulted a soldier in General Mallory's army."
One of them tried to speak with authority but belched when he said
Mallory's name, negating any weight to his words.

The other man tried to stand tall and said," By authority of
General Mallory we hereby con con con fis . . . seize all your goods
for his army's uses."

Seeing no immediate threat, Malcolm spoke to the tavern
keeper again. "How long have these men been here?"

"Four days sir."

"Drinking the whole time?"

A nod.

"Drive away or steal from any other travelers passing by?

A nod.

"Do you have an extra cart and horse the Red Knight can use
to transport," he looked back at the drunks, "those men?"

Another nod.

Turning back to his party Malcolm nodded. His people,
without Hmway or Alleyu, quickly secured the four drunks, then
dragged them, yelling and fighting, from the tavern to the stables
where the tavern keeper helped secure them in a cart. He pointed
out their horses, which truthfully, looked the worse for wear, and
left. Malcolm was unsure if the horses would make it back to the
Red Knight's Keep. They managed to create a harness that put
equal stress on all four horses and moved the cart, now loaded with
four men and a driver, forward.

Alleyu would be very proud of us, thought Malcolm. Turning
he saw Hmway and Alleyu enter the stable.

Alleyu immediately went to the horses to assess them. She gave a nod to Malcolm after inspecting the harness. She began singing softly to the horses while tending their wounds and giving them carrots she had found in the kitchen.

One of Malcolm's men took the role of driver and would escort them back to the Red Knight's keep. One of the women in the party offered to ride the fastest horse ahead to alert the Red Knight and have help sent out. She promised, with a slight bow to Alleyu, to switch horses and be back before they departed with the sun.

Chapter Forty-Nine
ALLEYU MEETS THE MAN WITH THE AURA OF GREEN

It appeared the extra time they had saved that day had, in fact, saved the day for the tavern keeper. When Alleyu finished checking the horses, the cart driver was to set out immediately for the Red Knight's Keep with the four men. The drunks were already snoring and farting themselves in slumber - unconscious men would make for an easier trip.

As Alleyu worked on the horses, she chided herself for not having prepared potions for injuries to animals. She went looking for the tavern keeper to see if she could find some herbs to make a salve for some of the more severe wounds on the animals. Instead, she met the man with the aura of green.

For just a few moments, they only looked at one another. Then the man with the aura of green smiled and held out one of the saddlebags he carried. Alleyu smiled back and without hesitation, took the bag and began rummaging through its contents. It didn't take long before she looked up, saying, "Everything I need is here," but the man with the aura of green was already gone. She wasted no time looking for him but began making the salve and tending to the animals as she softly sang a song of thankfulness to the man with the aura of green.

The cart driver became impatient to depart. They had sent the fast horse rider on. The sooner the rider reached the Red Knight's keep, the sooner he'd have help with this load. But his impatience waned as he listened to Alleyu sing and tend to the horses. By the time she finished, he was humming the song of thankfulness too. The horses who had gentled under Alleyu's touch and caregiving were more alert, stronger, and ready to take up the task of transporting their wicked masters to their reckoning. He realized as he set off at a smart clip that the candlemark of care was a small price to pay for the rewards gained.

Inside the tavern Malcolm and the others had been served a delicious meal of mutton stew and dark bread. The ale was refreshing and not too intoxicating. Which meant Malloy's men must have been drinking excessively for hours. When the tavern keeper approached the table again to offer more stew and ale, Malcolm asked him if he was there alone.

The man hesitated before replying. "No sir. I have a wife and child. They be ill." He wiped his hands on his apron before continuing. "We thought they was on the mend but those men," he spat off to the side as if just the mention of them was a vile taste in his mouth. "They laid hands upon them," he faltered, "held me," he fought back a sob, "made me watch." He stepped away from the group, trying to regain his control.

Malcolm rose and went to lay a hand upon the man's shoulder. "How can we help?"

With such vehemence it made Malcolm drop his hand and step back, the man said, "Kill General Malicious and every cursed man who claims to be his soldier!"

Malcolm waited until the man turned to face him. It took several moments before the tavern keeper was calm enough to speak again.

"Sorry sir. Pardons."

"No ill done, sir. You are not alone in your feelings about General Malicious' group." Malcolm realized his whole party was listening now. "How can we help you, your wife and child?"

"Thank ye, but the man with the aura of green has come. Might even be here now. He's worked his miracles on them." The man turned to go, then stopped. "Would you like to meet my wife sir?"

Malcolm nodded and followed the tavern keeper behind the bar and off to a cozy room kept warm by the kitchen fires. The man with the aura of green sat bedside checking some healing injuries on the woman. On the floor, a young girl sat holding a kitten, who was purring loudly. One arm was braced and wrapped in a sling. The kitten tucked inside close to her heart. Her head was wrapped in a bandage, freshly changed. Bloodied cloth lay in a pile on the floor with other discarded evidence of the brutality suffered.

The tavern keeper waited until the man with the aura of green stood. "I'll collect and clean those Sir."

The man with the aura of green nodded a thanks. He handed the tavern keeper a small packet of herbs. "For tea, to help the healing." He turned toward Malcolm and gave him a slight nod and a smile. "How fares the Red Knight, Malcolm?"

Malcolm tried not to act as surprised as he felt. The man with the aura of green knew him. He'd never been tended by him . . . but he had help tend others whom the man with the aura of green healed. "Well, Sir, save the terror of the evil moving in our land."

The man with the aura of green nodded knowingly. Without asking or explaining he left the room and went out to the table where Hmway sat. He held out one hand to Hmway who looked up at him with his soulful eyes, hesitating only a moment before extending his wounded hand. "The blades were very dirty you must clean this thoroughly." He handed Hmway a small pot of salve and a bandage. "When clean, use these." Hmway nodded. The man with the aura of green waited but no more was said. He pivoted to go, then turned back and said, "Your wife is an excellent healer . . . and singer." Then he was gone.

Hmway hummed then sang, "Now I understand."

Alleyu had just returned and responded in song, "A healer in green. A sight to be seen." She collected a clean basin of water and soap and cleaned Hmway's hand. Soon it had salve and bandage applied. She sat down and looked for her empty stew bowl. Jokingly to Hmway she asked, "Did you eat my stew?" Before he could reply, a fresh bowl was set before her and she dug in.

Malcolm and the rest of the Red Knight's people sat in amazed silence. In the course of a few candlemarks: wicked soldiers had been contained, horses tended and healed, the sick recovering, the man with the aura of green come and gone. Now Hmway and Alleyu sat, apparently unaffected by any of it, having mutton stew.

Hmway rose and held out a hand for Alleyu, who finished her last bite before taking his hand. "We leave early so now it's time for rest." He and Alleyu left the company humming a lullaby which made each person nod sleepily and then head to bed.

Malcolm sat with the tavern keeper. They savored a final glass of ale together.

"Sir, I can not express my gratitude," the tavern keeper began, "How can I repay . . . "

"Please," Malcolm stopped him before he could continue, "I'm glad we arrived here when we did." He took a long pull on his ale before continuing. "The Red and Blue Knights are working on some solutions to our General Malicious problem. If asked, would you be willing to assist? Perhaps be one of the watchtowers that could alert others of oncoming troubles?"

"Indeed sir, anyway I can help. But how could I alert others? We be too far for a shout or even a short horse ride to be helpful." The tavern keeper looked both perplexed and eager to be of service.

"Well, my friend, that is the intent of this journey." Malcolm looked at the tavern keeper who didn't look any less confused. "In truth, we are preparing for war. New ideas of how to fight the evil that moves in our land are needed. New ways to secure assistance and prevent ill from happening are required. You can play a very important role in all this. Are you able? Willing? Ready?"

The tavern keeper sat up straight, pulled his apron and shirt back into place. "Aye sir. Tell me what I can do."

Malcolm and the tavern keeper spoke for another candlemark before Malcolm realized the time to depart was almost upon him. He rose and stretched. He headed out the front door at the sound of hoofbeats. His fast rider galloped up on a new steed. Both rider and horse seemed to be smiling. She slid off the horse's back, reins in one hand. Spying Malcolm she nodded and spoke quickly, "The load was delivered safely. Driver and cart will be returning shortly, fully loaded, as thanks for the tavern keeper's assistance." She turned to stroke her horse. "I need to brush down and cool this beauty off so we can join the walk shortly." The rider looked around then said to Malcolm. "Sir, there is nothing better than a fast run in the early morn!" The horse raised her head nodding in agreement. So did Malcolm. She turned and headed for the stables, not waiting for Malcolm's reply.

"I'll bring you out some mutton stew."

Over her shoulder she waved a hand, "Thanks."

Malcolm smiled. Then paused. What would become of this world he loved, the people he cherished, if evil won? He shook himself. "It can't" He spoke out loud. Announcing it to the world. "It can't!"

Chapter Fifty
WHERE DOES EVIL COME FROM? (RED KNIGHT)

In the absence of his Captain of the Guard and newest family members, Hmway and Alleyu, the Red Knight began to search in earnest for the cause of the evil that was growing in the kingdom. It had already been told to him that about a dozen of his people had defected to General Malicious' army. It was inconceivable to him how any person, especially someone whom he knew and thought he could trust, would willingly choose Malicious. As he inquired further, he found a stream of dissatisfaction running underneath his well-run Keep.

His move to disarm and dismantle Malicious' army had been unusually successful. At least two-thirds of the men they had captured had been malnourished, physically damaged or ill. Most of them suffered from severe trauma either physically or emotionally. It hurt his soul when he walked up to these men and saw them flinch or look at him in terror, for no other reason than that he was the man in charge. He found it easier to help in the hospice, changing bandages, applying salve. There at least, he could talk to the people he helped. Put them at ease with soft words and a gentle touch. It seemed that as their bodies healed, with care, so did their distrust and fear of others. The emotional pain never seemed to leave them completely. It was tattooed on their souls, untouchable, unreachable.

There were those who seemed to revel in the pain and sorrow they caused. They sought out ways to do harm for no other reason than causing distress. Even in their imprisonment, they worked against those feeding them or offering them help of any kind. They were just as likely to spit in your face when handed food as to eat the food. These individuals were unable to accept kindness, acknowledge their wrong actions, or accept responsibility for the harm they caused. Malicious had drawn these types, mostly men, but also a few women, to him like flies to a refuse pile.

The Red Knight was hoping to integrate some of Malicious' people into his own Keep and lands. Or return some of them to their own homes and families. He was surprised at how many confessed to joining Malicious' army because they owed a debt or service to him. Many were taken from their families and lives without time to say goodbye or pack a good pair of shoes. The Red Knight had hope for these people. As they regained weight and strength and healed their external wounds, they seemed willing to accept responsibility for what they had done for Malicious.

The Red Knight's tradespeople were working on a contract, that included restitution for some of the damages these people had caused. Each knew which farms they burned, which businesses they had stolen from and then destroyed, and the people they had physically assaulted. Malicious had made sure their actions were written on their soul and often their bodies. This contract could be taken with them and offered to those they had harmed the most. It limited their liability because, in truth, Malicious was responsible, but they had participated and must make amends.

The contract became a much more complicated problem than expected. If a person took responsibility for their actions and made a contract with an aggrieved party, they both must honor it and not take advantage of the other. So far it had been used only twice. In the first attempt, both parties participated fully and fairly. The farmer said he would need more help to restore next year's crops, but offered to pay the offender for his work after the agreed upon retribution payment was met. Unfortunately, the second attempt was disastrous! Three men together approached a business owner. They had stolen most of the goods and burned down the building. The restitution was to help rebuild the building and each repay one-sixth of the lost product over two years. The business owner was supplying materials for rebuilding and paying for half of the cost of the stolen goods. The rebuilding went fine, but the repayment schedule collapsed before it began. The business owner wanted more than agreed upon and the men refused to pay. After a terrible brawl at the local tavern, all four ended up in jail for a fortnight.

A different version of the contract also included a commitment to their families, changing the fundamental way they understood relationships and the harm their actions had caused. This part of the contract caused the most problems because relationships can not be dictated by a contract.

He harkened this contract back to the oath he swore when he became the Red Knight, or when he married Beatrice. He knew that most people had no formal ceremonies or contracts for relationships. It was a practice of the wealthy, done to secure resources within relationships. The Red Knight hoped that the contracts would be one of the tools that would help defeat the evil, but instead they only caused more problems.

The Red Knight began interviewing the families of those who had defected to Malicious. He spent time with the various individuals responsible for the operations of the Keep, trying to uncover issues and discover problems previously unseen. For the most part, his was a happy Keep. People enjoyed their positions and those didn't had the opportunity to seek alternatives. Everyone had food and shelter. Several years ago Beatrice had reorganized the formal school process and most all participated through their early teens, providing them with enough education to read, write, do sums, and explore a little outside their own worlds before deciding whether to remain within the Keep. The trade guilds had set up apprentice positions and passed on their skills and talents to the next generation, regardless of which family they came from.

He did find that all those who had defected had made frequent trips to Center City, where the King's Castle was located. All trips occurred since the Princess had fallen ill and after the Magician had come to rebuild the hospices and train healers. Surprisingly, most had either been treated in the new hospice or taken a healer training program, and all mentioned a man called the Magician

Chapter Fifty-One
UNCOVERING EVIL'S ROOTS

Sarah was enjoying setting a formal dinner in the Keep. She loved having the Blue Knight and the Head Counselor in her kitchen, but then she didn't get to show off her culinary skills. They both liked simple fare and were not given to waste food or resources without cause. Tonight, she had a score to cook for! She kept everyone who worked in the kitchen busy. More bread was being made. Pie production was at peak efficiency. She'd consulted with the butcher and learned that an injured lamb had been freshly killed and would make a perfect feast for tonight. She sent out for a harvest of vegetables.

The Blue Knight was not much of a drinker, but since this was a special evening, a toast or raised glass would only be appropriate. She had one keg of wine brought in and prepared. She debated whether to decorate the room but determined it would seem too officious. She knew the discussions would be serious enough without hanging the weight of the Knighthood and Kingdom around them.

Sarah sent the Keep seamstress to find the Head Counselor and see if she needed a gown for the evening. She would not have her Mistress looking less than official and beautiful. She was taken aback when the seamstress she asked seemed displeased with the prospect of helping the Head Counselor. She didn't have time to give it much thought until after she found another seamstress whose response was much more excited and enthused about the prospect of helping the Head Counselor.

As she returned to the kitchen she made a mental note. Was the first seamstress another like Simon? Why? She thought back over the past several months and found nothing out of the ordinary, except that the girl had volunteered to go to Center City at every opportunity. Sarah had figured she had a beau in town. When the seamstress returned, she always spoke of a person called the Magician and his work on the hospice and healer training. Now that she considered the woman's actions, Sarah remembered that the girl was a little obsessed with the man.

It had been a busy, productive afternoon. By the time the even' repast was upon them, she was nearly spent, but pleased with the results. The Blue Knight wandered in, still dressed in his working garb, distracted.

"Sarah, about the meal tonight." He stopped and looked around the kitchen. "I guess I told you to expect extra people." He sighed deeply, looking far more tired and worried than she'd ever seen him.

"Yes Sir. We're set for twenty, but I have room and food for more, if needed." Sarah looked intently at her knight. "Are you all right?"

The Blue Knight finally seemed to focus and looked at Sarah with a wan smile. "Yes, yes, sorry. I am a bit distracted by the day's events."

"As to be expected Sir. But have no fear for tonight. All is taken care of. You and the Mistress can have no worries." She waited for a response, but receiving none continued, "It's time to change to your evening uniform Sir. I had a seamstress check in with the Mistress to make sure she'd be appropriately dressed for the evening also."

At the mention of Minerva, the Blue Knight seemed to snap back to consciousness. He gave Sarah a quick hug and spoke as he left the room. "Thank you Sarah. For everything." Then he was gone.

She spared only a few moments staring after him before turning back to make sure all the preparations were complete and the meal was ready to be served.

The meal was a grand success. There was plenty of food for all. A feast, set in an atmosphere of comfort and ease, which allowed the evening to progress into its real intention: discovering the root of evil.

The Head Counselor had opted for a simple but beautiful fabric, which she wore draped over her shoulders and as a skirt covering her withered legs. She did not cover her wheeled chair. The Blue Knight had found a jacket that matched in color. He wore a vest with the Blue Knight's crest. One of the Mountain Folk had made a drape for the back of the Head Counselor's chair which was a beautiful representation of the mountains. The two made an impressive couple.

The table seated twelve of the Blue Knight's most trusted leaders and seven of the Mountain Folk. The Chief Engineer, Mud, sat next to the Head Counselor. He had spent most of the meal stuffing his face and then speaking to her with a full mouth. She hoped he was not spraying her with food bits. But it was important for him to be here and be part of the conversation ahead, so she tolerated his eating habits.

The intermixing of peoples did not seem to pose a problem. The conversation had flowed. The food was delicious. The real purpose of the night was ignored for as long as possible. Finally, the Blue Knight indicated that the wine be served. When all had a glass, he rose.

"Thank you all for joining us this evening." He looked around the room smiling and making eye contact with everyone, as was his style. "Before we get to the serious portion of the evening let us all raise a glass." He waited for all to do so. "To our kingdom and all its people."

226

The Head Counselor raised her glass and her people followed. She had assured them that they would not succumb to the rule of a King and Kingdom, who had rejected them so easily. Lifting their glasses was in respect for the Blue Knight. She had also insisted that the evil within the Kingdom threatened them as well. If this evil was to be defeated, the Mountain Folk would need to be part of the battle.

Everyone at the table took a sip and set their glasses down. This was not a night for imbibing.

The Blue Knight began, "We all know there is an evil moving throughout our land." There were murmurs and nods around the table. "We know one source of the evil. General Mallory, or Malicious, as he is now known, and his band of thieves and scoundrels, which he calls an army."

At this, an outcry arose. Some slapped the table, others stomped their feet, some shouted 'Malicious be downed'.

The Blue Knight waited until the crowd settled and the nervous energy had been spent. "But there is another source. Much more pernicious. Much more disguised and dishonest in its intentions." He paused to take in a breath and consider his next words carefully. "It has infected our people."

He heard gasps from some at the table. This was not news to anyone, but stating the fact out loud and acknowledging that it was within the Blue Knight's own Keep was still unsettling.

"The Head Counselor and I have spoken to all of you here at this table. We have determined, I hope correctly, that you all remain without the taint that is spreading."

Those gathered voiced agreement and concern at this news.

"Please understand we must root out this evil at its core. Find the seed from which it grows and destroy it. It is a subtle creature. If we remain unaware of it, it can deceive and destroy us before we even know we've been touched." The timbre of his voice expressed his concern.

He waited for the mumbled comments and discussion around the table to cease.

"I hold up my own ignorance and lack of attention as an example." He paused and then lifted his cup to take a sip. The Head Counselor gently stroked the side of his leg once under the table, unseen by others. When he set his glass down, he was steadier and his stance wider so one leg touched her chair. "Simon, one of my own here in the Keep has been infected. It happened before we left on the King's Quest, but I did not note the little changes and growing differences in his attitudes and actions: Acts of tiny harms, attitudes of insensitivity toward others. When he lost his leg during the construction project, he had the very best care. In fact, his life was saved by the quick actions of the Mountain Folks. But he harbors ill will against them and my wife, their Head Counselor."

This shocked many at the table. Those who knew Simon had noticed changes since his accident, but he had been cloistered for the most part since his return, so they had not seen enough of the changes personally to take note of them as something significant or evil.

"Simon speaks of change. The need to purge the unwanted." The Blue Knight stopped to take in a deep breath. "I believe if I placed him in Malicious' hands he would join, without hesitation, but even more troubling is his attachment to someone called the Magician."

This caused some to rise to their feet. Shouts of "No", "It can't be". "Speak truth – no" and more arose. The Blue Knight waited, watching, looking for any who may have also fallen under the Magician's spell.

"We need to examine ourselves, our family, our friends. This is a disease which will kill us if it spreads. It can not be seen, save in the changes we see in those we love."

Murmuring spread.

"This is *not*, for lack of a better term, a vendetta against those we disagree with. Our intentions are not to bring harm or separate out anyone because we wish them ill, or simply don't like them. This is a search for evil. The evil makes a person feel different from you. The evil makes them respond with harm instead of compassion. I, I'm not sure how to describe what we are looking for exactly." He taps his chest over his heart, "but you'll feel it here."

Silence covered the room. The weight of what had been presented settled upon those within. Some were not at ease with even the notion of evil within. Others seemed to be analyzing and already making comparisons in their heads. Others were rejecting the notion that a loved one or friend could be tainted by this evil.

Surprising everyone, including herself, Sarah was the first to speak. "If we notice someone who seems to have changed, what do we do?"

The Blue Knight looked thankfully at Sarah. "I would propose we gather them together at another meal, such as this." He stretched out his arm over the table and guests. "With a few of us, untainted, interspersed, listening, asking questions, checking to see if it is, in fact, the evil we fear or just an ill-conceived spirit that brought them to this table. If it be true evil, then . . . " He could not go on, because he had no answer for what to do with them.

One of the farmers stood up and asked, "Do we know any cause for this?"

The Blue Knight hesitated and the Head Counselor touched his arm, asking for permission to speak. He nodded.

"So far, those we've identified have all made visits to Center City and had contact with the hospice, healer training, or someone called the Magician." She paused, scanning the faces in the room.

Murmurs arose again, someone shouted out, "We all go to Center City."

"We do not believe it is Center City or its people, but the connection to the hospice and healer training of which the Magician has been in charge." She spoke calmly, trying to reassure while expressing her concern.

More murmuring. Another voice spoke, "So if we've received healing we're tainted?"

"No. If you were treated outside Center City or the new hospices. It is not the healing that taints, but we think . . . " She hesitated because her thoughts were merely suspicions and if she led them down a wrong path, more time could be wasted and people falsely accused. "We believe it is contact with the Magician and his people, they are the cause of this infection."

Chapter Fifty-Two
BLUE & RED KNIGHTS JOIN FORCES

It was only a day and a half after leaving the tavern when the Red Knight's people entered the Blue Knight's Keep. They were greeted warmly and ushered into the Blue Knight and Head Counselor's study.

In truth, the Red Knight's people were a bit surprised at the lack of reaction to Hmway and Alleyu, even though they were both tall, dark-skinned, wearing a bright orange wrap and stood out in a crowd. Instead, it was the Red Knight's people who were surprised to find the Keep was filled with activity. They had heard of the Blue Knight's marriage to the Head Counselor of the Mountain Folks, but they had not expected to meet any of her folks. But here Mountain Folks were working side-by-side with the Blue Knight's people.

People without limbs, people who were blind, people in wheeled chairs all living and working like everyone else. What caught most of the Red Knight's people's eyes was a little girl with a woman and man on either side, touching her shoulders, each holding a kitten, engaged in a very serious discussion. It only took a few moments to realize the adults were blind, the child was not. She was clearly in charge of their walk, even though she was still a child. The threesome moved across the busy courtyard without incident or distress, settling against the far wall with a basket of wool and weaving tools. The woman took up the weaving and began instructing the girl. The man was tasked with handling all three kittens as they worked.

One of the guides the Blue Knight had sent to them noticed their attention and commented, "That's Joseph, Mary and Joy. I don't know the kitten's names yet." His listeners waited for more, but he offered nothing. They were left to wonder. "Follow me, the Blue Knight and the Head Counselor are anxious to see you." He

231

moved through the courtyard, greeting many, giving everyone in the Red Knight's party a sense that the world they knew had definitely changed.

The guide entered a large building and led them down a short hallway, stopping only to knock on a door before opening it.

"Welcome, welcome!" The Blue Knight ushered them in, indicating seats around the fireplace where the Head Counselor sat, in her wheeled chair. "You made good time. No trouble?"

"Well Sir Knight, we did encounter some of General Mallory's men abusing a tavern owner." The Captain of the Guard raised one hand, "Fear not, they were already too far in their cups to be of any problem. They are now in the hands of the Red Knight."

"Aah, I feel there is more story to tell, but first introductions." The Blue Knight moved to stand beside the Head Counselor. "This is the Head Counselor of the Mountain Folk. He laid a hand upon her shoulder, sighing with deep contentment, and went on, "And my wife, Minerva."

Minerva, the wife smiled and laid her hand upon his, squeezing it gently. Minerva, the Head Counselor, turned slightly to face those gathered and said, "Please let us know who you are."

The Captain of the Guard proceeded to introduce everyone, saving Hmway and Alleyu until last. "And these are the caretakers of our desert, Hmway and his wife, Alleyu."

When they were introduced, the pair sang and hummed a brief greeting song. When they had finished the Head Counselor wheeled over to them and touched two fingers to her heart. "Well met, fellow travelers. Welcome to my home."

Hmway hummed while Alleyu leaned over and gave the Head Counselor a hug and whispered something in her ear. She nodded as they parted and big smiles lit up all three faces.

"I'm sorry to bring our introductions to a quick end, but we have serious business to discuss." The Blue Knight spoke gently but with authority. Looking around the room at those gathered he asked, "Who's first."

Each had something different to share: the capture of Malicious' army, the condition of those captured, the man with the aura of green's appearance, both at the Red Knight's Keep and also at the tavern where they had stopped. They outlined the reorganization of the Red Knight's Keep, the landholders being organized into small alert and militia groups. Also an explanation of how they were preparing and protecting the livestock, horses and people. It was several candlemarks before they paused and gave Hmway and Alleyu a chance to speak.

"Hmmmmmmmm," Hmway hummed. "We have been working on a song." He tapped his leg gently, marking out a beat.

Alleyu began humming the melody. Everyone stilled and listened.

"A song of overcoming, success, and joy," Hmway continued. "It is meant to be a vehicle for uniting, strengthening and giving courage in this unsettling time."

Then Alleyu sang the song, softly the first time, then a little louder. On the third refrain, Hmway joined her and motioned for others to do the same. By the fifth repeat everyone was singing the chorus, having learned the words and embraced the message.

"That is exactly what we need!" The Head Counselor said a little breathlessly. "I haven't sung in years, but it sure felt good."

"Indeed, indeed," the Blue Knight spoke up.

He had refrained from singing until the final round, unable to hold back any longer. His tenor voice had deep bass undertones.

When he finally sang, Hmway harmonized with him, and the song soared.

"Well, let's get you fed and refreshed before you meet with our people here. We have a lot to share!" That said, he opened the door and found Sarah and several of the Keep staff waiting outside.

"Pardon, Sir Knight," Sarah spoke in a hushed tone. "What was that song you were singing?" Those gathered around her leaned in to hear his response.

"Our new anthem. *THE* new anthem for our kingdom." The Blue Knight answered with deep conviction.

"Beautiful!" Sarah whispered.

Someone else in the gathered crowd spoke up, "When do we get to learn it?"

Others chimed in with "Yes, when?"

The Blue Knight raised his arms to still the group. Chuckling he answered, "After dinner, this evening." Turning to Sarah he asked, "Is the even' meal ready for our guests?"

"Just waiting on you Sir Knight," Sarah replied a bit more sassily than was appropriate. Correcting her tone and demeanor, she tried again. "Sir Knight, your meal awaits."

She stepped back out of his way and shooed the others back to their tasks. She waited in the hallway as the guests exited the study, giving a nod and smile to each. To the few she knew, she reached out to touch a hand or arm. The last to leave were the tall, dark, visitors. The woman was pushing the Head Counselor's wheeled chair and they seemed to be in a deep discussion. The man had a gentle hand on the woman's shoulder guiding her away from obstacles, humming softly.

Sarah watched as they entered the dining room before finally returning to the kitchen with a amused smile on her face. "First, he brings home a wife, now a new anthem and desert people. The world is changing!"

Sarah provided a feast for all gathered. The conversations had been lively and spirits high.

Since the Head Counselor arrived, Sarah had noted how people seemed more relaxed and open with one another. Surprising since the Mountain Folk had always been outcasts, the unwanted. Now they had become people again. They were open and willing to forgive those who had cast them out. Thankfully the Blue Knight's people had started asking questions, instead of staring or making false assumptions. Everyone seemed more willing to listen to one another, even to those whose opinions differed from their own.

It was a different world indeed.

Chapter Fifty-Three
BLUE KNIGHT PRESENTS A NEW LANGUAGE

It had been another fine meal. *I'll have to make sure to thank Sarah,* he thought. After two nights of feasting, the Blue Knight was ready to settle in for a quiet evening and some alone time with his wife, but that was not on his agenda tonight. He looked around the table thoughtfully. He was amazed at the collection of thirty people who were all different, but not really so different at all.

"Why does it take a crisis to bring people together?" He mumbled under his breath.

"Because we don't take the time to gather when things are going well," the Head Counselor answered him just as softly as he had mumbled.

He leaned over and gave her a kiss on the cheek. "What do you say we change that," he looked around the table, "when things settle down."

She stroked his cheek, and he leaned into her touch. "I think that's a marvelous idea, love," she leaned closer, "But we need to start this evening meeting or I won't be able to move before it's done." She smiled. It was a smile filled with pain, the pain that haunted her body every day.

The Blue Knight rose and tapped the table, waiting for everyone to give him their attention. "Friends, visitors – new friends, although I believe this has been a pleasant evening for all, we now have a less pleasant task ahead."

He paused and looked down to see Sarah delivering the pain tea to the Head Counselor. He nodded to her and gave her a smile of thanks. He saw Minerva already consuming the tea without hesitation, which spoke volumes to just how much pain she was in!

He mentally shook himself, pulling his focus back to the crisis at hand.

"We are fighting an evil, seen and unseen. Our physical enemy is General Mallory and his army and a man called The Magician and his minions. Our rooting out our unseen enemy, the evil spreading throughout the land, is why we are here."

Many around the table nodded and slapped their hands on the table.

The Blue Knight continued, "As you can see we have some of the Red Knight's people and two leaders from the Desert People are with us tonight." Smiles all around. "They have much to share, as do we. We have all responded to this evil in different ways. The Red Knight has created a militia of sorts, having confronted General Mal ..." he stumbled, sighed, and continued, "What the Power! The man is just evil, let's call him as he acts: Malicious!"

A round of boos and hisses went up around the table, more pounding and foot stomping too. The Head Counselor laid a hand upon the Blue Knight's arm for just a moment, helping him gain calm more quickly. He raised his hands and brought the room back to calm also. When he had lowered his arms, he laid a hand upon her shoulder and waited for her to speak.

"As you all have surmised by now, I am of the Mountain Folk," she began.

A few of the Blue Knight's people snorted and chortled, a few mock- exclaimed "No! Really?"

She had the good humor to dip her head for a moment and smile. "Surprising as that is," she went on, "we have been creating a language, or more correctly adapting a language that has been in use for many years." She nodded to Doug and he moved to the far end of the room standing next to the Red Knight's Captain of the Guard. She asked Doug a question for the Captain of the Guard with hand language. Doug in turn, verbally repeated the question, listened to the reply then used hand language to tell her his answer. Everyone, not already in the know, was quite puzzled.

"I asked Doug to ask the Captain of the Guard a question. His answer was: Blackie." She looked at the Captain, who had a shocked look on his face. "Captain, what was the question I asked?"

He smiled and replied, "What is the name of my favorite horse?"

"And the answer?" she asked.

"Blackie."

There were gasps of astonishment and disbelief. "How did they do that?" "How can wiggling your fingers talk to someone?" "They set that up before we ate." "I wonder if I can do that?"

"The Mountain Folk have used hand language for many years to be able to communicate with all types of people, in all types of conditions, removing barriers." She paused to let that sink in. "We have created a new hand language specifically to handle the battle ahead." She waited until the murmuring died down. "It is not intended to be a complete language, just the essentials one might need in a time of crisis, a battle, or whenever you may be prevented from communicating like you usually do."

She looked at one of the servers and nodded. The server excused herself briefly and returned with two poles and two whistles. She gave one pole to the Blue Knight and one whistle to the Head Counselor. When she leaned down to hand her the whistle, the Head Counselor asked, "Is all ready in the courtyard?" The woman nodded and left with a pole and whistle.

"But as helpful as the hand language is, if you can not see another's hands, it is no more effective than speaking. So," she paused for effect, appreciating the full attention she had and the looks of expectation on everyone's face. She turned the person sitting next to her. "Give me a number and direction."

The woman considered then said, "37. Northeast."

The Head Counselor took the pole and pounded: loud, soft, loud, soft, loud soft, then tapped the pole with her spoon quickly. She then took the whistle and let out two distinct sounds. Then she waited.

From somewhere in the Keep, those at the table heard the pounds and sounds repeated, once and then again. A few moments later a young lad came jogging into the dining room and approached the Head Counselor. He bobbed a bow and breathed out, "Mistress, 37 coming from the Northeast."

There were gasps of surprise around the table. Someone asked the woman who'd given the directions if she was part of this trickery, which she denied vehemently. Someone else called out. "Again, do it again." They followed up with another number: "Four score" and direction "South". Again the Counselor tapped out and whistled. Again the same sounds were repeated elsewhere in the Keep. Again, a young lad came jogging into the room, up to the Head Counselor. A bob and bow, "Ma'am we're being invaded! 80 coming from the south." This time the response from those in the room was stunned silence.

After giving everyone enough time to process what they had just witnessed the Head Counselor spoke. "As you can see, we now have two forms of communication. One is silent using our hands for visual communication. One uses sound for distant communication."

The Blue Knight continued, "We believe that with this language we will be able to wage war against evil. These tools of communication will give us an element of surprise. We will be able to subdue our foes and prevent the senseless violence and destruction that Malicious is causing."

Cheers and shouts went up in the room. More foot stomping and table slapping.

The Blue Knight spoke over the voices, "That may help defeat our physical enemy, but we also need powerful tools to defeat the evil within." A quiet settled over the room. "We need something to bring us together. Something to reassure our spirits. Something that reminds us of who we are and what our kingdom is meant to be."

An uneasy silence fell.

Apprehension kept the room still. The Blue Knight motioned Hmway and Alleyu to his side. They began to sing. The new song of the new kingdom. They sang it once, twice the room sat mesmerized. On the third go, the Blue Knight and Head Counselor joined in as did the Red Knight's people. By the fourth round, all were singing, and the fifth round ended with a triumphant cry.

The Blue Knight let the euphoria calm before speaking again. "If we can rekindle our spirits and reclaim our wayward neighbors, I believe we can overcome the evil that seeks to steal our kingdom."

A thoughtful silence held the room.

He waited several long moments before he spoke again. "Tomorrow, the Red Knight's people will join ours. They will teach us the anthem and their military strategies. We will teach them our hand language and sound signals." He took a deep breath. "When they leave we will establish way stations between our two lands which will open continual communication between the Red and Blue Knights Keeps."

He wanted to pound on the table, just barely resisting because he saw the Head Counselor looking at him with what only could be described as admiration and love. He straightened his stance slightly, and in his most knightly voice stated, "We will no longer be taken by surprise, subjected to senseless violence, nor suffer harm, because we no longer stand alone."

A cheer went up in the room. People stamped their feet. Slapped each other on the back. Raised a glass in salute.

He gave a wave of departure and turned to push the Head Counselor's chair out of the room. "On the morrow all."

He was glad to see she didn't resist and try to push herself, for he worried that the tea had not been enough. *There is too much to do. I hope she doesn't push herself too hard. Because without her, what is this all for?* He kept his thoughts to himself as he pushed her to their bedroom. They both needed a good night's rest.

Chapter Fifty-Four
DISCOVERING THE SOURCE OF EVIL

The next few days in the Blue Knight's keep were a beehive of activity. There were voices singing, poles banging, whistles blowing, people laughing and concentrating. Their hands were waving and anyone looking from the outside would have thought they'd all gone mad!

It was a miraculous event taking place. Red Knight and Blue Knight people, Mountain Folk, Desert folk, all working together. Learning from one another. Coming to know each other not as *others* but as friends, compatriots, members of the same kingdom all striving for the same good, a greater good for all.

The Blue Knight was paying careful attention, watching for anyone who hesitated. Anyone who didn't seem to be able to relax and work with those different from themselves. Or a person who could only find fault with whatever task or person they were working with. By mid-morning he had gleaned about a dozen who seemed unable to engage. He had set up a room with mending and tool-sharpening tasks with a male and female counselor. As he drew an individual aside, he asked if they had any skill sewing or working metal, and all admitted to some. He asked if they could help him with special tasks and sent them to work in the room set apart. The counselors guided their tasks and conversations, observed and watched their actions. The Blue Knight hoped by nightfall they would have some idea of what, or who, had caused these people to behave differently from the rest.

The next evening, one fast rider after another arrived to report small scrimmages with General Malicious' people. Malicious' army was defeated every time, but the incidents were becoming more frequent.

More surprising was a warning that arrived from the man with the aura of green. "Do not trust any of the new healers." That was all, no explanation, no alternatives. The Blue Knight was so frustrated by this mysterious message he contemplated harming himself to entice the man with the aura of green to his Keep. But he need not have fretted because the Head Counselor's pain and need for help brought the man with the aura of green to their door.

He had come in to refresh himself before the even' meal and found Minerva and the man with the aura of green in their bedroom. He was giving her a back massage and the grimace on her face showed how much pain she was in. He slapped his forehead; he hadn't given her a back massage since the Red Knight's people arrived. How could he be so thoughtless! He started to speak but the man with the aura of green shook his head, so he stopped, stilled at the door. It was several minutes before the grimace gave way to a sigh and then a word of release. The man with the aura of green ceased his labors and knelt before her.

"Ask, don't wait." He spoke loud enough so the Blue Knight could hear.

"I," the Blue Knight started to protest and explain, but again was stilled by only a shake of the head.

"Tell Sarah to double your dose."

Minerva grimaced but nodded, another sign of how much pain she was in.

The man with the aura of green stood and turned to the Blue Knight. "The Magician is the source of evil which is spreading. He has been training healers. He has the King's ear." He turned to go.

"Wait!" The Blue Knight reached out to touch the man with the aura of green's arm but dropped his hand before he made contact. "I don't know this Magician. Why can't we trust the healers? What are we supposed to do?" He looked and felt helpless. Lost like he'd never been before in his life. He reached out again. "Did I harm my wife?" He asked in a soft, pleading voice.

The man with the aura of green took a step toward the Blue Knight and laid a hand upon his shoulder. "No." He looked over at the Head Counselor and shook his head slightly. "She knows her limits." He looked back at the Blue Knight. "She should ask, but don't wait for her to do so."

The Blue Knight let out a heavy sigh of relief. "Then sir, please. What of this magician?"

The man with the aura of green dropped his hand. "That is not my disease to heal." He turned and left without another word.

The Blue Knight stood there for several moments. Unsure of what was ahead. What was his responsibility? He had failed his wife; would he fail his kingdom?

"Rupert, can you help me into bed please." Minerva's voice had a slight quiver. She was trying very hard to keep the pain out of her voice.

The Blue Knight started, his trance broken, he turned and moved quickly to Minerva's side. "Of course, love." He scooped her gently out of her chair and set her on the edge of the bed. He helped her undress. When she was about to don her sleeping gown he asked, "Can I get the fleece and some warming stones and give your back a little more relief tonight?"

She was almost in tears and choked out, "That would be most appreciated love."

She lay back and he covered her, kissed her forehead, and said, "I'll be right back." He hurried to the kitchen where he found Sarah with a tray already filled with a fleece wrapped in warming stones and a cup of healing tea.

"The Mistress doesn't let us know when she's in too much pain. I thought she might need a little extra tonight."

The Blue Knight gave Sarah a quick hug and kiss on the cheek. "You are a wise woman, Sarah dear. Thank you." And he hurried back to their bedroom.

Sarah watched him go. Wiping her hands on her apron she said to no one in particular, "If anything happens to that gal, it will be a death for all of us."

Chapter Fifty-Five
REPORTING TO THE RED KNIGHT

The next few days passed quickly. When the Red Knight's people returned to their Keep with poles, whistles, and a new hand language, twelve of the Blue Knight's people had come with them. Some were to establish waystations or watch towers between the two Keeps. Some went to gain more insight into military preparedness. For all that the intention of their journey was a deadly serious purpose, they were a light-hearted group, feeling revived and ready for what was ahead.

They had an uneventful journey back. Four independent waystations and watcher towers were established. Twice they came upon a home or farm that had been recently destroyed. One was deserted, at the other they found a family burying their father and oldest son. The party stopped to help. They restored what they could and left some supplies with the family. They also taught them the danger whistle and left a whistle with them, explaining that within earshot there was a watchtower that would hear them and alert both the Red and Blue Knights and help would be on the way.

Most of the family looked skeptical and did not listen or learn the whistle, except the youngest girl. She took the whistle as her own and practiced, practiced, practiced until she had it perfect and then took sole possession of it, by putting it on a string and wearing it around her neck.

One of the Blue Knight's people leaned down and whispered in the young girl's ear. He stood upright and held out an arm. The girl hesitated then reached up and grasped the man's arm firmly and smiled. He grasped her arm and held it for a few moments. Then he dropped it and joined the departing party. He looked back only once, to see the young girl standing alone in the path watching them go.

When they arrived at the Red Knight's Keep the reception was as it had been at the Blue Knight's Keep. The few Mountain Folk who were part of the group were accepted without question. The training for hand language, pole, and whistle messaging went smoothly and almost everyone could be heard humming or singing softly the new anthem.

The Red Knight asked Hmway and Alleyu to join them for a quiet evening in the study. Beatrice sat next to the candle lamp working on a piece of embroidery. Bartholomew was pacing. Circling the room, hands behind his back, slapping them together occasionally. After the fourth pass Beatrice, without looking up from her work, asked, "Something on your mind?"

"Hmm? Yes, that sounds good." The Red Knight continued to pace.

"Bart!"

"Hmm? Sorry, I'm a little preoccupied.

"Who would have guessed Sir Knight." Beatrice's tone was a bit mocking but more concerned. "What, pray tell, has my beloved Red Knight in such a state of mind?"

He stopped and sat down beside her, absently inspecting her handiwork. "Lovely, dear." Then he sat back with a frustrated huff.

"I've just been informed that more fighting has occurred. This time with loss of life, as well as property." He stood up and began pacing again. "I just don't understand where all these people are coming from and why they are doing so much senseless harm!" He flopped back into his chair and looked at her with such despair that she set her handiwork aside and reached out to him.

"My love," she waited until he looked at her, really looked at her, not around or over her. "Bartholomew, evil has no explanation.

All we can do is try to head it off before it does more harm." She took both his hands in hers. They dwarfed hers but she held them like they were a child's. "Sir Red Knight, you and the Blue Knight have made great strides in combatting this evil. Together you will do even more. Do not ask for troubles that are not yours." She shook his hands making him look down at them, then back up at her. "If evil is all you look for, that is all you'll see. Look for the good." Again she shook his hands once then lifted them to give each a kiss on a knuckle. "I think you're missing your songbirds."

At that moment there was a knock on the door and Hmway and Alleyu entered.

Both the Red Knight and his wife rose to greet the travelers. Beatrice and Alleyu embraced. Bartholomew and Hmway grasped arms, then Hmway pulled him into a strong hug, humming softly a soothing melody.

"Welcome home," Beatrice ushered them in and motioned for them to sit. "I have tea and biscuits." She picked up the teapot and at Alleyu's nod began to pour.

After they had all taken their first sips of tea the Red Knight asked, "How fares the Blue Knight and his people?"

Hmway gave him one of his bright smiles and hummed a happy tune. "Well, my friend, well." He took another sip of tea. "And the Mountain Folk!" He smiled again, now with even a twinkle in his eye. "Amazing, wonderful people. So talented." His humming became louder and all listened. When he stopped he set down his tea cup and turned to face the Red Knight. "Much good is happening. "

The Red Knight leaned in, waiting for more, but Hmway remained silent. "Excuse me Hmway, is that all you have to report from your journey?" He worked very hard to keep the edge out of his voice. He waited, trying to be patient.

Finally Alleyu spoke, "The evil is definitely within your land. Both you and the Blue Knight now know of its existence and are working to identify and eliminate it." She paused selecting her next words carefully. "It won't be easy but you will win the struggle."

Again, the Red Knight waited for more. He started to rise, then fell back, sighing heavily. "My friends, you give me no solace!" He rose and started to pace, dismissing Beatrice's look of disapproval with a shake of his head. "I need something more." He waved his hands. "Something tangible!" He stopped and stared at them. "How can I fight something I can't see?"

Beatrice gave her husband a moment of relief by saying, "We have identified a group of people who have been to Center City and either visited the new hospice or did some healer training there." She looked at her husband but he let her continue. "There is an underlying sense of discontentment in them. Their families have no explanation for their dis-ease."

Hmway and Alleyu nodded. "The Blue Knight has found the same," Hmway stated.

"But what of this continual onslaught of violence, people causing harm and destruction, without cause or purpose?" He breathed out heavily, "Where are these people coming from? They are not our people!"

Hmway rose and stood beside the Red Knight. "Weeds in your garden."

The Red Knight stared at him, dumbfounded. "What?"

Hmway sighed, something he rarely did, and looked at the Red Knight like he was a child, not understanding a simple concept. "Your King has let evil influences, weeds, into your Kingdom, garden." He waited for the Red Knight to register comprehension.

Finally the light dawned and he nodded in understanding.

Hmway continued, "You need to weed your own garden first." He waited for the Red Knight to acknowledge his words.

"Deal with the discontented people in my own Keep?" Puzzled the Red Knight asked.

Hmway nodded.

"Prepare for the outsiders."

Hmway nodded.

"My wise friend, do you have any suggestions or words of guidance for me?

Hmway smiled. "Sing." He smiled broader. "Talk." He began to hum the new song Alleyu and Beatrice created. "Create contentment."

The Red Knight sighed, then smiled. He began to sing the song. Hmway, Alleyu and Beatrice joined in. On the second round there was a knock at the door and the Captain of the Guard, a woman, and three of the Mountain Folk came in and joined the song. When they had sung their fill, the real conversations began.

All present shared about the exchange of information and new languages created and being taught. It turned from dusk to dawn before they concluded their discussions. More changes in all their lives were on the horizon. The evil still grew.

Chapter Fifty-Six
PREPARING FOR WAR

The signal towers were set. The watchers are in place and trained. A new song of unity, *Peace will Succeed, Joy will Overcome*, or *Peace & Joy* for short, was being hummed or sung by everyone in the Red and Blue Knights' Keeps. Those who had never borne arms had received elementary training in fighting. They were shown how to use the tool they felt most comfortable with as a weapon or in defense. Some now wielded their rakes and hoes like pikes and spears. Others used axes and scythes like swords. The tools they used every day had now become weapons or defenses. A new sense of ownership, commitment and companionship had settled into the day-to-day activities.

A stray look was no longer ignored. A disgruntled snort or sigh was acknowledged and addressed. Those who isolated themselves were brought into the light. Those who spoke ill of others or the world were heard. Their concerns were brought to the knights or family members, some put into what had come to be called "protected custody". Both Keeps had created a holding area, a jail, where the truly dangerous or disenfranchised could be sequestered away from the general populace.

Additionally, no one was allowed to travel to Center City without a watcher. The watchers were a group of people with minor healing talents trained specifically to watch for the seeds of discontent that may be planted in individuals around them. Over the course of several weeks, numerous outsiders and the local healers trained by the now infamous Magician were identified as the source of the problems arising in the Kingdom. Yes, they did teach some of the healing arts, but never enough for full cure and always creating an underlying sense of disenchantment in the healing, the King, or the individual's sense of self.

Despite the work of the knights, the evil continued to spread. The interpersonal evil, or what some were calling discontentment, was diminishing within the Keeps of the knights, but remained unchecked in areas not under their direct supervision. Center City was a particularly disturbed place, fueled by the physical violence of General Mallory's militia and by the number of people who came in contact with the hospice. Yet the King had not responded.

Few knew that after the Knights had arrived home from their quest for the King, the man with the aura of green had taken the Princess out of the Castle. The Knights had assumed that she had been taken out of the Kingdom. None knew if she was alive, safe, or ever to return. The disappearance of the Magician shortly thereafter went mostly unnoticed.

Meanwhile the Kingdom simmered. General Malicious was mustering his troops, calling to arms all the disgruntled and those who thought themselves downtrodden or abused by others. He also found a fresh source of fighters entering through the Forest Lands the Green Knight seemed to be ignoring. And since the departure of the Magician's entourage, those ready for a fight seemed to be multiplying. The question was: Where was the Green Knight? (Only the other Knights knew he was in the Castle looking after the King.) The real question was: Where was his son?

Chapter Fifty-Seven
MALICIOUS PREPARES

The Red and Blue Knights' people were becoming more and more adept at anticipating attacks and preventing too much damage or harm being done. Even with the continued appearance of outsiders who sought only ill, the Knights appeared to be winning the battle against evil. Malicious knew he had to do something to turn the tide of evil back in his favor.

General Mallory stomped around his office, knocking over random items as he could. His aide followed behind, setting things to rights so he could knock them down again on his next pass. The General stormed, his words heated and frustrated. The aide did not listen because there was no point, it was all madness! He just had to make sure he was attentive to the mood and could anticipate the violence when it came. He ducked as Malicious whirled in place, arms outflung, head back, screaming. He backed into a corner of the room, crouching, waiting for Malicious to move on to his next rant.

"Worm!" Malicious shouted.

"Yes, Sir." The aide stood up, back against the wall, trying with all his soul not to look as afraid as he felt.

"Call all my officers." He paused, "No, call ALL my soldiers!"

The aide nodded, adding, "Yes Sir." He was afraid to ask the obvious questions: Where? When?

"I want everyone in the yard within a candlemark," he raised an arm as if already directing the gathering bodies. "No make that two candlemarks. Send out riders to all my outposts and have them gather here."

"Yes, Sir." The aide trembled but had to ask, knowing he'd be punished either way. "Can all gather in two candlemarks, Sir?"

Malicious turned on him and he shrank further into the wall and lowering his head below Malicious'. Malicious glared at him. Should he punish the man for challenging him or allow it to be the right question, saving him from having to wait for the outliers later? He backhanded the man, more lightly than normal. "Three candlemarks. I said three!" He raised his hand to strike the man again but let it fall. For now his fury was spent. He needed to focus on his plan.

As the aide scuttled out of the room, Malicious sat at his desk and made mental notes. He mumbled, "Perhaps a thousand, no Red has half mine. Five hundred, but only half under my direction. Trouble, these foreign instigators, are more trouble than they're worth. Just a waste of energy if they don't follow directions."

He rose and circled the room. Not knocking over things but patting them as he passed. "Worm, thinks I don't see him picking up. Ha. I see everything." Having finished the circuit of the room he sat again. "No defenses at the Castle. King is a babbling fool!" He slapped the table and chuffed a laugh. "A fool for the taking."

The aide knocked on the door. "Come!"

"The word has been sent. Troops are gathering. Fast riders sent to those afar"

Malicious interrupted him before he could continue. "Good. Out."

The aide backed out the door, happy to have avoided another blow.

Chapter Fifty-Eight
TIME FOR CONFRONTING EVIL – BLUE KNIGHT

The Blue and Red Knights each rose early and went to their special spots. The Blue Knight climbed the highest tower, from where he could see out beyond the walls of the Keep. The Red Knight went out into a far pasture and sat under the trees watching the horses graze and the sun rise. Both men were seeking answers to questions they didn't know who to ask. What did we do that let this evil invade our land and people?

How can we purge it from us?

The Blue Knight watched a circle of children playing with long sticks. Striking the ground then making a hand sign. He smiled. He could not hear the sticks but counted three strikes and what looked like a number in the hand signal. His smile turned to chagrin. The children learned quickly, much more quickly than their elders. It would help them communicate with the Mountain Folk. He sighed, but why did they have to learn it now? Why hadn't we all been learning this all our lives? If, no, WHEN the evil is gone, will our minds and hearts still be open? Will my love, my heart, still be welcome?

He had hoped his little escape would have raised his spirit, but instead, he was drawn further down into despair. "Oh, how I wish the man with the aura of green had a cure for this ailment of the heart." He spoke aloud, not expecting a response and was startled when he got one.

"Our hearts are only as strong as we let them be."

The Blue Knight spun and found the man with the aura of green standing with him in the tower. "Why are you here? Is it Minerva? Has there been a battle? Harm to more innocents?"

The man with the aura of green raised one hand stopping the Blue Knight's questions. "Easy." Lowering his hand slowly he added, "Breath."

The Blue Knight took a deep breath. "Please, is my beloved all right?"

A nod. Then a raised eyebrow.

"She was sleeping when I left. I will be sure to give her a back massage when I return."

A slight upturn on one side of the man with the aura of green's lip, noting that Rupert had taken the chiding for not paying closer attention to her well.

"Then if not her . . . why are you here?" It took all the Blue Knight's composure not to shake the man with the aura of green and demand an answer.

"I was tending your wife." Again he raised an eyebrow, but this time it was a rebuke. "She does not share how much pain she has."

The Blue Knight turned to rush to his beloved, but the man with the aura of green stopped him with only a slight touch on his arm.

"We need to talk."

The Blue Knight stopped, torn, wanting with all his heart to go to Minerva, beg her forgiveness for his thoughtlessness, yet he honored the man with the aura of green, so he waited.

"You are tending your own house well."

The Blue Knight waited, becoming more anxious as the moments passed.

"What of your King?"

The Blue Knight was puzzled. It took him several moments to comprehend what the man with the aura of green was asking. "The Green Knight is with the King." He turned back to look out the window that faced Center Town and the King's castle. "The Magician has left." Turning back to the man with the aura of green. "General Malicious is waging attacks throughout the land." He paused, suddenly understanding. "The King is unprotected!"

A nod.

"Great Power! How could we be so self-consumed?" He turned again to leave the tower and was again halted by a touch. He bit back a harsh response and took a deep breath. "Is there more?"

"You must go alone."

Halted, the Blue Knight stood mutely puzzled. "Without any of those we've been training?"

A shake of his head.

The Blue Knight pondered, then started. "Without the Head Counselor, Minerva, my wife?"

A nod.

"Why? She is wiser, braver, as much a leader as I. I need her!" It came out almost like a plea.

Another shake . "She needs time to recover."

The Blue Knight's shoulders hunched and his words came out almost a sob, "I've pushed her too hard! Expected too much! Not giving any thought to what she might need!" He turned to face the man with the aura of green. "Please, tell me what I can do!"

The man with the aura of green laid a strong but tender hand upon his shoulder. "Attend her and let her heal. You must go alone."

The Blue Knight could not contain himself any longer. He rushed down the tower steps and into the bedroom he shared with his wife. Sarah had just finished replacing the heating stones and the fleece cover.

"Good timing Sir. You can help me get my Lady back into bed."

Minerva began to protest, but Rupert swept her up gently and laid her carefully upon the warm fleece. He covered her both with kisses and another warm fleece before placing the quilt upon her.

From beneath the covers Minerva gave a little chuckle. "I feel like a small child, all wrapped up tight with warmth and love." One hand emerged, then the other. She took the quilt and pulled it up to her eyes so that all Sarah and Rupert could see was the twinkle in her eyes. "Sarah, you have much more important things to do than attend to me."

"Nay Mistress, at this moment there is nothing more important than you," Sarah responded while she bundled up the cold fleece and stones. "Shall ye be seeking the fast break in bed this morn?"

Before Minerva could answer Rupert replied for them both. "That's a marvelous idea Sarah. We'll both play the wastrel this morn. Do I need to slip into the kitchen to grab our meal or have you found someone to replace Simon?" He hesitated only a moment over the mention of Simon.

"Nay Sir, all is taken care of. Give me a half candlemark or so and there'll be another 'round with your meal." She turned and left before another word could be said. For she too, had a moment's discomfort at the mention of Simon. Once a child of the Keep who now was possessed by the evil none could name, or purge from their midst.

The Blue Knight watched Sarah, the keeper of his household, depart. *Another person I don't know what I would do without...* He turned to the bed and found Minerva watching him, thoughtfully, with Head Counselor, or perhaps just a wife's eyes. Before he could speak she asked, "What did the man with the aura of green say?"

Although he was surprised, he need not be, his wife was a very intuitive person, and the Head Counselor was wise far beyond her years. He started to hedge, not wanting to confess the truth of it, but knew she would see right through him. "I need to go alone. You need time to recover and heal."

She nodded and patted the empty bed beside her. "Come keep me warm. You can give me that massage you promised." The twinkle was back in her eye. "We may have just enough time before our fast break arrives." Rupert leapt into the empty bed and tunneled under the covers to give his wife the massage he'd promised and a little bit more.

Chapter Fifty-Nine
TIME FOR CONFRONTING EVIL – RED KNIGHT

The Red Knight watched the sun rise. He pulled an apple out of his pocket when his steed wandered over to him.

"Ah, you found me! I wondered if you'd be out this morn." The horsed nudged the hand with the apple. "Ah there now. You and I haven't had a good run in many a morn. This is supposed to be a treat after we have a run."

His horse lifted his head and shook in left and right in a definite indication of NO, then he opened his lips and puffed in the Knight's face. The Red Knight let out a deep heartfelt laugh. "Don't know why I even try. You know I can't deny you." He stretched out his hand and felt soft lips delicately pluck the apple from his palm.

He stroked his steed's neck. "My friend, what is this world coming to?" The horse leaned into his touch and nudged him gently. "You and I are not soldiers." He wrapped both arms around the horse's neck and laid his head upon it. "I just want to run with you, sing songs with Beatrice and enjoy my days." A tear wet the horse's mane, and the steed stood very still. "Can you tell me why, my friend . . . " He released the horse and wiped his eyes. Stroking the horse's cheeks and looking in his eyes, he asked again, "What did we do to bring this evil upon us."

For several long moments all was still, but his trusted steed had no answer.

He mounted the horse bareback and trotted over to the watchtower. He spoke with the night's watcher. All was quiet. No disturbances or strange travelers. The Red Knight proposed a trial. He was going to race to the next watchtower. He wanted this tower to alert them of his coming and mark his time. Before the watcher could respond, he and his steed were off.

It felt so good to be on his mount. Just the two of them free to run as fast and far as they wanted. Beneath him his steed moved faster and faster, flexing his muscles and stretching his legs. Head up and mane in flight, the horse seemed as pleased as the man to be together and running free.

It was several leagues to the next watchtower and both man and beast drew up with relief and exhilaration at the tower's door. A woman burst out the door, "Less than half a candlemark Sir Red Knight." She took the reins from him and walked the horse over to water and some feed, already starting to brush him down. "He's a fine one Sir." She brushed expertly and the horse leaned into her strokes. "If I may say so, he looks like he might be one of my family's pedigree." She stroked the horse's cheeks, "and you know you're a fine one too, don't ya." The horse gave her a snort and took another bite of hay. "To what do we owe the honor of this visit Sir Knight? The other watcher only told me you were coming and to mark your time! Twas a good time too!" She had stopped brushing while she talked and the horse gave her a gentle nudge. She laughed and began brushing again, "Sorry Sir, but you aren't the only honored one here." The horse snorted again, which the Knight would swear sounded like "Of course I am!"

The Red Knight watched the woman tend his horse and listened to her rapid patter. He was waiting for her to take a breath and let him speak. He chuckled at his horse's antics and felt his spirit rise, a bit. The woman finished the brushing and turned to look at the Red Knight.

"Half a candlemark you say?" He tried to keep the humor out of his voice.

"Aye Sir. If I'd known you'd be so fast, I would have counted tics, but for most it's a three candlemark walk at a brisk pace. We're pushed out a bit from the Keep because it was figured that the Keep would most likely have horses to respond on, others are an easy two candlemark walk, less if you run or have an animal to ride."

The knight was working very hard to keep a serious look on his face. This young woman and her unfiltered joy of life was doing his soul good. Before he could speak, she began again.

"We don't often get two special visits within the turning of a day." She indicated over her shoulder with a thumb. "Alleyu is in inspecting all our animals. She a miraculous healer and has an understanding of animals that rivals even my own da."

The Red Knight tried to ask a question but she continued unceasingly. "Hmway has gathered everyone to teach us our new song." She looked a bit longingly over in that direction. "I'm not much of a singer and someone has to keep the watch." Her high spirits returned. "But I would have missed you if I was there, so all the better for me!"

"Have you a name?" the Red Knight asked, a full smile on his face.

"Eey, my ma would tan my hide for forgetting to introduce myself and to a knight even." She wiped her hands on her breeches and stretched out one to the Red Knight. "They call me Bubbles. I have a family name but nobody uses it, so I don't see the point of telling."

The Red Knight reached out an arm and grasped Bubble's wrist and she did the same. Before he could withdraw his arm, Bubbles took his hand and turned it palm up to inspect. "Good rein hands, but it's been a while since you and the Master here." She slapped the horse's rump and got a tail swipe. Chuckling she went on inspecting the knight's fingers. "Lyre?" He nodded yes. "Did you help write our new song?" He didn't know how it was possible, but she was even more energetic than before. "Tis a might fine song. I think it inspires us all: *Peace will Succeed, Joy will Overcome.*" She finally released his hand and gave the horse another pat. "But I just call it *Peace and Joy.*"

The Red Knight couldn't quite believe the spirit of this woman. Unfiltered, unflinching, unwilling to let position sway her open heart, she shared her joy of life and the world with all who happened to come within her reach – literally! "I can not take credit for the song. My wife and Alleyu are the composers. Hmway and I may have filled in the tune a little."

"Good on you then!" Again she looked back toward the gathering. "My replacement will be here in just a few tics. I can take you over."

"Thank you Bubbles. I can find my way. Just point me in the direction of where Alleyu is checking the animals." Bubbles pointed and the Red Knight headed in that direction with a wave.

"Sir, your horse," before she could finish her sentence the steed was following his rider, head up, tail erect, and with a twinkle in his eye. "A fine beast, fine beast indeed!" Bubbles said as she watched them walk away.

Under his breath the Red Knight said to his horse, "Show off!" But it was said with love and good humor. The horse nodded once.

It didn't take long to find Alleyu. Every animal from the surrounding countryside was lined up waiting for her attention. The Red Knight wondered how long she had been at this. What time had everyone arrived? Last night or this morning? He acknowledged those who waited in line. Some he knew by name or trade. Most, he just gave a nod. When he finally came to Alleyu he found her with a very pregnant sow and concerned owner.

"Do you have a grass field where the other animals have not been?" Alleyu asked. The man nodded yes. "Then for the next

263

several days let her roam free there. Alone, unless you have other pregnant pigs?" The farmer rung his hands and indicated seven more with his fingers. "Ah, then all the pregnant sows should have access to this field and *only* them. Make a temporary shed with some clean straw where they can rest. The more good greens and real rest they get, the healthier the piglets will be when they arrive."

The man nodded, looking relieved and appreciative. He offered Alleyu the chicken he had under his arm. She declined politely saying, "Have many healthy piglets which I can visit next time I am here." The farmer cajoled the sow away from Alleyu. It was quite content to stay beside her and only left when she whispered in its ear. Looking up she saw the Red Knight and hummed a greeting to him.

"Looks like you have the countryside of animals waiting for you," he said and gave her a brief hug and hummed greeting.

She sighed a bit wearily. "I'm afraid I did not know what I was offering when I agreed to take a look at one woman's horse." She looked at the line of people and animals still waiting for her.

"Have you eaten?"

She shook her head.

"I'll find some food and when I get back you take a break."

She smiled at him a bit condescendingly.

"No, I'm not taking no for an answer. If you don't fuel the healer, she'll have no fuel for the healing."

Before she could say or do anything else, he turned away. She hummed a thanks as he departed.

It didn't take long for him to secure some food he knew she'd eat. He'd noticed that his steed had stayed by her side, inspecting the next animal to approach. He would swear the two of them were having a conversation. When he brought the food, she did take a few moments to eat and sit down alone. Before he went to find Hmway he asked. "When did you get here?"

"This morning."

"But I was up with the sunrise. I did not see you or Hmway leave."

"Ah," it came out a clear note. "We could not sleep and knew there was a need that we had to attend to, so we left early. We were here by sunrise."

The Red Knight did the calculation in his head. Bubbles had said it was a three candlemark walk. Hmway and Alleyu walked more briskly than most, so maybe two candlemarks and some tics, making it well before sunrise. "That's very early." He paused, watching her. "Should I be concerned?"

Alleyu finished her food and smiled at him. "Thank you for the fast break. It was what I needed. You are right. I should not deny myself sustenance. But now I have work to do. We can talk on the walk back."

"But I have my horse . . ." He trailed off. Knowing she would insist they all walk back. This time his horse followed. He too knew the Red Knight would not ride back. "Don't even think about it." The horse shook his head. "We go home together. Riding or walking." His horse snorted. "Maybe I'll find an excuse to leave early." The horse gave him an affirming nudge.

The Red Knight walked toward the gathering where he could hear singing. Hmway stood head and shoulders above the crowd of people. His deep baritone voice rang out. As those gathered learned the words and melody, Hmway's voice ceased to be a soloist and became part of the harmony. When everyone seemed to know the song Hmway announced, "One more time for your Red Knight." The people took up the song without him, and it was glorious!

"Well, done! Well, done!" The Red Knight greeted and acknowledged those gathered. The crowd slowly dispersed, humming and singing. Everyone returning to their usual tasks and duties.

"You were out early today." The Red Knight stated to Hmway.

Hmway smiled and hummed a greeting.

"Should I be concerned about what had you moving so early this morning?" The Red Knight knew he had to ask the right question or he would get no useful answer.

Hmway paused, humming quietly, contemplating the right way to answer the Red Knight. "It may be time for us to return home." He gave a small shake of his head to stop the Red Knight's response. "You are family. But we miss our people."

The Red Knight's spirit crashed. With all the self-control he could muster, he kept his own counsel and waited for Hmway to continue.

"I know you struggle with the evil within your kingdom." Hmway's usually positive hum turned pensive, a little dark. "But you now have more tools to fight it." Hmway stopped humming. "And there will be a fight."

The silence was deafening. The Red Knight could not remember a time when Hmway wasn't humming. Finally, he spoke. "And this is not your fight."

Hmway began humming a melancholy tune and nodded. "In my home, I would defend you with my life as I know you do here for us." His tune uplifted a bit. "But this is not a fight to protect family. It is a fight for your king." His tune became serious. "Not our king."

The Red Knight listened. So much was being said within Hmway's tune and his words. It took several long moments before he finally acquiesced. "I know." He took several breaths. "Thank you, my friend." They had come back to Alleyu just as she was finished with the last animal. "We'll miss you." Alleyu took only a moment to comprehend Hmway's song, the Red Knight's words."

"It is time?" she asked. A nod from Hmway. She laid her cheek upon the steed's and whispered in his ear. His ear twitched but he did not move. Then she took both of the Red Knight's hands and sang him a blessing. She got on her tip-toes and kissed his cheek. "Come see us soon."

The Red Knight and his horse watched Hmway and Alleyu leave for their desert home.

It was not till Bubbles approached that they stopped staring after the departing duo. "Sir Knight? You be needing anything before you depart? Want me to have them message the Keep you're returning?"

The Red Knight mounted his steed. "Thank you Bubbles. No need to let the Keep know." Then they were gone. The horse took the lead and soon they were galloping, full speed. Both knew they could not run away from the loss they already felt, but they would give it a good try.

Chapter Sixty
WHAT OF OUR KING?

It was midday when the Red Knight returned to his Keep. It was alive with activity. He found Beatrice directing several sewers. He looked at the piles of bandages, slings, and patches. He waited until she had finished giving a very specific set of directions before touching her shoulder to get her attention.

"May I have a moment of the Mistress' time?" Bartholomew leaned down and gave his wife's upturned lips a soft kiss.

"Aye, my love, but just a moment, we have lots to do and little time," Beatrice responded.

"I've been out for a ride. What's happened?"

Beatrice waved at the Captain of the Guard and turned her husband toward him. "Malcolm will catch you up. A spy in Malicious' camp reported in this morn." She patted his arm and turned back to her task.

The Captain of the Guard strode up briskly. Much to the Red Knight's surprise, he stopped and almost saluted him. "Sir!" Then he seemed to come back to himself and relaxed, just a bit, and spoke again. "A good day to you, Sir Knight. I did not know where to find you so I hope you are of a mind to understand why we've already taken action." The Red Knight stood bemused and motioned for the Captain to continue. "A spy on Malicious reported in this morn. Malicious is planning to attack the King and take possession of the Castle," he stared at the Red Knight trying to read his reaction before continuing, "He plans to make himself King!"

The Red Knight's face reddened and his temper flared. He looked for something to throw, kick, or hit. Instead, he fisted his hands and took three deep breaths. When he was calmer he asked, "Is there more?"

"Aye, but let me have the spy tell ye, Sir." He motioned to a dirty man across the courtyard. "I need to get back to gathering and repairing all the weapons." He hesitated only a moment before he turned away and returned to his task.

The Red Knight looked from his wife to his Captain of the Guard and then around the courtyard. After his first encounter with General Malicious he thought they had gained the upper hand, but the insidious ill-will that drove men to do evil seemed to be growing, not ebbing. The pain of Hmway and Alleyu's leaving now becoming just another part of the upcoming struggle. He sighed heavily. He considered returning to his steed and running, just running, until they could run no more. But he knew, he knew in his heart, that wasn't the answer. He sighed again as the spy approached and turned his sigh into a greeting and encouragement to tell all

Chapter Sixty-One
MALICIOUS' PREPARATIONS UNCOVERED

General Mallory watched out his window. Disgusted at the hoi polloi of ruffians, thieves, indigents, and (he scoffed) "soldiers" gathering. *I can't even begin to conquer this kingdom with this rag-tag lot!* he thought. "WORM!" He heard shuffling outside and panicked whispers. "WORM, NOW!" A few moments later a panting and breathless Worm entered.

"Yes, (gasp) my Lord (gasp) General."

Mallory watched the man, desperate for a breath, and more desperate not to be struck, trying to appease his Master. He turned back to the window. "Are my troops ready?"

"Sir (pant) not all have (pant) arrived yet. (Deeper breath) One group refused to come (a small step back and exhale)."

Mallory slapped his hands behind his back. Already feeling that uncontrollable anger rising as he watched the bodies outside become more unruly and disorganized. *I guess now is as good as any time.* he thought. "They better be ready Worm. We have work to do."

He grabbed a whip and hung it from his belt. He slipped his long knife into one boot. He watched out of the side of his eye as Worm cringed with every weapon he added to his person. Sword or axe? Power be damned – both! He strapped on his sword and swung his axe over his shoulder. He shrugged his shoulders to make sure he had freedom of movement. Adding one more knife to his belt, he marched past a cowering Worm and out into the mob he called his army.

The rabble in the yard pushed and shoved each other. They slapped and insulted one another. Some were ready to come to blows when the whisper of Malicious' arrival went around. An uncalm quiet moved throughout their numbers. A sharp slap, then a yelp, and a thud were heard before the group finally stilled.

General Mallory had backhanded a man, breaking his nose and knocking him unconscious. He had another man grab the unconscious man's leg and drag him to the center of the yard where Mallory now stood.

General Mallory stood. Hands akimbo. Looking over the assembled rabble as if they were less than dirt and not worthy of his time. He waited. Till all stilled. And he waited. Till all began to shift and sway uncomfortably. And still he waited.

Till someone spoke. "Why'd you bring us here if we're just going to stand around?"

Mallory grabbed his whip, with a snap and a crack, had it around the speaker's neck, pulling him to the ground and then under his foot. The man struggled to loosen the whip around his neck, slowly losing all breath and going faint. Only then did Mallory release the whip and take his boot off the man's neck.

"Any other questions?"

All gathered shook their heads not saying a word.

General Mallory gave them a sneer. He took several long moments to walk around the yard. Looking everyone up and down, watching them cower and avoid his eye contact. Returning to the center of the yard he finally spoke. Softly.

"The time has come." Everyone leaned in trying to hear him. "You've been a miserable lot. Thwarted by the likes of these kingdom people." Some stepped closer, straining to hear. "Now is your time to redeem yourselves." He scanned the faces, seeing fear, confusion, and frustration.

Loudly he stated, "NOW IS OUR TIME!" A cheer went up. He scoffed at them. They had no idea what he was talking about, but he had them all like puppets on his string, ready to do his bidding, no matter what the cost – to them.

"Captains, to me. I will give you our battle plan and your next fight." He scowled when there was not an immediate response. Slowly a few people moved toward him. He saw some others arguing, over who was in charge he imagined, with one finally winning (or losing) either by word or fist and coming to him. It was all he could do to contain his disgust and not kill or maim everyone who stepped forward. He slowly rolled up his whip and placed it on his hip, adjusted his axe, and laid a hand upon the knife in his belt. Eventually, the captains ceased coming and half a score of people stood around him.

"This Kingdom is ours for the taking." Pointing at three, "You will move through the Red Knight's land doing as much destruction and harm as possible." Pointing out a different three, "You will cause havoc in the Blue Knight's land." Looking at the remaining four, "You will follow me and we will lay siege to the castle and the king, doing as much damage as possible to Center Town as we go!"

The group looked dumbfounded. They stood, statue-like, staring at Mallory.

Mallory struggled to maintain some calm. "What?" He glared at them. "What don't you understand?"

One woman who was taller and broader than most men spoke gruffly, "Mes peoples hadn eaten in days. Wes was promised food." The others nodded.

A small squirrelish man squeaked out, "And weapons. We've been fighting hand to hand. They's fighting back now!" The others nodded.

Mallory stared them all down before stepping out of the circle. He nodded to Worm who rushed to his side. "We'll have to feed and arm most of this lot. Sort it out." He walked away leaving Worm to sort it out.

~~~

The man with the aura of green wandered among Mallory's followers. Casually kneeling beside the unconscious man with the broken nose. He checked his breathing, labored from the dislocated nose. He moved the nose back into place, receiving a pained grunt from the man. Upon hearing the man's breathing ease, he wandered casually out of the yard.

Only the Red Knight's spy noticed the man with the aura of green. He tried to follow, but quickly lost sight of him. Glancing over one shoulder, he continued out of General Mallory's camp. He'd hoped to steal a horse, but all the ones he saw were so ill-tended, broken, and too pathetic to ride at a walk, much less a gallop. When he got to the road he had to make a decision: Red or Blue Knight's Keep? If he hurried he might make the fast break at either. He heard shouting behind him and decided to head for the Red Knight's Keep although it was a bit further away. They had people who were more skilled in weaponry. If he were followed, he'd at least have a chance with them, if he got close enough. Malicious had already destroyed the closest watchtower twice. He knew he was on his own. He began to jog. Despite his hunger, it was the best he'd felt since he'd been sent to spy on Malicious.

At the next watchtower, he'd sent word of his coming. He was given a horse, bread and cheese for the rest of the journey. The watchtower guard had suggested he take a bath before entering the Red Knight's Keep. The spy just smiled, then said, "There'll be time for that, but only if I get there in time." The watcher wished him well, and under his breath said, "I hopes the horse don't throw ye. Yaowww what a stench!"

The rest of the spy's journey was uneventful. He did apologize to the Captain of the Guard when he greeted him at the Keep gate and let the horse be led away for a good rubdown and wash. The Captain led him to a steaming tub with soap and a change of clothes. As he stripped off the exterior physical layer of Malicious' filth, the deep rotting soul of the evil still clung to him, and he knew it wouldn't scrub away easily. The Captain of the Guard did not leave his side and expected him to tell all even as he was scrubbing behind his ears and private parts.

When he finished telling his tale the Captain told him to have a good soak, asked if he needed more hot water, then told him to get a meal when he was done. With all formalities done the Captain took only a moment for a personal aside.

"Well done, my son. Your mom and I sent the good Power your way every day. I'm glad to have you home." Then he was gone.

The spy settled in to soak, with a slight smile and a single tear, thought. *Thanks, Da. I'm glad to be home too. I only hope it's not too late.*

Chapter Sixty-Two
PREPARATIONS & CREATIONS

The Blue Knight and the Head Counselor held counsel in their marriage bed. Plans were made. Options created. Assurances given. But eventually the stalwart Head Counselor asked for the pain tea and a much-needed nap.

After the tea was finished, a massage was given. The Blue Knight kissed his wife once more before slipping away. He hadn't planned to depart on the morrow; he had hoped for another week, but warnings had come via the watchtowers: General Malicious was on the move. Even more worrisome, he was heading toward Center Town, where the King's castle and King resided.

Neither the Red or Blue Knight had gotten any word from the Green Knight or his son. The Green Knight had stayed with the King, but everyone knew the Castle and King were without any guards to protect them. The Red Knight had planned on sending out a small group before daybreak on the morrow, but that effort was thwarted when another small community near his Keep had been attacked.

Fortunately, the watchtowers worked just as they'd hoped. Alerts were sent out. Those in danger took steps to protect themselves and their neighbors came to their aid. The watchtowers had given their intended targets time to prepare and defend themselves. They had stopped six bands of marauders from doing too much harm or destruction.

Little real harm had been done, some property was damaged and lives were temporarily upturned. Once the intended victims began to fight back Malicious' people cowered and ran away. Many were caught, but few contained, most got away, to do harm another day. Discussions about how to detain and contain these marauders became a top priority. The gangs were not led by General Mallory, but they shouted his name and claimed all for his use and domain.

What was more unsettling was the fact that those attacked often saw one or two neighbors in the band of marauders. When they tried to call them out to bring them away from Malicious' thugs, they faced hostile shouts and angry faces. Parents, spouses, and siblings all tried to bring their loved ones around, to no avail. Seeing those they loved, lost to Malicious, was perhaps the greatest harm done. Though seeing family members within these groups disheartened all, it did not deter them from their plan to capture and secure all who were under General Malicious' command.

~~~

The Blue Knight sought out the building trade leaders. "How can we create secure, temporary cages that will hold Malicious malcontents until we find a more permanent solution?" He'd barely finished asking before plans were being discussed and existing options being reviewed. He did not wait to hear their solutions; he knew that when they had a viable structure and building plan they would present it to him.

Next, he approached the metalworking trade leaders. "We need more weapons to defend, and, unfortunately to kill. They pondered for several moments then one asked, "Permanent or temporary?"

"The Power willing, temporary? Why?" the Blue Knight asked.

The same woman replied, "If it is only temporary, we can rework blades from plows and reapers. We can fashion blades onto wheels and augment other tools we use to farm, to build, and cook," she paused to check with those gathered. She received nods and looks of approval. The gears of creativity were spinning for all now.

A man spoke up, "When you speak with the farmers have them collect their tools and bring them to us." He started to turn away and then added, "We can use their help too." Once more he turned away, then back. A bit more humbly and said, "Thank you Sir Knight."

The Blue Knight nodded and was on his way to the farm leaders. There he discussed how quickly the crops could be gathered and where all the stored food could be kept safe. He explained the idea of refashioning tools into weapons. Then he asked if help was needed to gather the food and secure it. He mentioned coordinating with the metalworkers, because they needed help too.

As he walked back to the Keep on the eve of dusk, he saw many people still hard at work. Lanterns lit the hillside and fields as food was collected. A long line of sheep and horses heading to the yards could be seen. The fires in the metal shop burned hot and bright. The clanging and ringing of metal being reformed sang its own song. He paused to watch some builders create a temporary cage.

It was a fascinating collection of woven sections and poles that slipped into one another. He couldn't understand how it stood or would be secure, but that was a thought for another day. His mind was as weary as his body. It had been a busy day. He made one more stop, however, at the watchtower. He had heard the pounding and whistles and seen people running through the Keep, but no one had come to find him. He stood a few more moments, waiting for someone to come looking for him, but none did. He sighed and entered the Keep's kitchen.

"Evening Sir." Sarah pulled out a chair and set a bowl of steaming meat stew on the table holding out the spoon to him. "Sit. The Mistress wanted to make sure you ate and sat a minute before you did anything else."

The Blue Knight took the spoon and dropped into the chair without comment. After three or four good bites he reached for the cider Sarah had placed beside him. He drank deeply. "Thank you Sarah. I needed that!" He took several more bites before speaking again. "How is Minerva?"

"Faring as well as an ailing body can." Sarah shook her head. "That woman endures too much silently. After you left this morning she slept most of the day and when she woke wanted a full report of the day's goings on." She smiled as she spoke. "Amazing woman, your wife!"

"Don't I know it Sarah!" He took several more bites and even lifted the bowl to his lips to drain the remains. Then he turned serious. "I have a favor to ask."

Sarah paused in her fixings. "Anything, Sir."

"When I leave," he had to pause because he was choking on his words, "please take special care of her."

Sarah turned to face him. "You're going without her?"

The Blue Knight nodded. "I was told to do so by the man with the aura of green."

Sarah looked concerned.

"He said she needs to recover." He paused again. "I've asked too much of her."

Sarah crossed her arms and waited.

"At least you'll have help managing while I'm gone."

Sarah gave him a soft snort

He looked longingly in his empty bowl, avoiding eye contact with Sarah.

"Sir." She waited until he looked at her.

278

"We will tend the home fires and wait with open arms for your return. And, yes, with the Mistress' help things will go very smoothly. But know this, Sir Knight. She has a mind of her own. You can ask nothing of her but what she is willing to give." She paused a moment longer. "Yet, still, she gives too much."

The Blue Knight gave her a quick hug and left so she couldn't see the tear that escaped.

The rest of the Keep was alight with activity and creativity.

~~~

Despite having to send out four different defense groups to battle some of Malicious' gangs, the Red Knight's Keep was abuzz with activity. Occasionally, a group of pole talkers would stop in the middle of a pathway, pound out a beat then sing the new song, encouraging everyone nearby to join in. They would end the sing-along by pounding ten times and a shout.

Despite the tasks at hand and the fact that Malicious was on the move, everyone chose to find the good in each action and word. The Red Knight saw families sitting together sharpening tools that could be their weapons. Cooks caroling the new anthem while serving food. He was sure it was adding joy and uplifting spirits at every meal.

The Captain of the Guard had created what he called "Seek and Prevent" groups. With six to eight well-trained fighters, some were hunters with good tracking skills, others had learned all the pole, hand, and whistle signals. Their mission was to see if they could anticipate the next attack from Malicious' minions. If the Knight's people were forewarned, they could head off, if not all, at least a good number of individuals and capture them with minimal harm to anyone.

One of the Seek and Prevent groups had gone to the Blue Knight's Keep with some information about a possible attack. While they were there, they saw the builders making cages. The team liked the idea of quick set-up cages and wanted an opportunity to test one. The Blue Knight's builders had come up with an ingenious quick-build cage. With three fully woven sides (the weaving was done with cloth, wood, and any other pliable materials) that each slid onto four large poles planted into the ground, the fourth side had a hinge on one side so bodies could enter and leave. The weavers had created sixteen completed sides in just two days and were waiting for more materials to continue. The building folks were having a bit of difficulty finding trees large enough to use. They had only found eight suitable trees and were waiting for more trees to make more cages. They needed the Green Knight and his forester. One of the metal workers had been making hinges and had modified a latch into something that could attach to separate pieces and still lock.

"There are other ways of keeping people in check," stated one of the Seek and Prevent members. "We can't be standing around, singing, while Malicious is doing harm." So the group decided to offer classes. They were surprised at how many people joined the classes to learn the hand language, pole pounds, and whistle notes. Those who learned then volunteered to be watchers. Quickly, the watchtowers were fully patrolled day and night. The Seek and Prevent groups had more information and soon Malicious' malcontents were hardly effective and filling up the new cages.

The Knight's healers agreed to tend to the wounded bodies of Malicious' minions as well as their people. Very shortly, with the help of the Seek and Prevent groups and watchtowers, the number of life-threatening wounds were minimal and people rarely saw the man with the aura of green. The emotional wounds were proving much harder to heal.

Despite all the positive steps taken to stop the physical violence and destruction, the Magician trained healers surfaced here and there, spreading discontent and emotional strife. Once identified and confronted, they gave up easily, claiming, "This isn't my fight. I just do what the Magician taught me." When the first evil healers confessed, expressed regret and repentance, they were released. Those who'd allowed them to leave had expected them to leave the Kingdom completely – but they did not – they showed up in another community, healing. Every time an evil healer showed up again, they had become more subtle, and it became harder to root out their insidious evil intentions. It was decided that all, healer or soldier, would be contained until a workable solution could be found.

The evil healers objected strenuously to being caged with the soldiers. They argued that they were not like the stinking, foul lot that Malicious called his soldiers. They asked to be manacled to any tree or structure far away from the stench and foulness of these individuals. The Kingdom's people wanted to expect the best of others, wanted to trust others, especially if they were healers who should be helping people. It was decreed that Magician healers should be separated from Malicious' soldiers. They had to be manacled and treated with a bit more dignity than Malicious' soldiers.

Unfortunately, this too failed. The Magician's people were escape artists as well as healers, actors, and who knows what else. They extricated themselves from this confinement easily. The only positive aspect of these situations was that after their second capture, most of them did not return to another community's healing center. As good as they were at escaping, they did not tempt fate a third time. No one knew where they went.

Chapter Sixty-Three
MALICIOUS' FRUSTRATION

Despite his best plans, Mallory's army was failing to cause the havoc and harm he intended. His despicable lot was no better than a wet blanket thrown at a forest fire. Completely useless. Even when they did cause some damage, the knights' people rose up again and again. Half a fortnight had been wasted and what had he accomplished? He cursed and slammed his hand against the wall, causing the whole building to shutter.

Worm crept into the room. "Did you need something General?" He lurked at the door, hoping to make a quick escape if possible.

"Are my troops ready?"

"All are armed. All are fed. We've tended the wounded and prepared them to fight again." Worm paused to take a breath before continuing with his report, but Malicious broke in.

"How many?"

"Twelve score." Worm cringed even as he spoke. It was a pathetic number. He had not informed the general about how many had joined the raiding parties and been captured.

Malicious turned slowly to face Worm. "Two hundred and forty?" He paused watching Worm move further out the door.

"Actually, 223 Sir."

Malicious barely controlled his urge to hurt Worm. "Then why did you tell me two hundred and forty?"

"That-that-that was the count last night. I was just updated." Worm tried to get behind the door and still be visible. He knew it was only a matter of tics before Malicious struck out.

Malicious stood straighter, adjusted his clothing and weapons. He cleared his throat. "Prepare my army for the march to Center Town."

"Sir?"

Malicious stared Worm down. "Problem?"

"It-it-it's midday General. Perhaps only three or four candlemarks more before daylight is gone." Worm waited, but Malicious was not going to make this easy for him. "You'll have to set up camp an extra night if you leave now." Again, he waited for Malicious to respond, but Malicious left him hanging. "Wou-wou-would-wouldn't it be better to wait until daybreak?" He had backed all the way out of the general's office now and was tensed to run as soon as the Malicious moved. As an afterthought he added, "Tonight can be the last meal you have to feed them. Make them scavenge for their own food on the march."

This last statement was the one that saved Worm's life that day. Malicious paused, giving it thought. Finally he spoke. "Ready my army." Worm's shoulders sagged even more if that was possible. "We leave at daybreak." With that he snapped out with his whip, grabbing the door handle and slamming the door in Worm's face.

Worm slid down the exterior wall and curled into a fetal ball, breathing deeply. Under his breath you could barely hear him chanting, "Living for one more day, one more day. I'll live for one more day. Power save me."

Inside Malicious re-curled his whip and chuckled. That worm is getting smarter. I didn't even catch a toe this time. As he replaced the whip on his hip, he turned to the window, watching the activity in the yard. It was not the army he had planned on, but he would make do. The King was unprotected. The Knights were occupied with the raiding parties he'd sent out. This conquest was still doable.

Chapter Sixty-Four
TO ARMS

The Red Knight and the Captain of the Guard rolled up the map and grasped each other's forearms.

"We've done all that we can to prepare. Now it is time to take the fight to Malicious." The Captain said as he released his Knight's arm. "Sir, I believe we will be the victors of this fight."

The Red Knight sighed heavily, "I know we're prepared. I know we've made plans and alternative plans. I know we have the Power on our side." He sighed again. "But we shouldn't have to be doing this at all."

The Captain of the Guard smiled ruefully. His Knight, how he ached for his Knight. Since Hmway and Alleyu's departure his spirit had been subdued and could not be raised either in joy or ire. "Nay, Sir, we shouldn't." He took the map and departed. He wanted to spend some time with his son before he had to leave. At least he didn't have to send him back to spy on Malicious. Power be blessed, he had come home whole and sound. Now he was going out to fight against Malicious. No matter how the Captain tried to convince him, he refused to stay with his mother. Of course, he could not deny his son, he just hoped they would quickly be joined again at home.

The Red Knight surveyed the yard. It was a bustle of activity and he could hear the anthem being sung here and there. "Thank you Hmway and Alleyu!" he breathed out and sighed. When would he see them again? Would he see them again? No, he had to stop thinking about them and focus on the task in front of him. Even so, he gave up a silent prayer for their safe travels home. No matter how much his heart broke at their departure, he knew they would have had to leave some time, and better now than after the battles began.

In the yard, four different groups were getting organized, outfitted, and given instructions for the upcoming confrontations. Two groups were heading for Center Town on the morrow. Two groups were meant to clean up the miscellaneous strays of Malicious' army and help the Blue Knight's builders construct more of the ingenious temporary cages to keep them contained.

The Red Knight was on the path to Center Town and the King. How different this journey is. Not seeking good via the man with the aura of green, but confronting evil caused by the man known as General Malicious. Was this an ending or a beginning?

~~~

The Blue Knight was lingering with the Head Counselor in the kitchen. He had used every moment of the past seven days with his wife preparing for the struggle ahead and spending time with her. His builders had created amazing temporary, quick build, cages for containing Malicious' strays. All his people were now armed with a weapon so they could protect themselves and subdue an attacker. The tools the weapons had been made from remained in substance and could be revived after this mess was all completed.

The Blue Knight was very proud of his people. After the amazing decimation of General Malicious' army by the Red Knight, without a single loss of life and only minor injury to his people, he had worried he would not be able to adequately fulfill his role as knight in this struggle. But his people, his glorious, inventive, creative, hard-working people had created the things they needed most, Together with the Red Knight's people, they would catch and contain one source of evil that was in their land.

"Love?" A gentle hand upon his arm. "Love, where are you?"

The Blue Knight started, having been so lost in his thoughts, he had to be drawn back not only by word but also by touch. "Sorry

Love," he gave his wife a wan smile. "Your knight is off gallivanting, in his own mind." He chuckled softly and turned to kiss her and their lips met. Soft, warm, inviting lips, that drew him in and aroused his passion. When they broke apart, gasping a bit for breath, they heard Sarah chuckle. "I'd say get a room you two, but the whole Keep is yours, so who am I to speak!" She chuckled again. "I hope you always love each other as you do now."

Minerva was beyond the stage of blushing when it came to her Knight and their affection for one another. But Sarah never failed to make her feel like a young girl, head over heels for her first love. Because, although she was not young, this was her first love and the depths of it were infinite.

"Need us out of your kitchen, Sarah?" Minerva asked. "I think I have a meeting to attend in a few tics. Is it possible to get one or two more bites of that lemon pie?"

Sarah held up an empty pie tin. At Minerva's crestfallen look, from behind, she produced a small bowl with the scrapings out of the pie tin. She watched the whole room light up with Minerva's smile. "I know ye Mistress, nothing goes to waste." She handed Minerva the bowl and once again marveled at how much this woman had changed all their lives.

She watched her Knight push her Head Counselor out of the kitchen and couldn't be prouder or filled with more love and respect if she tried. "Come home safely Sir," she whispered as they left.

~~~

As the Blue Knight pushed the Head Counselor to her meeting, they chatted about nothing in particular. Just as she was about to enter the meeting room she laid a hand upon his and asked. "Tell me love."

He hesitated, then spoke from his heart. "I know it is my duty as a knight to defend my King and our Kingdom. I know General Malicious has only evil intentions. I know that I can do nothing less than what the Power has laid out for me. Yet . . ." He knelt beside her so they were eye to eye. "My heart wants to give all that up," he lifted one of her hands and kissed it tenderly, "for you, love." He continued to look into her eyes.

She reached out with her free hand and stroked his cheek. She felt the stubble that was growing into a full beard and his warmth as he leaned into her hand. "My Knight. We would not have met if you hadn't been doing your duty." He started to speak but she brushed a thumb across his lips. "My Knight. I could not love you any more, or share my love any less, if we had eons of time together." She took time to take all of him in, sealing his image in her memory. "Sarah and I will keep your, our home safe and ready for your return." She put all the force of her Head Counselor look and authority into her next words. "And you will return."

He rose and kissed her tenderly and then with more passion until she pushed him away. "Go, go," she breathed heavily, "I have a meeting to conduct and I will not have you undermining my authority with your passion." She grabbed him and brought him back for another passionate kiss before firmly pushing him away and wheeling forward into the room, leaving him standing, watching, hoping that what she said would be true.

~~~

One of the builders approached him. "Sir, we're all loaded up and ready to meet with the Red Knight's people." He waited for the Blue Knight to respond, when he didn't he continued, "Is there any special message or instructions you wish for me to take from you?"

The Blue Knight finally turned and faced the man. He laid a firm hand upon the man's shoulder. "Go with all speed and safety.

Take no unnecessary chances and return to your family and our Keep quickly." He smiled warmly at the man, hoping he was projecting a sense of assurance he did not feel. "You have built marvelous things. I could not be more proud."

The man beamed under his Knight's praise. With a slight bow of his head he said, "We'll be off then. See you soon, Sir Knight."

"Soon, indeed, soon." The Blue Knight gave him a wave and turned toward his own group of travelers. His path was leading him back to the King and General Malicious. His last trip for the King led him to the Head Counselor, Minerva, now his wife. *This trip can only lead to heartbreak and confrontation,* he thought.

Chapter Sixty-Five
AN ENDING?

The Storyteller stopped, took a deep breath, then a long pull on the draft, which she emptied. She looked into the empty pint mug but waved off the barmaid who approached with another.

"It is time to end our tale tonight."

There were heavy groans and shouts of "No", "Just a little more", "You can't stop now", "What of the White and Green Knights?" "When will you finish?" "Please, tell us more!"

The Storyteller smiled but waved aside all pleas for more. "Trust me, my friends, I have plenty more to share." Cheers started up in those gathered, and over their hope, she continued, "Tomorrow."

The cheers turned to groans and eventually yielded to the fact that the rest of this story had to wait for another day.

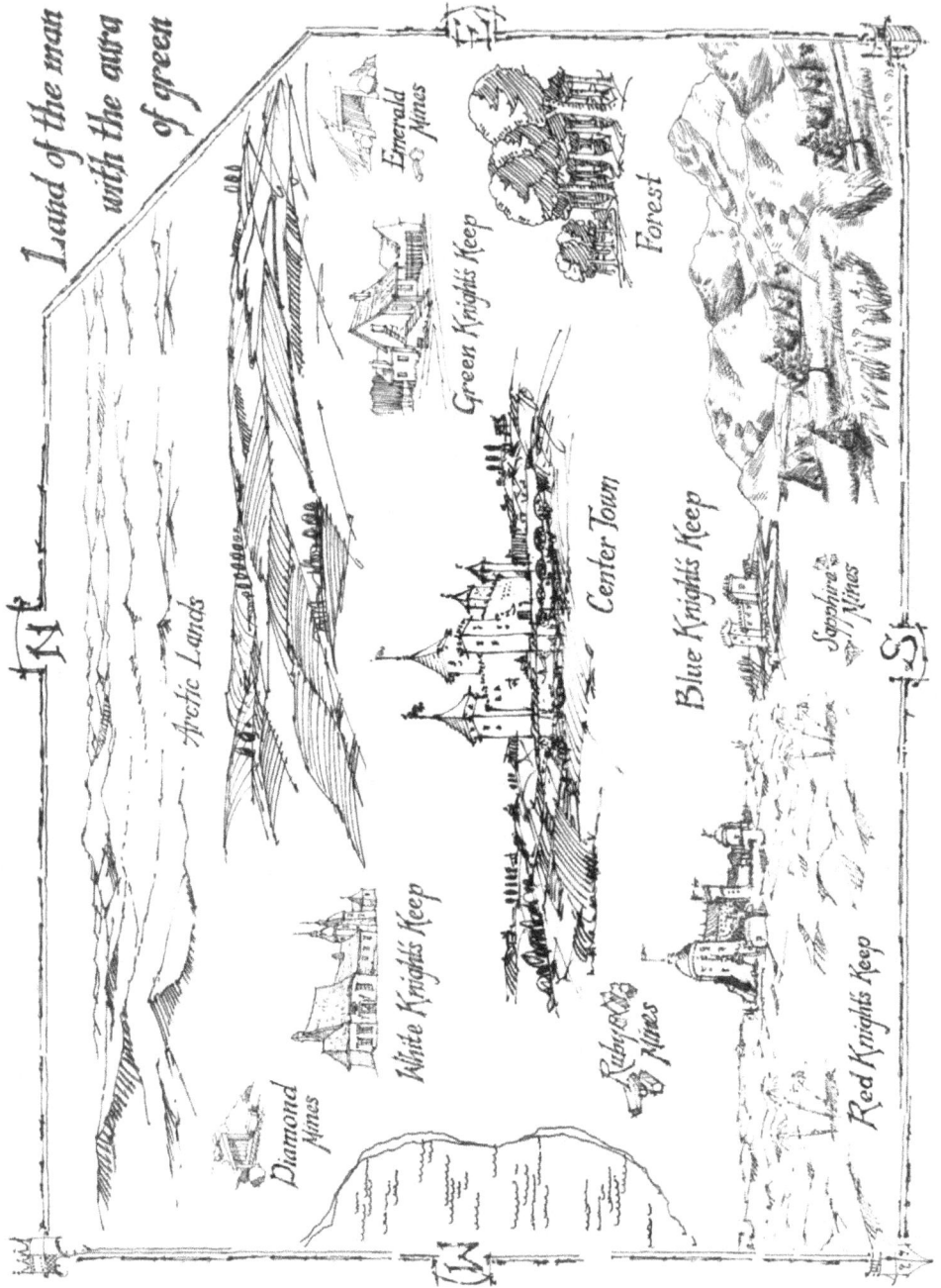

Land of the man with the aura of green

Arctic Lands

Diamond Mines

White Knights Keep

Emerald Mines

Green Knights Keep

Forest

Center Town

Ruby Mines

Blue Knights Keep

Sapphire Mines

Red Knights Keep

The people in the man with the aura of green's home

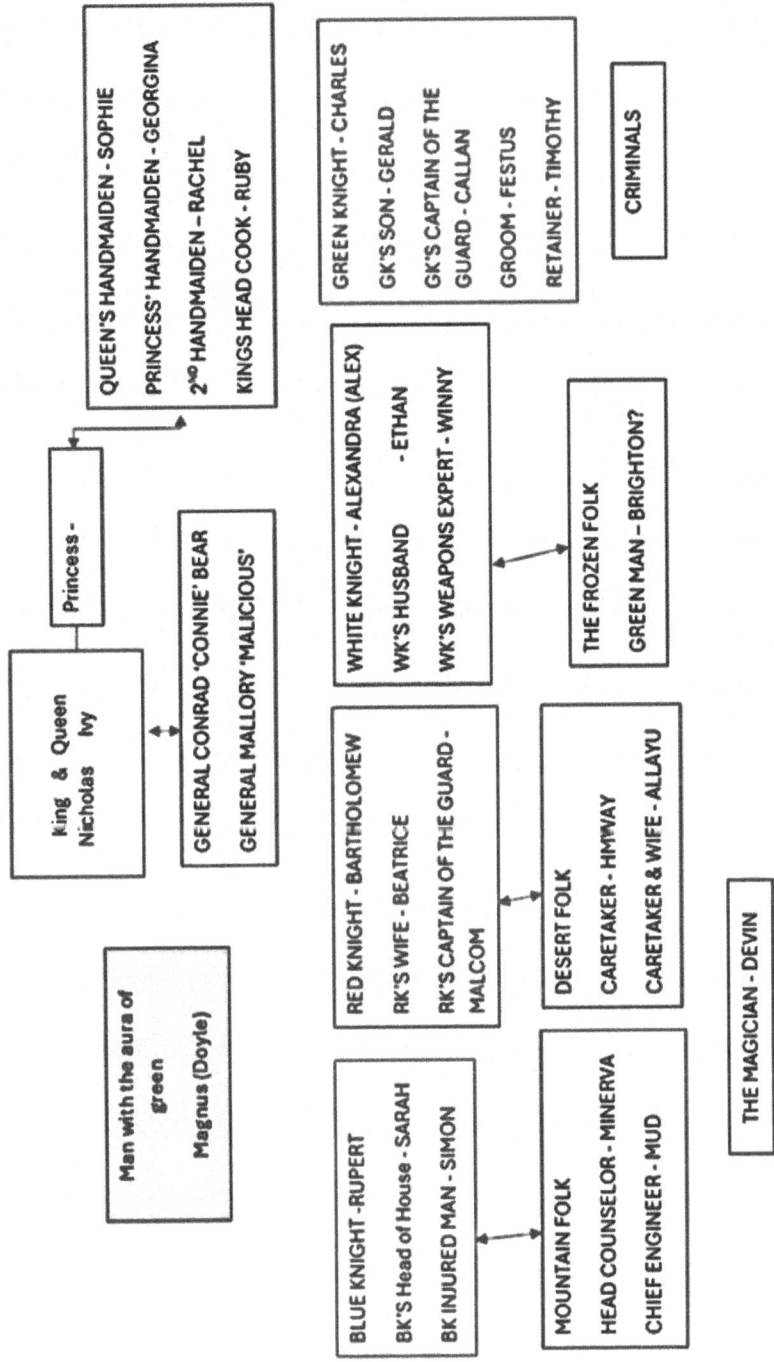

Man with the aura of green
Magnus (Doyle)

King & Queen
Nicholas   Ivy

Princess -

QUEEN'S HANDMAIDEN - SOPHIE
PRINCESS' HANDMAIDEN - GEORGINA
2ND HANDMAIDEN – RACHEL
KINGS HEAD COOK - RUBY

GENERAL CONRAD 'CONNIE' BEAR
GENERAL MALLORY 'MALICIOUS'

GREEN KNIGHT - CHARLES
GK'S SON - GERALD
GK'S CAPTAIN OF THE GUARD - CALLAN
GROOM - FESTUS
RETAINER - TIMOTHY

CRIMINALS

WHITE KNIGHT - ALEXANDRA (ALEX)
WK'S HUSBAND   - ETHAN
WK'S WEAPONS EXPERT - WINNY

THE FROZEN FOLK
GREEN MAN – BRIGHTON?

RED KNIGHT - BARTHOLOMEW
RK'S WIFE - BEATRICE
RK'S CAPTAIN OF THE GUARD - MALCOM

DESERT FOLK
CARETAKER - HMWAY
CARETAKER & WIFE - ALLAYU

THE MAGICIAN - DEVIN

BLUE KNIGHT -RUPERT
BK'S Head of House - SARAH
BK INJURED MAN - SIMON

MOUNTAIN FOLK
HEAD COUNSELOR - MINERVA
CHIEF ENGINEER - MUD

Rise Up

Rise up! A new day's be - gun. Rise up! So much to be done.

Rise up! To meet our fate.___ Rise up! A new day's be - gun. Rise up! So much to be done.

Rise up! To meet our fate. Rise up! A new day's be - gun. Rise up! So much to be done.

Rise up! To meet our fate.___ Rise up! Rise up!

Nev - er a day too dark or gloom - y, nev - er a strug - gle too hard or loom - ing. Our spi - rits will pre - vail

O - ver dark___ ness! Rise up! Rise up!

Rise up! Rise up! Rise up! A new day's be - gun.

Rise up! So much to be done. Rise up! To meet our fate.___ Rise up!

Rise up! Gath-ered we strive and gath-ered we ov-er-come. Rise up, rise up in hope we will suc-ceed.

We will con-quer all,___ with har-mon-y and grace!___

Rise up! A new day's be-gun. Rise up! So much to be done.

Rise up! To meet our fate.___ Rise up! Rise up!

The time will come when chall-leng-es won, Ev-il, pain and grief will___ be un-done.

Voic-es in the heav'ns will all cry RE-JOICE! Re-joice! A new day's be-gun.

Re-joice! So much to be done. Re-joice! To live our fate.___ Rise up!

AFTERWORD

The legends of the man with the aura of green are many. So are the tales of the knights. The tale of the White and Green Knights will be forthcoming shortly.

The confrontation with General Malicious will come and the fate of the Kingdom with be determined.

As the series continues you will learn more about the man with the aura of green, other characters mentioned in volume 1 but not 2, and even more.